When in Rome

When in Rome

Nicky Pellegrino

First published in Great Britain in 2012 by Orion Books,
an imprint of The Orion Publishing Group Ltd
Orion House, 5 Upper Saint Martin's Lane
London WC2H 9EA

An Hachette UK Company

1 3 5 7 9 10 8 6 4 2

A CIP catalogue record for this book
is available from the British Library.

ISBN (Hardback) 978 1 4091 3376 6
ISBN (Trade Paperback) 978 1 4091 3377 3
ISBN (Ebook) 978 1 4091 3378 0

Typeset by Deltatype Ltd, Birkenhead, Merseyside

Printed in Great Britain by CPI Group (UK) Ltd,
Croydon CRO4YY

The Orion Publishing Group's policy is to use papers
that are natural, renewable and recyclable products and
made from wood grown in sustainable forests. The logging
and manufacturing processes are expected to conform to
the environmental regulations of the country of origin.

When in Rome

Our Lady Of Grace

On every door there is a photograph. They show us as we used to be – not weathered or worn; not bent by age and nearly finished with life. On some doors there are photographs of smiling brides linking arms with long-gone husbands. On others, women holding babies or young girls in white Communion gowns. We were beautiful, strong and healthy. We were young.

Here in the Our Lady of Grace Rest Home we live behind those doors. There is a photograph pinned to mine just like all the rest. They took it from the old frame now tucked away with the other remnants of my life in the bottom drawer of the wardrobe. Few of the staff ever pauses to look and none have asked me about it. They must assume the man beside me is my husband but, of course, he never was. It would have been impossible.

He is smiling and so handsome it could break your heart. His dark hair has been parted at the side and marshalled into a neat quiff, his shoulders seem broad thanks to sly padding in his smart suit jacket. To me he looks tired but then I know the story behind the photograph; I remember everything about the time it was taken far more clearly than I recall what happened last week or even yesterday.

I never tell anyone his name. The older ones, if they had heard of him, might not believe it and the young ones wouldn't care. Perhaps sooner or later he'll be recognised, for he hasn't been forgotten, I'm sure of that. But really, who would put us together? Who would imagine that once my

I

life tangled with his and changed entirely?

Some day I may share my story if I find a person with time to listen. But I won't blurt it out in the middle of a brisk bed bath or try to talk as my pillows are plumped and my coverlet straightened and they ask, 'How are you feeling today Signora?' They never bother to wait for a reply.

My story doesn't begin with him, anyway. It starts with a woman leaning out of the window of an ivy-covered building in Trastevere and calling down into the narrow street below: 'Serafina … Serafina … Sera-feeen-aaaa.'

Golden Days

'Serafina ... Serafina ... Sera-feeen-aaaa.' My mother's voice could be heard through closed doors; it reached down flights of stairs and, when she leaned out of the window of our building in Trastevere, echoed all the way down to the narrow street below.

It was me she called most often since I was the eldest of her three girls. When laundry needed taking to the *lavanderia* or food fetched from the market or ribbons tied in my sisters' hair, mine was the name she shouted. 'Serafeeenaaaa.'

My mother was still beautiful then. Even wearing a faded housedress with her dark hair pulled back from her face and caught in a clump at the nape of her neck, she looked impressive. She had full lips painted the colour of coral and eyes shaped like a cat's, which she would line carefully with black every evening before reaching for the shiny white handbag with the gold clasp and going out for the night.

Her clothes were beautifully tailored – dresses with wasp waists and full skirts, little gypsy tops that showed off her shoulders. Most things she had made on the sewing machine she kept in our bedroom. My mother might have been a seamstress except she had found another way to make money, a way that she preferred.

In the evenings it was her habit to leave my sisters and me with the dirty dinner dishes and enjoy a leisurely *aperitivo* with friends in the nearest bar before they all went to work. We were used to being left alone. Mamma expected us to tidy up then go to bed early but of course we disobeyed her.

Some nights we pulled out the magazines she had brought home and stared at pictures of movie stars: Rita Hayworth, Ava Gardner and our own Gina Lollobrigida. What might it be like to be so famous and so beautiful?

Mamma didn't mind us looking through her magazines but she might have been cross if she had seen me pull her precious records from their sleeves, put them on the turntable and carefully lower the needle. She had so much music: American jazz, Neapolitan love songs, even some opera. But my favourite singer, the one whose voice cut a slice from my heart and left me shivering with pleasure, was Mario Lanza.

'He isn't even a real Italian,' my sister Carmela always sneered. 'And look at him in this picture – he's chubby.'

'But listen to him sing,' I argued. 'Is anything more beautiful?'

'If you play that record too many times you'll wear it out and then Mamma will know what you've been up to,' Carmela told me. She was fourteen, the age I had been when I was taken out of school so I could help look after her and my littlest sister Rosalina.

Carmela herself had a beautiful voice. Even singing along to Mamma's records it sounded fantastic. Often in the warmer months, after collecting her and Rosalina from school, I would walk them up to Piazza Navona where Carmela would sing for the tourists.

She had a favourite place to stand, right beside one of the fountains. As soon as she opened her mouth people gathered and began to drop coins into the straw hat we put on the ground. Sometimes Rosalina and I harmonised, for we could sing a little too. But it was Carmela who had the real talent. We dreamed that one day she'd be discovered and then we'd all be rich.

Once the crown of the hat was covered with lire we'd stop to count it up. If there was enough money we would treat ourselves to ice creams or Coca-Cola then go to see a movie.

Musicals were what we preferred, often watching the same ones over and over. I'd seen *Serenade* so many times I think I knew it off by heart. And it was the same with *The Toast of New Orleans* and *Because You're Mine* – all the Mario Lanza films.

'You're in love with him, aren't you?' Carmela accused.

'So what if I am?' I replied.

I couldn't see anything wrong with being in love with a movie star. Mario Lanza was better than any real man I had met. His eyes sparkled, his smile was kind. To sit in a darkened auditorium staring at him on the screen was comforting. And when he sang 'Be My Love' it felt genuine and perfect, the way romance was meant to be. He was so different to the Roman boys who stared as I walked by, chasing me with catcalls and whistles. Or the too-friendly older men who must have known I was my mother's daughter.

I suppose I was a pretty girl. I had my mother's lips and liked to think my grey-green eyes came from my father, although I had never seen a picture of him. My hair was sleek and dark, swept back in a high ponytail. I wore wide skirts, well-pressed blouses buttoned to the neck, a narrow belt around my waist. And I was taller than other girls, however much I rounded my shoulders to bring myself down to their level. No wonder people stared.

Mamma was proud of my looks. She used to paint my face with make-up and exclaim at how much older it made me seem. She covered my eyelids with shimmery gold and stained my lips pink. I always scrubbed off every scrap of it as soon as she would let me.

I wonder if Mamma ever guessed what Carmela, Rosalina and I did with our summer afternoons. She may have chosen not to notice. Most days she slept late and then took a long bath, plucked her eyebrows, painted her nails. Even if she had known that my sisters missed school altogether at times, she might not have cared. So long as we could count well enough to tell if we were being short-changed at the market in Testaccio, Mamma was happy.

The only thing she insisted was that we all study a little English. She'd learned to speak some herself for the Americans during the war and made us practise a new phrase every day. Already it had come in useful. The tourists listening to Carmela in the Piazza Navona seemed to like it if we greeted them in their own language, wishing them a happy holiday. Often they would laugh and hand over a few more coins.

'I was born singing,' Carmela would call out to them. 'Stay and listen to more of my songs. I know lots of American ones as well as Italian.'

And then she might sing 'Be My Love' because she knew it was my favourite, effortlessly hitting the notes, her voice like sweet peaches and warm honey.

'The minute I look old enough I'll find a job as a nightclub singer,' Carmela promised as we sat beside the fountain eating our ice creams. 'Some day my voice will make me famous. And then I'll buy a big palazzo near the sea and we'll all live there together when I'm not making records and movies.'

'I don't want to live in a palazzo by the sea,' Rosalina complained, licking the drips of pistachio running from her cone. 'I want to stay here in Rome and sell *gelato* in Piazza Navona.'

'You'd eat more of it than you sold,' I told her, laughing. 'Your stall would never have any *gelato* left.'

'Yes it would,' she insisted. 'And I'd be richer than Carmela because I'd have all the best flavours. Then I'd get a big apartment in Trastevere and we'd have our own beds instead of having to share.'

Every night the three of us went to sleep squashed into the same double bed. When Mamma came home, often very late, Rosalina was lifted out and placed on a mattress on the floor because she was the smallest and slept most soundly. Waking to find herself there in the morning she always grizzled and

6

tried to push herself back beneath the covers with us.

Our apartment was so very tiny, just two poky rooms in a crumbling building; one where we all slept and the other a sitting room with a gas burner where I cooked dinner each night. The space was damp, dark and cluttered with our belongings. We didn't even have a bathroom – only a shared room at the end of the hall where we washed and used the toilet. Perhaps we might have found something nicer if we had been prepared to move to another part of the city but Mamma always refused.

'We are *Trasteverini* … we live in the heart of Rome,' she told us. 'Why would we want to be anywhere else?'

She loved the maze of narrow streets, the tall terracotta buildings with arched doorways and plants scrambling over walls, the overhanging laundry, the old signora sitting out-side her front door shelling peas and soaking up the morning sun, the men who set folding tables on the cobblestones and argued over card games for half the afternoon, the gaudy street-corner shrines. Mamma liked the life of Trastevere.

Every Sunday she took us to morning Mass in the ancient church in Piazza di Santa Maria. Always we slipped in a little late and took our places in the back pews, staring down the rows of columns towards the shining mosaics above the altar. Mamma wore a scarf to hide hair as bright as burnished copper and fastened her dress modestly at the throat. She bowed her head and closed her eyes while she prayed. Well before the service was over she gathered us up, and with a finger held to lips, herded us back outside. Many years later I understood why. There were men in Santa Maria that may have felt awkward to see my mother there and wives who might have guessed why.

As soon as we were out in the piazza, she would pull the scarf from her hair. 'Which café shall we go to, girls?' she'd call, already gayer and more like her usual self. 'Serafina, isn't it your turn to choose? Where would you prefer?'

7

Our Sunday treat was being allowed to sit with Mamma, shaded by sun umbrellas or in a booth beside a bar, and order whatever we wanted from the menu. We took turns to pick which café we would visit. Rosalina loved the one in Piazza di Santa Maria because usually there were children she could play with beside the fountain, Carmela liked to try a different place every time and my very favourite, as all my family knew, was hidden away down a narrow alley and felt as though it hadn't changed in centuries.

Mamma spoiled us on Sundays, treating us to deep dishes of *gelato* and too many cakes while she sipped at her espresso and smoked a cigarette. Often she might buy a copy of *Confidenze* magazine from the kiosk in the piazza and, as she leafed through, she would criticise the stars whose pictures we all pored over. 'See this Sophia Loren ... such a shame about her nose ... so sharp and her nostrils are too large. Pity, eh? And Gina Lollobrigida, lovely but look at her hair, it's always a mess.' She smoothed her own hair as she said it. 'You'd think with all her money she could do something with it.'

'You should be a movie star, Mamma,' Rosalina told her through a mouthful of cream-filled *cornetto*. 'You are much more beautiful than the signora in the magazine.'

Mamma laughed and pinched my little sister's cheek affectionately. 'Would you like it if I was famous, *cara*?'

'Could I be famous, too? And Carmela and Serafina?' my sister asked.

'I suppose so ... why not?'

'Then yes, I would like it,' Rosalina decided.

It was Carmela who found the gossip item tucked away inside Mamma's magazine. 'Oh, look, there's something here about Mario Lanza.' She frowned as she tried to make out the words. 'I think it says he's coming to Rome.'

'Let me see.' Like Carmela I was a slow reader and made hard work of it. Tracing each line with my finger, I mouthed the words slowly. 'Mario Lanza is rumoured to be filming a movie in Italy called *Arrivederci Roma*. He will be arriving here from his home in America along with his wife Betty and his four children ... Oh and look, there is a picture of them at the bottom of the page. Don't they all look beautiful?'

My mother stared at the magazine for such a long time. I wondered if she was putting herself in the photograph beside Mario, imagining herself in the stylish coat with draped sleeves that his wife wore, hand in hand with perfect children in matching outfits.

I waited, expecting her to find some criticism to make, but for once it seemed she couldn't.

'Do you think we will get to meet him, Mamma? Ask for his autograph?' Carmela always pretended not to care about Mario Lanza but even she seemed excited. 'Maybe if he's staying here in Rome we'll hear him sing?'

Mamma shrugged and muttered, 'Perhaps ... We'll see', which meant she thought it was unlikely.

Once we had eaten our fill of sweet things, we left the café and followed the winding lanes of Trastevere back to our own street. Mamma liked to rest on Sunday afternoons, slathering her face with cold cream to soften her skin and rolling curlers in her hair before lying down for a nap. 'Give me some peace, girls,' she'd mutter. 'It's such a lovely afternoon, why don't you take a walk somewhere? Just be sure you're back in time to cook your sisters some pasta, Serafina.'

I never appreciated how much freedom we had, walking from one side of Rome to the other, going wherever we pleased. When we were thirsty Carmela would take the hat from her head, put it on the ground and begin to sing. Soon enough it was filled with enough money for us to find a bar and buy bottles of ice-cold *aranciata*. If we were among the thick crowds of tourists near the Colosseum or the Pantheon and Carmela was in good voice then the hat filled so much faster and we could afford slices of pizza or *tramezzini*, the triangles of soft white bread filled with savoury things. We might even take a tram ride home.

Usually as we neared our apartment we would hear Mamma's voice well before we saw her, lighted cigarette in hand, leaning out over the narrow terrace where we grew our herbs and tomatoes, calling out my name.

'Serafina ... Serafina ... Serafeeenaaaa.'

My Destiny

I cut out the article about Mario Lanza from *Confidenze* and for safekeeping hid it in a box where I put all the things that were mine. There wasn't a great deal in there. Just a red scarf I didn't want Carmela to lay her hands on, the gold chain with the holy medal I had been given when I was a baby and some birthday cards with Mamma's writing on them. Everything else we shared. The clothes I had outgrown were passed down to my sisters, shoes as well if they weren't too worn. Rosalina's doll had been held in my arms once, her pink ribbons tied in my hair.

I didn't want the others to touch my magazine clipping, though. I liked looking at the photograph of Mario Lanza holding hands with his daughters. They were sweet little girls wearing clean white twin-sets, shiny leather shoes and ankle socks. The caption said the curly-haired one was called Ellisa and she seemed shy, with eyes cast down, while her elder sister Colleen looked taller and more confident.

I never had a papa to hold my hand like that, so firmly and so proud. If Mamma knew who our fathers were she hadn't told us. I suspect she had no idea. There had been so many men and none more than a way for her to make a living.

Never once did Mamma bring a man home to our apartment. Perhaps she rented a room somewhere or went to their hotels; I never dared ask. Back then I didn't know enough to be ashamed of what she did. To me it seemed normal. Throughout the war it had been what fed Mamma and me while other families were starving. It kept her glamorous when other women grew faded and neglected. She never had rough skin on her feet or hair in places it shouldn't be. She and her friends shone with hoops of gold and walked on high heels. They left lipstick stains on every glass they drank from and smelt of L'Air du Temps and Acqua di Colonia. What they did every night after they left their favourite table at the corner bar was never much talked about.

Carmela had been born during the war. Her complexion was fairer than mine and she liked to think her father was an American soldier. Rosalina looked like a real Italian with chocolate eyes and skin that tanned deeply in summer. I still remember Mamma's despair at falling pregnant with her and knowing the seams of her body would stretch and money would be scarce again.

Whoever fathered me might have come from Mamma's hometown. She was born on the plains beneath Vesuvius where her father was a marble cutter. As soon as she was old enough she fled to Rome and now she rarely talked about the person she'd been in the time before Trastevere. But there were things she hated that made me think her family had been poor – cheap cuts of meat that needed to be softened with hours of cooking, clothes that were patched and badly mended, chipped plates and anything second-hand. What Mamma liked was newness and sparkles; she loved reasons to smile. I have never known another woman so certain of what it took to make her happy.

Asking her about our fathers never got us anywhere. Carmela was the one who really itched to know. She was fascinated by anything American: music, movie stars, the tourists we saw. 'Some day I'll go and find my papa,' she promised me.

'Where would you start? You don't even know his name.'

'I'll make Mamma tell me.'

'Perhaps he'll have another family by now and won't want to know you.'

She shrugged off my words. 'There's no point worrying about that. First I need to find him.'

Until I saw that photograph in *Confidenze* I hadn't understood why she cared so much. What could a father give me that I didn't have already? But the picture showed me how a family was meant to look – everyone together, smiling and in their best clothes, hands held in hands: Betty with their sons, Mario and his girls.

'I think I'd like to find my papa too,' I told Carmela.

We were sitting pressed against the railings of our tiny terrace, warming our skin in a shaft of evening sunlight, and Carmela was painting her fingernails with something she'd stolen from Mamma's dresser.

'What do you think he's like?' she asked me.

I closed my eyes and tried to build an image of a man with grey-green eyes walking at my mother's side. But his face was blurry and I couldn't imagine ever having held his hand. 'Who knows?' I said at last.

Carmela tried to help. 'You're beautiful so surely he'd be handsome. And he must be tall because you didn't get your height from Mamma. Do you see him yet?'

'Nearly ... No, not really.' In my head the man had become Mario Lanza and I knew for sure he couldn't be my father.

Carmela held out her scarlet-tipped fingers so the polish would dry without smudging. 'Pretty colour,' she said, satisfied.

'You'll have to clean it off before Mamma sees it.'

'Maybe.'

'She'll be furious at you for wasting her nail polish.'

Carmela looked sullen. 'It's not a waste. It looks good on me.'

Down below us the knife sharpener was calling for business and the street was starting to fill with people. If I craned my neck I might have seen Mamma sitting outside the bar with a glass of something to fortify her for the night ahead.

She had left an hour or so earlier with her nails painted the same stolen scarlet and a new gold charm bracelet on her wrist. By now all her friends would have admired it.

'Do you think we'll be like Mamma?' Carmela said suddenly.

'What do you mean?' I asked, surprised. I had never imagined any of us would take the same path she had. 'Why would we be like her?'

'She thinks we will. I heard her joke about it one day. She was talking with her friends and they were laughing and saying once they'd put their daughters to work they'd have more time to rest.'

'But Mamma didn't mean it, surely?' The idea horrified me.

'Why wouldn't she? Surely you must have realised it. You are old enough now, Serafina, so the time can't be too far away.'

'Never,' I told her. 'Never ever.'

Carmela looked down at her scarlet nails. 'What then? How will you live?'

I had never thought beyond the things I did each day: sweeping the floor and making the bed, shopping for food and ironing our clothes, wandering the streets of Rome with my sisters and finding ways to amuse ourselves.

'I have no idea,' I admitted.

'You ought to think about it,' she warned me.

'I suppose your plan is to sing?'

'Of course.' Carmela looked at me, her sharp little face serious. 'Will you help me, Serafina?'

'Yes, if I can. But how?'

'We have to find out when Mario Lanza is coming to Rome. I want to sing for him. If he likes my voice then who knows what he might do? He may put me in his movie. Perhaps he'll even help me get to America.'

'But, Carmela, you're too young ...' I began.

'I'm going to sing. If you won't help me then I'll find a way to help myself.'

I envied my sister her certainty. Even as a small child she had known exactly what she wanted. It seemed so very unlikely she would ever get to meet Mario Lanza, never mind sing for him, but still I promised to help.

Later, in bed, a sister on either side of me smelling of hot milk and clean hair, I worried about what Carmela had overhead. Surely Mamma didn't expect the three of us to choose her life, to blacken our lashes and pencil our brows and follow her out onto the streets. And yet what else could I do? Apart from keeping house and looking after my sisters, I had no skills or learning. I had left my childhood behind and must have been sleepwalking not to notice.

I lay awake worrying until I heard a key turn in the lock and the creak of our front door. Beside me Carmela shifted and sighed and Rosalina sucked on her thumb.

Mamma was moving around the sitting room. She poured herself a drink, most likely red wine from the bottle she'd opened at dinnertime. There was the click of her lighter as she held it to a cigarette and the scrape of a chair as she sat down. My mother never came to bed straight away, no matter how late she got home. First she needed to relax for a while. And when she did roll onto the mattress, nudging me over with her hips to make more space, there would be a muskiness clinging to her skin, cigar smoke too, perhaps, and the sourness of the wine on her breath.

'Mamma,' I whispered as she pushed open the bedroom door.

'Serafina, aren't you asleep yet?'

'It's too hot,' I lied.

'It's late ... you'll be tired in the morning.'

'Mamma, where have you been tonight?'

'Where? Oh, the usual places. It was a good night. Tomorrow perhaps we'll go and buy some fabric to make you a new dress.' She grunted as she shifted Rosalina onto the mattress. 'You need something pretty – in green, perhaps, to match your eyes.'

'Yes … maybe.' A new dress was tempting.

She lay down and closed her eyes. Already her voice sounded sleepy. 'Spaghetti straps,' she murmured. 'A sweetheart neckline.'

I barely slept that night and when I did my dreams were vague and frightening. The next morning my head ached and my mouth felt gluey. I had no patience with my sisters, snapping at Rosalina for taking too long to strap her feet into her sandals and fighting with Carmela about the scarlet polish on her fingernails.

'You can't go to school like that,' I told her.

'I don't want to anyway. I'd like to sing in the Piazza del Popolo then walk in the gardens.'

'Not today.'

'It's not fair,' Carmela whined as I soaked a ball of cotton wool in nail polish remover. 'Why should I have to go to school if you don't?'

'Because Mamma said so. Today she's taking me to buy fabric for a new dress and I don't have time to go walking all over the city with you.'

'So what? We'll go without you, won't we, Rosalina?' As always my sister was headstrong.

'No, you're going to school.' I seized her hand and began scrubbing her thumbnail clean. 'I'm taking you whether you like it or not. But I'll make you a promise – on the way back I'll buy as many magazines as I can. Don't you want to know if there's more news about Mario Lanza?'

'Yes, I suppose,' she conceded.

Carmela stilled for long enough for me to wipe away the rest of Mamma's scarlet. With her fingernails bare and ordinary, she sulked all the way to school and I was glad to see her swallowed up in a crowd of other girls, someone else's problem until lunchtime.

Relieved to be free of her, I walked to the market at Testaccio to shop for food. Moving quickly from stall to stall, I was careful to search out bargains, filling my basket with tomatoes too ripe for anything but a salsa, the waxy end of a wedge of Parmesan that would still be good in soup, bread that was cheap because its crust had been singed dark brown, tiny artichokes that would have to be eaten soon.

Each evening I cooked for the family, making dishes Mamma had taught me, peasant food she must have once learned from her own mother and the Roman dishes she liked best. With so little space and only a gas burner there were limits to what I could manage but still I did my best. I fried salt cod with onions, made salads of bitter chicory and anchovies, or bowls brimming with pasta creamy with egg yolks and salty with bacon. When my sisters tasted the food and smiled, it made me feel happy.

With my basket so heavy, the walk home from Testaccio always felt long and slow. I envied the girls buzzing past me on scooters, sitting side-saddle with their hair flying in the wind. Once or twice I rested my shopping on the ground, regretting the promise to buy magazines. *Tempo*, *Novella* and *La Settimana* – I needed them all since I had no idea which one might carry news of Mario Lanza.

All was silent in our apartment and Mamma was still sleeping. Careful not to wake her, I moved about quietly, starting a sauce for dinner, chopping an onion and frying it slowly with some fatty trimmings of beef the butcher had sold me for next to nothing. Once the tomatoes were diced and simmering with a dash or two of olive oil, I spread the magazines over the table and began to work my way slowly through them, searching for the name Mario Lanza or, even better, another photograph.

Distracted by the horoscopes and sketches of the latest

fashions, I didn't get far. Half an hour passed as I struggled with the words, and then Mamma emerged, wrapped in a faded orange silk robe. She looked worn out. For the first time I noticed wrinkles beginning to crosshatch beneath her eyes and a few strands of grey streaking her hair.

'Make me some coffee, *cara*,' she asked, husky voiced and already reaching for her carton of cigarettes. 'And a slice of that bread with a little jam, if we have any.'

Pulling a chair to the open window, she sighed and lit a cigarette.

'Are you tired, Mamma?' I asked, cutting the bread and spreading it thickly with a preserve of apricots.

'I'll feel better once I've eaten and had a bath. We're going shopping, aren't we? Don't we have to find some fabric in a pretty green for you?'

'Spaghetti straps and a sweetheart neckline,' I reminded her.

She rubbed her eyes and smiled. 'That's right … you'll look so sophisticated. A woman at last, eh, Serafina?'

Serenade

Often I imagined how it might be to meet Mario Lanza; how his eyes would twinkle and he'd prefer me to all the other girls asking for his autograph. I daydreamed as I walked, helplessly lapsing into thoughts of him when I should have been concentrating on other things.

'Look where you're going, Serafina,' Mamma scolded. 'It's not like you to be so clumsy.'

We spent the morning shopping for fabric, pulling out roll after roll of slithery silks in jewel colours with me shaking my head at every one. Finally, Mamma stopped asking for my opinion and bought a bolt of the shiny rayon she liked best – a green with white polka dots so bold I couldn't imagine wearing it.

'Most girls would be grateful to get a new dress,' my mother grumbled. 'What's wrong with you, Serafina, eh?'

I couldn't admit why I preferred the flower-sprigged cottons and the girlish pastel shades. There were too many other things Mamma and I had never said to each other standing in the way of that.

As we browsed around the shops, her mood improved. She bought some diamante earrings shaped like daisies, a pair of dark sunglasses and some gold sling-back sandals, pulling the cash from her handbag and counting it out carefully before handing it over.

'So many packages to carry and it's getting hot,' she sighed. 'Let's take a taxi home. We can stop at the bar, see if any of the girls are there, have a rest and a drink.'

'But Carmela and Rosalina need picking up from school,' I reminded her.

Mamma seemed unconcerned. 'Your sisters have a key to the apartment, don't they?' she asked.

'Yes …'

'Well, in that case surely Carmela can look after things. It's time she started helping more. She's old enough.'

'They'll be expecting me. I always go to meet them.'

'Carmela will work it out,' Mamma insisted. 'She's not stupid and she knows the way home perfectly well. Don't fuss so much, *cara*.' My mother hailed a taxi. It was the first time I'd ever travelled in one and I slid across the smooth leather seats, captivated by the white curtains to pull across the windows for privacy or shade. As we drove towards Trastevere, my mother hurriedly fixed her face, pressing powder on her nose and cheeks, colouring her lips and smoothing her eyebrows into an arch.

Pulling up outside the bar, she rolled down the window and called out loudly, making sure everyone noticed us stepping from the smart car and weighed down with so many packages.

Two of her friends were sitting at the outdoor table they thought of as their own, sipping at glasses of ruby-red Campari.

'Ciao, *bella*,' they called to my mother. 'Come and show us what you've been buying.'

'Lovely things.' Mamma smiled. 'I spent too much, of course.'

They made space for us at their table, kissing our cheeks, waving at the waiter for more drinks and chattering excitedly at the sight of all the treasures we had found.

'Oh, darling, how pretty,' Mamma's best friend Gianna said when she pulled out her new earrings to show them off. 'But not real diamonds, no?'

'Of course not. Just costume jewellery but still very stylish.

Now let me show you the sandals. These are special.'

Mamma's friends were nowhere near as beautiful as her and they knew it. She never seemed to mind their envy – in fact, I think she enjoyed it. When she'd had an especially good night she found a way of making sure it didn't go unnoticed. There would be some new trinket for them to admire, a fragrance to sniff from her wrist, once even a winter wrap trimmed with real fur.

These were women who wore the wealth they had: gold rings on their fingers, chains around their necks, the very latest fashions. Some rented places far shabbier than our apartment, but so long as they looked good when they stepped out of their front doors they didn't seem to mind.

All of them were captivated by the shininess of Mamma's new gold sandals. Gianna pushed her feet into them, fixed the diamante daisies to her ears and struck a photo model's pose. I looked on awkwardly, unused to being part of things, not quite sure how I was meant to behave.

Perhaps sensing my discomfort, they made an effort to include me. Gianna took the daisies from her ears and clipped them onto mine. Slipping off a couple of rings from her own fingers, she passed them across the table.

'Serafina, you look so plain,' she declared. 'You need some jewels. Try these on. And perhaps a necklace, too. No? But a girl your age needs to start thinking about her appearance. Trust me; no man likes a woman who doesn't bother to make an effort.'

'Gianna,' my mother murmured, 'leave her if she doesn't want to try them.'

'Why would she not want to? Every girl likes to look pretty. Put them on, Serafina,' she urged.

The jewellery looked out of place on me. My hands had only ever been for cooking meals or washing dishes; my fingernails were ragged, my skin reddened and rough.

'You should let me give you a manicure.' Gianna held out

her own fingers to be admired. 'See how I take good care of my nails. I always rub a little oil in the cuticles, keep them filed to the same length and paint them pretty shades. Things like that are important, Serafina, you'll see.'

'She doesn't care about manicures,' Mamma told her, waving at the waiter for another glass of Campari since she had swallowed her first so quickly. 'She isn't ready for things like that yet.'

Gianna stared at me. 'But how old are you?' she demanded.

'Nineteen,' I admitted.

'That's old enough to wear a little make-up and some jewellery,' she declared. 'By the time I was your age I'd left home and—'

'No, Gianna,' my mother said in a low voice and with a warning shake of her head.

Sulky at being silenced, Gianna took back her rings, sliding them onto her fingers. 'If you change your mind about the manicure, the offer still stands,' she murmured.

I smiled but only because it seemed polite. My mother had been right – I didn't want nails that were slick and fake with colour, or to crowd my fingers and throat with metal and move in a cloud of perfume so heavy I could taste it. I had no interest in being like that. Not at all.

Mamma's second glass of Campari went down much more slowly. As she sipped and lit yet another cigarette I tried not to picture my sisters on the school steps waiting for me. I only half listened to the chatter around the table – the talk of where was the best place in the Via Veneto these days and who had been seen with who the night before.

I was pleased when my mother drained the last drops from her glass and decided it was time to go home. 'I have to start on a new dress I'm making for Serafina. I'll see you girls later though, no? We'll have another little drink this evening.'

My sisters had found their way home and were perfectly fine, just as Mamma had promised. Rosalina seemed especially thrilled by the adventure of being free to walk the streets without me. 'We went through the Piazza di Santa Maria and the waiter from the café came out and gave us lollipops,' she said excitedly. 'Mine was lemon flavoured. He asked us to say hello to you, Mamma.'

'Mmm,' my mother replied. She was spreading the green polka-dot fabric across the kitchen table, the pins already in her mouth.

'We came straight home,' Rosalina promised. 'We only stopped to say hello to the man at the newspaper kiosk. He told us Serafina had already been past and bought lots of magazines from him.

'That's nice, *cara*.' Mamma sounded distracted. 'Why don't you girls give me some peace now? Go out on the terrace and enjoy the sun. Take your magazines to look at. Practise your reading.'

We did as we were told, Rosalina only pretending to read because the print was far too small for her. As for Carmela, her fingernails were scarlet again. I noticed them as soon as she turned the first page. She flicked out her tongue when she saw me staring.

'You'll get into trouble,' I hissed.

'I don't care.' My sister held up a copy of *Novella* to block me from view.

I had never noticed before just how many dense columns of words there were in those magazines. Usually we skipped over them, interested mainly in the pictures. But now I had to concentrate, searching for the columns of Hollywood news dotted among the romance stories and fashion spreads.

As Mamma cut the fabric and set her sewing machine humming, I waded through the print until my head ached.

Rosalina grew bored. 'Can't we go back to the piazza? See if the waiter will give me another lollipop?' she whined.

'No, not until we've finished with the magazines.' Carmela was determined.

'But this one's too difficult to read and I don't like it,' Rosalina complained.

'Well, swap with me, then,' Carmela said impatiently. 'Just try not to be so annoying.'

'Girls,' my mother called over the noise of her sewing machine. 'Don't think I can't hear you.'

It was me that found the photograph of Mario Lanza in *Tempo* magazine. It was from his most recent movie, *Serenade*, where he played a singer who loses his voice and falls into the depths of despair. In the picture he was scraping his fingers through the wet clay of a sculpture and wearing an agonised expression.

I scanned the words that accompanied the picture then read them through a second time to be certain I'd understood. 'Oh no, this is terrible news.'

'What does it say?' Carmela demanded.

'That Mario Lanza has lost his voice like he did in *Serenade*. He can't sing any more.'

'Lost his voice?' Carmela sounded disbelieving.

'Listen to what it says,' I told her.

'*Is life imitating art for Mario Lanza? The celebrated tenor has not sung live since pulling out of his Las Vegas concerts last year, citing a sore throat and disappointing his many fans. Critics declared his last album,* Lanza on Broadway, *the worst he had ever released and there are now rumours he has lost his voice entirely just like his character from the movie* Serenade.

'*Born in the city of Philadelphia, Lanza is the son of Italian immigrants. He has been hailed as the new Caruso and seemed destined for greatness. But for some time there have been concerns that the tenor is forcing his voice, especially in the upper register, and this combined with recent bouts of ill health may have ruined it completely which would certainly be a tragedy.*'

Carmela looked shocked. 'If he can't sing any more then

24

surely he won't be coming to Rome to make a movie. Does the article say anything about that?'

'Nothing at all.'

My sister reached for the magazine to see for herself.

'Forcing his voice in the upper register ... What does it mean?' I asked as she read.

'I think it must mean the high notes. That he is pushing himself to reach them.'

'So he's straining his throat and making it sore?'

Carmela shrugged. 'Perhaps. But it makes no sense to me. He's a big star. Why would he risk everything and ruin his voice?'

'In *Serenade* he can't sing because he's heartbroken,' I reminded her. 'Then he falls in love with the beautiful Mexican woman and his voice is restored.'

'That's just a movie. In real life something else must be wrong – a more serious problem than heartbreak.'

'Surely a voice like that could not be lost? It's a gift from God.'

'I don't know,' Carmela admitted. 'Perhaps he's injured it in some way. Poor Mario Lanza. I can't imagine opening my mouth and being unable to sing. If it's true then his life might as well be over. What is he without his voice?'

Ave Maria

Carmela had always been fascinated by Mamma's things – the corsetry that nipped in her waist and held her belly flat; the boned bras to shape her breasts. Sometimes she tried them on, stuffing the spaces her body couldn't fill with tissues and parading through the apartment in satin and lace. Mamma didn't seem to mind her playing dress-up. Nor did she scold when she noticed the scarlet polish on her fingernails or complain when Carmela disappeared one afternoon and returned with her hair cropped like Audrey Hepburn's in *Roman Holiday*. It didn't matter what my sister did, it seemed she got away with it.

But it wasn't Carmela who was being given a new dress with narrow straps to show off tanned shoulders; a bright green dress covered in white polka dots with a skirt cut in a perfect circle so it flared when the wearer danced in it. I saw the expression on her face when Mamma stood me in front of the mirror, checking it fitted the curves of my body.

'Remember that dress will be mine when you outgrow it,' Carmela said. 'Try not to rip or stain it in the meantime.'

I was sure she was wrong. This frock would never be handed down. It was my mother's gift meant just for me.

'What do you think?' Mamma smiled at my reflection in the mirror. '*Bella*, eh?'

'Yes, it's very beautiful,' I agreed.

My mother was quick and clever with fabric, but with this dress she had taken her time, determined there should be no stray stitches or wobbly seams. It looked smart enough to have come from any exclusive shop on the Via Condotti and in it I was a different version of myself, the tip of my ponytail touching my bare back, my breasts swelling above the sweetheart neckline.

'Can I try it on?' Carmela begged. 'Please?'

Mamma laughed. 'It won't fit you, *cara*. You don't have the figure – not yet. In a few years' time, perhaps.'

'But it's wasted on Serafina. She never goes anywhere nice enough to wear a dress like this one.'

'Perhaps now she will,' my mother said lightly. 'Who knows where this dress will take you, eh, Serafina?'

I turned my back so Mamma could unzip me.

'No, no, leave it on,' she insisted. 'You must come with me, show all the girls how perfect you look. Just for a drink, *cara*, that's all. So everyone can see what a fine job I did with the dress.'

Carmela insisted on helping me get ready. She loved Mamma's little jars of creams, the soft pouf to dip into loose powder, the lipsticks in gold cases and most of all the pancake make-up from Max Factor of Hollywood that the advertisements claimed was Elizabeth Taylor's favourite.

'Can I come, too?' she wheedled, spreading make-up over her cheeks and admiring her reflection. 'Just for a glass of Coca-Cola if I promise to be good.'

Mamma smiled and shook her head. 'Sometimes you're so like I was at your age, Carmela … so like me.'

At the corner bar there were yellow sun umbrellas fluttering in the breeze and American rock 'n' roll music was turned up loud. All of Mamma's friends were there, clustered round their favourite table, and they called for more Campari the moment they saw us coming. The waiter put a segment of orange in mine, and a coloured paper umbrella that poked above the rim. 'Your first cocktail,' he announced, planting it on the table with a flourish.

Everyone made such a fuss, admiring the dress, making me twirl so they could see the flare of the skirt. They pulled my hair from its ponytail, exclaiming when it fell into soft waves around my face.

'Enchanting,' Mamma declared.

'Yes, much better,' Gianna conceded.

The Campari was bitterer than I'd expected but the drink was pleasantly fizzy and I sipped carefully so it wouldn't drip down my new dress. As soon as I had emptied the glass, they ordered me another.

'Your second cocktail,' the waiter laughed and I finished that one more quickly, enjoying the way it was helping to blur and soften everything.

One of the women placed a gold bangle round my wrist and I didn't complain, even though I hated the feeling of gold warmed by another woman's skin. They teased my hair and glossed my lips in red. I even allowed Gianna to file my fingernails and blow cigarette smoke in my face. It felt as if we were having a party, a nice time.

Then my mother glanced at the light leaching from the sky and down at the watch on her wrist. 'It's getting late,' she said and all the gaiety stopped.

Faces were powdered hastily. Gianna spritzed more perfume on her wrists and pressed them behind her ears. 'Are you coming with us?' she asked.

Mamma replied on my behalf. 'No, not tonight,' she murmured. 'Serafina is going back to her sisters now.'

Gianna threw me a look – half amusement, half disdain – then dismissed me with a shrug of her shoulders. 'Of course, run home with the children. The rest of us will go to work.'

Run I did, hitching my skirt in my hands, my head pounding with the alcohol I had drunk, not stopping until I was standing outside the entrance to our apartment.

Inside Carmela was playing a Mario Lanza record; I could hear his voice through the closed door. He was singing 'Ave

Maria', the sound so clear and pure. I closed my eyes and stayed there, remembering how in his movie *Serenade* the song marks the moment Mario realises his lost talent has returned. He begins the first few bars hesitantly then lets his voice go free and soar until the whole church rings with it. I had heard that recording of 'Ave Maria' a hundred times or more but that night, pushing the door ajar to listen better, the music seemed like a miracle.

'Who's that?' Carmela called, turning down the volume. 'Serafina, is it you? Why are you standing outside like that?'

'I was listening to Mario Lanza,' I told her. 'Turn up the sound and play "Ave Maria" again so I can hear it from the beginning.'

She and Rosalina had pulled the pillows from the bed and were sprawling on the floor listening to the music. I joined them there, hearing the crackle as Carmela lifted the needle and placed it gently back at the beginning of the song. To start with there was church organ music and then Mario softly joining it, singing each word as if it were precious. His voice grew stronger, filling our whole apartment; and it seemed to fill me, too – I felt it in every part of my body.

When the last note had sounded, we were all quiet for a few moments. And then Carmela asked the question that had been in my mind also while Mario was singing the prayer.

'What do you think he sounds like now? I wonder if he can still perform "Ave Maria" as beautifully as that.'

'Surely he can.'

Carmela stared at the record sleeve with its glossy photograph of a handsome man dressed in a black evening suit, caught mid-song, his head thrown back and his hand gesturing.

'Not if he's lost his voice like that magazine said. I wish we could find out if it's true.'

Lying on her back, Rosalina kicked at a pillow impatiently.

'Who cares? We can still listen to him, can't we? We have all of Mamma's records. Stop talking and play "Nessun Dorma". That's the one I like best.'

She was right in a way. Even if he had been silenced we still had his voice right there in our apartment. In the weeks that followed I played his songs until the neighbours hammered on the walls for me to stop. I liked the opera arias as much as the show tunes, didn't care if he sang in English or Italian, so long as it was his voice, as whole and true as it had ever been.

The polka-dot dress stayed on its hanger. I didn't wear it to join Mamma at the bar a second time. Instead, every night after she had gone to work I curled up with my sisters and we listened to Mario Lanza. His voice always reached me, pushing away the worries that pressed on the edges of my mind. It stopped me thinking about a time when I would have to wear polish on my nails and rings on my fingers. It shut out the future. My world was his singing and his smile, and nothing else mattered so long as there was a record turning on the table.

Be My Love

The famous tenor Mario Lanza has arrived in Napoli aboard the liner Giulio Cesare. *Thousands of cheering fans waited to greet him as he walked down the gangplank and he was taken by limousine to an official reception where he was made an honorary citizen of the city. Afterwards he made a brief visit to the tomb of the legendary opera star Enrico Caruso and told the press how happy he was to be in Italy at last. Tomorrow Signore Lanza and his family will travel onwards by train to Rome where they are to stay at the Bernini Bristol Hotel in Piazza Barberini.*

I was alone listening to the radio and washing our dirty clothes in the kitchen sink when I heard the announcement. Mamma was at the hairdresser's having the grey I'd noticed dyed away and my sisters were at school. There was no one to share my excitement that Mario Lanza was in Italy. Soon he would be right here in my own city, breathing the same air as me. I gave a little squeak and dropped the underwear I'd been rinsing back into the sudsy water.

Knowing she'd be just as thrilled, I was impatient to tell Carmela. Surely she would want to go to Piazza Barberini first thing in the morning and wait outside the hotel until the great tenor arrived. Her plan was to pretend to be an autograph hunter and then surprise him with her singing. She was convinced he would recognise her talent and it would be the beginning of all the good things that were going to happen to her.

On the radio they were playing one of his recordings to celebrate his arrival – 'Santa Lucia', a Neapolitan favourite. It was all I could do to finish the laundry and peg it out on the line strung across our terrace. Then I had to mop up the pools of spilt water and put some cannellini beans in a pan to soak before I could change into clean clothes and go to find my sisters.

Waiting at the school steps with the other sisters and mothers, I held back from sharing the news. 'Mario Lanza is here at last,' I wanted to say. 'I've listened to his songs, seen his movies and now I may have the chance to see him in the flesh.' I imagined the blank looks among those who didn't appreciate his singing and saved my excitement for Carmela.

By then it was late May and already the heat in the city was building. I wondered what Mario might do with his time here this summer. Would he spend the days with his family at the beach and while away his evenings at the expensive cafés in the Via Veneto? Would he eat pasta or American food? Would he sing in public and still have the voice to do it? Now he was here, anything seemed possible.

By the time Carmela appeared, I was desperate to tell what I knew. 'Mario Lanza has arrived. He is in Napoli,' I called out as I spotted her in the column of girls filing from the school entranceway. 'Can you believe it? We've waited so long for this.'

I had imagined how she might greet the news, jigging in excitement, demanding to know all the details and chattering about her plans to meet the famous singer. Instead, Carmela's dark grey eyes seemed steely, her face set and calm, her voice steady.

'When will he come to Rome?' she asked.

I told her what little I knew as we walked home, Rosalina lagging behind us.

'This is my chance,' Carmela said once I had finished. 'I have to meet him.'

'Shall we go and wait for him at his hotel, do you think?'

'No, let's go to the train station. I want Mario Lanza to see me the moment he arrives in Rome.'

'We should get there early. There are bound to be lots of his fans wanting a glimpse of him at Stazione Termini. If we're late we won't get a good spot and he'll never notice us.'

'Fine, let's go early.' Giving me a sideways glance, Carmela added slyly, 'I'm going to wear the polka dots.'

'No.'

'Please, Serafina.'

'That dress is mine.' Even though I rarely took it from the rail, still I didn't want my sister to have it.

'Just this once. I have to look good and none of my own clothes are right.'

'It won't fit you properly.'

'I'll make it fit, you'll see. When Mario Lanza steps off the train at Termini the first thing he'll see is a girl in polka dots and the first thing he'll hear is my singing.'

Carmela was so determined, I couldn't say no. The minute we were home she rushed to try on the dress. It didn't look as bad as I'd imagined. Perhaps it was a little long and she would have to pad out the hollows of her chest with cotton wool but the shade of green suited her and the style made her look years older.

'What are you going to sing for him?' I asked. 'Something Italian or an American song?'

'American,' she said with certainty.

'Which one?'

'"Be My Love", of course.'

I could picture the scene. The train arriving, the crowds cheering as Mario Lanza appeared for the first time, then the sound of a young girl's voice and everyone falling silent to listen. Surely he would be impressed and want to know her name. Perhaps he might even invite Carmela back to his hotel and ask her to sing some more for him.

The same thoughts must have been running through my sister's head as we lay side by side struggling to get some rest that night. Both of us tossed and fidgeted until Mamma complained that we were stealing her sleep.

In the morning Carmela was the first out of bed for once. I smelt coffee beans grinding and heard the low drone of the radio as she listened for more news.

Careful not to wake my mother, I crept out to join her. 'Is there anything?' I asked.

'Not yet.' Carmela looked tense. 'Will you keep listening while I go down the hall to the bathroom?'

There was another Lanza song playing, an American one called 'Because You're Mine' and I wished it had been 'Be My Love' since that would have seemed a better sign. Turning up the volume a little, I finished making the coffee.

When the music stopped, the announcer began:

At a reception yesterday at Napoli's beautiful Internazionale restaurant, the American tenor Mario Lanza and his family were welcomed officially to Italy. His co-star, our own Renato Rascel, entertained him with some music, including a song from the film they will soon be making together. Signore Lanza himself did not sing but he told reporters he was looking forward to his new life here and had felt instantly at home in Italy.

Then they played more music, this time Renato Rascel singing an Italian song. His voice seemed frail in comparison to Mario's and I felt sorry for him. Carmela spent a long time in the bathroom and when she reappeared I noticed she smelt strongly of Mamma's perfume. I didn't say a word; nor did I try to stop her painting her nails scarlet or smoothing make-up on her face. Once she was ready, I helped her into my polka-dot dress and watched while she strapped her feet into my mother's gold sandals.

34

Rosalina whined at being woken so early, complaining too when she was hustled out of the apartment without any breakfast. Only the news that she wasn't going to school silenced her; that and a whispered promise of creamy pastries coaxed her quietly enough from the apartment for us not to disturb our mother.

Walking all the way to Termini would have taken much too long so we paid for a tram instead. Even so, I could feel Carmela's impatience as it lurched to a stop at the Porta Portese, people crowding off and on.

'Don't worry, we won't be late,' I reassured her.

'We have no idea what time he's arriving so how can you be certain?' she asked sharply, her nerves showing now.

Arriving at Termini it felt like an ordinary morning; men in business suits pouring from trains, stopping to throw back an espresso or buy a newspaper, then hurrying to their offices. There was no sign that today was different, that soon the great American tenor would arrive, the man they said was surely the new Caruso.

We found the platform and a place to settle and wait. For a while there was no one there but us and I wondered if we'd got it wrong and Mario Lanza wasn't due to come at all. Gradually, though, people began to cluster in groups around us. By lunchtime, when I went to buy slices of pizza and bottles of mineral water, I had to fight my way back through a thickening horde to find my sisters.

All sorts of people were there among the crowd: grand-mothers, young women and middle-aged men; I even heard English voices. Every time a train from Napoli pulled into the station we seemed to surge and move as one, and I held tightly to Rosalina's hand, scared she might fall and be crushed underfoot.

By late afternoon, with still no sign of Mario Lanza, the three of us were becoming impatient. Around us people were sharing the food they'd brought: rough bread filled with salami and olives, coarse chunks of Parmesan, bags of boiled lupin seeds.

'It doesn't seem like he will ever come,' I said to Carmela. 'Perhaps we should go home.'

'No.'

'But Rosalina's tired and Mamma will be getting worried.'

'You go, then. I am staying here,' Carmela insisted.

I couldn't abandon my sister and anyway I wanted to see Mario Lanza just as much as she did. So we waited and waited.

It was evening by the time his train arrived. By then the crowd had swollen and there was no space to move. People were waving banners and chanting, 'We want Mario.' Reporters and film cameramen were swarming onto the platform. As the train drew up there was a huge and deafening cheer from everyone.

'I can see him, I can see him,' I shouted to Carmela who was standing on her tiptoes struggling for a view.

It was the most wonderful moment. As his train drew in there was Mario Lanza leaning out of the open window, blowing kisses to the crowd: his face so familiar from the movies I'd seen, his grin wide and happy. Once it halted he held up each of his children in turn so they could wave to us. I thought they looked older and bigger than they had seemed in the photograph I had clipped from *Confidenze* but still I recognised them straight away – Colleen, Ellisa, Damon and Marc. The little girls were wearing pretty white hats and both were smiling. The boys seemed more timid. Finally his wife Betty appeared beside him, waving a white-gloved hand, looking beautiful and so stylish.

The crowd was roaring louder and louder and, when I felt Carmela jogging my arm, I had to lean down to hear what she was shouting. 'We must get closer,' she told me. 'Push through, push.'

I tried but it was hopeless. As Mario Lanza stepped from

the train he was engulfed. Reporters bombarded him with questions and autograph hunters waved their notebooks in the air. Flashbulbs were popping and people were holding up microphones to his face. No one noticed the small girl in the polka-dot dress or heard a single note when she tried to sing.

Still we waited, hoping the crowds would tire and Carmela might get her chance. But the cheering showed no sign of dying down. If anything, more people were gathering, attracted by the noise and fuss, until we were hemmed in and half crushed by the press of bodies.

'Mario, we love you', 'Mario you're wonderful,' they were calling to him. 'Let me kiss you, Mario.'

A pack of fans followed the singer right out of the station and into the piazza. We were pulled along whether we wanted it or not. Every glimpse I got of him he seemed thrilled and excited, turning to wave again and again, shaking people's hands and signing his name on the scraps of paper they gave him.

He loved the crowd and can't have wanted to leave. As he was being led to his car, he stopped and broke away, heading to a nearby horse and carriage instead. To everyone's delight he climbed aboard and, standing above the sea of heads, waving his arms in the air, he called out more greetings to the crowd. It was exactly like one of my favourite scenes from his movie *The Great Caruso*.

At last I had a better view. I could see he was wearing a smart dark suit, his tie slightly crooked, and he looked handsome but rather tired. It was a thrill to have such a great and famous man right there in front of me. Mario Lanza, in the flesh. Forgetting about my poor sister, I joined in the cheering.

By the time he'd torn himself from the crowds and been driven away, it was extremely late; the sky was inky and the piazza in front of Termini layered with dropped streamers and banners. Clutching a yawning Rosalina between us, we walked slowly back to the tram stop.

'We'll go to his hotel in Piazza Barberini; we'll try again,' I promised a disappointed Carmela. 'There won't be such a great crowd next time.'

But she was tired and had lost her spirit; she didn't want to be consoled by me. 'Perhaps,' she said. 'We'll see.'

I had never seen my mother as angry as she was when we got home that night. Her skin was washed pale, her mouth a thin line. She must have spent hours pacing the apartment, pausing now and then to lean from the terrace and scan the street below. Mamma knew what Rome could be like once it got dark and had imagined the worst. There was no way she could leave, not while she had no idea what had become of us. She had wasted a whole night when she might have been working and her purse was empty. But what she seemed most furious about was the sight of Carmela in my polka-dot dress with her own gold sandals on her feet.

'What do you think you're doing? Take them off,' she cried, thrusting rough fingers down the front of the frock to tug out the cotton wool that was padding out my sister's bust.

At first Mamma shouted and then she began to cry, a strange gasping sound I had never heard before. Rosalina joined in noisily, still clinging to my hand as tightly as she had when we were caught in the crowd. As for Carmela, she lowered the lids of her eyes and stayed quiet until it was over.

'It was my fault,' she admitted as Mamma stripped off the dress and left her in her underwear. 'I wanted to see Mario Lanza. I didn't know he'd be so late. I'm sorry.'

'And was it worth it?' my mother asked bitterly. 'Was it worth all the trouble you've caused me?'

'I wanted to sing for him. I didn't realise there would be so many people and so much noise.' Carmela's tears came hot and fast. 'I'm sorry, I'm sorry.'

'Stupid girl,' Mamma said but her tone was less harsh.

'I thought if I were the first one he heard he might remember me. But I couldn't even see him properly. And now ... now ...' She leaned her head against my mother's chest and sobbed out the words. 'Now you're so angry with me.'

'But, *cara*, I was worried,' Mamma explained, wrapping her arms around Carmela and rocking her slightly. 'I kept telling myself you were sensible girls and nothing bad had happened but I couldn't imagine where you'd gone. Do you have any idea how late it is?'

'Past midnight?' Carmela guessed.

'Later than that, much later. Go to bed now. We'll talk about this in the morning. You too, Serafina. You have your share of blame for this, I'm certain, but now is not the time to discuss it. We're all exhausted.'

As my mother tucked us into bed I heard Rosalina's voice, tired and still muddy with tears. 'Past midnight,' she said wonderingly. 'I've never been awake as late as this before.'

'No, and you won't be again,' Mamma told her. 'Not for a long time.'

She clicked off the light, shut the door firmly and went out onto the terrace to smoke a last cigarette for the night. Pressing our faces into the pillows we didn't dare even whisper to each other. None of us wanted to hear Mamma shouting again or see her tears.

From the way their breathing changed I could tell my sisters had fallen asleep quickly but I was beyond being tired. Lying awake, I remembered Mario Lanza standing on the carriage, his arms above his head like a champion, warmed by the appreciation of the crowds. I was tall enough to see him more clearly than most. I had even heard his voice. 'Thank you. I love you!' he had cried in English and Italian. 'I love you all.'

By now he would be in his suite at the Hotel Bernini Bristol. There would be fine furniture and flowers, perhaps even champagne. The little children would be sleeping soundly and he and his wife would be looking out over the domes and rooftops, toasting their future here in Rome.

Fools Rush In

Marisa Allasio, the Brigitte Bardot of Italy, is to star opposite Mario Lanza in his new film Arrivederci Roma. *Signore Lanza told our reporter he was lucky to get such a talented actress and she is sure to be a big hit. Recording of the musical soundtrack is expected to begin soon at the Vatican's Auditorium Angelico Studios.*

'Marisa Allasio.' My mother said the name scathingly. 'Why do they not get the real Brigitte Bardot for their movie instead of the pretend one?'

'She is very beautiful,' I argued, turning up the radio in case there was more news of Mario.

'But he is a big Hollywood star. This reporter must be a *cretino* to believe every line the film studio feeds him. Surely the truth is they can't afford anyone more famous? Marisa Allasio ... beh,' Mamma said dismissively.

Since the night we'd scared her by getting home so late, my mother had spent more time with us and been stricter. Most days she collected my sisters from school and supervised their homework. If we wanted to leave the apartment during the afternoon she demanded to know where we were going and exactly when we'd return. All of our freedom had disappeared. There had been no chance to go to Piazza Barberini and stand outside his hotel waiting for Mario Lanza to appear. All we had to keep us going was the occasional radio announcement and snippets of news in magazines, and they didn't tell us much.

The more trapped she felt the more determined Carmela became to find a way of singing for him, although so many other girls would be trying to do the same. With every day that passed her chance seemed to slip further away. I knew how frustrated she must feel but like me she understood it was better to stay quiet until Mamma tired of being so attentive and relaxed her grip on us.

It took some weeks to win back our freedom and by the time we managed to get there, Mario Lanza and his family were long gone from the Hotel Bernini Bristol. The concierge refused to tell us where to find him but Carmela was crafty. She pinched poor Rosalina so hard she started up an ear-splitting squealing until, purely to be rid of us, the concierge muttered, 'Try the Excelsior on Via Veneto.'

It was only a short walk to the Excelsior, stopping along the way to buy a lollipop to soothe a still fractious Rosalina. Outside the hotel we found a few autograph hunters clustered on the pavement and I asked whether they expected Mario Lanza to arrive or leave any time soon.

'We're waiting for him to return,' they told us. 'Usually he comes back at lunchtime.'

One of the women already had his signature. Proudly she showed it to Carmela. 'I'm collecting them,' she explained. 'I'm hoping he'll come soon so I can get another one.'

Carmela shrugged, not caring about a name scrawled on a piece of paper. For her meeting Mario Lanza was only ever about the singing. But I was interested. The woman wouldn't let me touch her autograph book, agreeing only to hold it up so I could take a better look. Still I could see his writing, the letters looping in violet ink, the name quite legible, a little intimate piece of him.

'I'm going to ask if he'll sign a photograph this time,' the woman confided. 'Then I can put it on my wall at home.'

We waited for hours in the glare of the sun, bored, hot and thirsty, all of us lost in our own thoughts. When the car drew up we were the last to notice. Suddenly there was a flurry of excitement and, calling his name, the autograph hunters surged forward.

Mario Lanza's chauffeur climbed out first, smartly uniformed and wearing a grey cap emblazoned with the words 'Titanus Studios'.

'Get back, get back; give Signore Lanza some space,' the chauffeur ordered and, opening a large black umbrella, held it up to shield the singer as he emerged from the car.

He was smiling, of course. Ducking free of the umbrella, he seemed pleased with the small crowd, shaking hands and signing autographs. I was near enough to see him very clearly. His eyes were darkly shadowed and his brow etched with lines, his cheeks fuller than they seemed on screen and there was a small pouch of flesh beneath his chin. In all of his movies Mario Lanza looked smoother and more polished than this. Yet still to my eyes he was beautiful.

Carmela stood back from the crowd, patiently waiting her turn. Only once he was moving towards the hotel entrance did she begin to sing 'Be My Love'. My sister's voice was strong and steady, as warm as it had ever been. She sang for him with all her body and I was pleased when he paused to listen, waiting for her to hit the high note at the finish before beginning to clap.

'*Brava, brava*. You sang it beautifully. Well done,' he called.

Before Carmela could reply, he had swept up the steps, through the entrance of the Excelsior and was gone. Neither of us could believe our moment had passed so quickly. Dazed, we stood among the autograph hunters, staring at the door he had disappeared through.

'What now?' I asked.

'We follow him, of course,' Carmela said, determined.

'We can't ...' I began but already my sister had launched

43

herself past the doorman and into the lobby. All I could do was grab Rosalina by the hand and follow her.

Inside it was cool, hushed, perfumed, even the air felt exclusive. Chandeliers hung from vaulted ceilings and uniformed men stood behind a long desk. A braver woman like my mother might have stalked across these shining marble floors with her head held high but I had never seen a place so grand. Already I felt as though we were being stared at and measured: our clothes, our shoes, even our hair, none of it coming up to scratch. There was no sign of Signore Lanza, only my sister standing in the middle of the lobby looking awkward.

'Carmela, let's go,' I hissed but she ignored me. Instead she approached the desk and said something to one of the dark-suited men who was busy writing in a ledger. I saw him push his spectacles up his nose, glare at her and shake his head. She turned and pointed at me but he shook his head again, more definitely this time, and resumed scratching on the paper with his fountain pen.

'But please,' Carmela said more loudly. 'My sister is here for an interview with Signore Lanza.'

Looking up, the man frowned. 'An interview, you say? *Va bene*, I will try to call the suite. It is pointless, though, they never answer.' Picking up the receiver he began to dial. The phone must have rung close on ten times before he gave up and put it back down. 'You see?'

'But they are expecting her,' Carmela insisted.

'I don't think so.'

'Please ...'

'I haven't had any instructions.'

Carmela stepped up to the desk and lowered her voice. 'Signore Lanza wants my sister to work as a governess for his children,' she lied smoothly. 'He won't be pleased if he has no one to care for them.'

A different expression crossed the man's face then: less

stern, hopeful almost. He glanced at me. 'You are really a governess?' he asked.

Trapped in my sister's untruth, I had to continue it.

'Yes.' I didn't quite manage to meet his eyes.

'And you are going to look after the Lanza children? All four of them?'

'I would like to.' This, at least, was not a lie.

The man made a sound that began as a sigh and turned into a dry cough. 'I suppose you can go up,' he relented. 'Not with these two, though. They must wait for you here.'

Carmela shot me a look, imploring and desperate. She pressed her palms together as though she was praying. 'Thank you,' she said to the man behind the desk.

'Fifth floor, the Cupola Suite,' he muttered, before turning back to his ledger. 'And good luck.'

Throwing Carmela one last furious glance I crept across the gleaming stretch of lobby towards the elevator. Like everything else in the Excelsior it was over-sized, the interior mirrored and embellished. As it propelled me towards Mario Lanza's floor, I checked my reflection, smoothing my hair nervously, making sure my fingernails weren't grubby and my clothes were in good order. I told myself I would find the courage to knock on his door and beg for another chance for Carmela to sing. Most likely he would send me away but at least I could try.

The lift doors opened with a soft hum and, stepping out into a carpeted corridor, I saw high double doors and a discreet gold sign that read 'Cupola Suite'. Daunted, I paused and might have turned back if the door hadn't opened and a small boy hurtled through it, his face red-stained with tomato sauce, his mouth wide open and screaming.

'Don't like it, want hamburger,' he shouted before barrelling towards me.

I recognised him at once, was surprised when no one bothered to come after him. The child was nearly at the elevator when I bent, arms outstretched, and stopped him with my body. 'Damon, where are you going?' I asked in my faulty English.

He gazed at me in surprise. 'How do you know my name?'

'I've seen a photograph of you.'

'Where?' he asked. A sweet little boy, he smelt of the soap used to wash his clothes and clean his hair.

'I saw it in a magazine. You were with your papa.'

Damon nodded as though it made sense. He looked very like his father, with dark eyes and a button nose. Taking his hand, just as I would my sister Rosalina's, I tried to lead him back towards the Cupola Suite.

"Don't want to,' he insisted, pulling against me. 'Mommy is crying and the spaghetti tastes bad.'

'Bad spaghetti in Italy? But that is a crime,' I said lightly.

He stared at me, his face serious, tipping his head to one side. 'Really?'

'Yes, of course.'

'Can we call the police?' he asked hopefully.

I smiled and offered my mother's stock reply. 'Perhaps. We'll see.'

At last the child allowed me to take him back, noisily whooping the sound of a police siren all the way through the open doors and into the foyer of the Cupola Suite.

That place was like nothing I'd ever seen: so vast, such richness and luxury, almost like a church. There was a frescoed dome, polished wood panelling on every wall, so much gold, velvet and softness everywhere. But the first thing that struck me wasn't the beauty of it all but the way it had been ruined: the clutter of dropped toys and discarded shoes, the clothes left in muddled piles, the cushions pulled from the furniture and strewn around the floor and the clamour of children crying.

I knew them from the photograph I'd pored over. The youngest one – Marc – was lying on the floor, beating his heels against a rug; the elder sister – Colleen – was wailing too. Only the younger of the two sisters – Ellisa – was sitting at the dining table, forking up spaghetti calmly as though this unruly scene was nothing out of the ordinary.

I realised there was a woman sitting alone on one of the couches. Her face was wet with tears and her eyes still full of them, her hair un-brushed, her robe unclean. She was barely recognisable as the same cool beauty that had waved a white-gloved hand from a train's open window as it pulled into Stazione Termini.

'Signora Lanza?' I asked hesitantly.

She turned and looked towards me but something seemed wrong with her eyes, they were glazed, unseeing.

'Are you all right?' I asked. 'Can I do anything to help you?'

Burying her head into a cushion, she ignored me. It seemed her children were meant to fend for themselves. A pasta bowl was upturned in the middle of the dining table, the sauce seeping over the fine wood. The sight jarred. Our table at home was only Formica yet still I'd never have left such a mess on it. Righting the bowl, I cleared up the sticky tangle of spaghetti and looked for a cloth to wipe away the sauce. Once I'd finished it made sense to pick up the dropped toys, fold the crumpled clothes and line the shoes neatly beneath a table. There was a satisfaction in restoring order to such a beautiful place that I'd never found tidying our little apartment in Trastevere.

Colleen had stopped crying and was watching me carefully. Ellisa kept eating and said nothing. As for Signora Lanza, she had balled herself up on the velvet-covered couch and seemed to be sleeping. It didn't seem right to leave her alone with the children. I hovered for a while, uncertain whether I should try to wake her or find help.

Damon reached up and touched my elbow. 'Can we call the police now?' he asked.

47

'The spaghetti seems fine to me,' I told him. 'And see how your sister is finishing all of hers. No need for the police.'

'But I'm still hungry,' he complained. 'I want a hamburger.'

'I want one too.' It was Colleen, her face still ruddy, streaks of tears drying on her cheeks. 'If you phone them, they will bring it. That's what Mommy always does.'

I wondered why there was no one to care for these children since their mother seemed so ill. Surely movie stars were meant to have a retinue of helpers to keep their children well fed and scrubbed, neatly dressed in matching clothes and ready to be photographed. Where were the nurses, the nannies and tutors? Something was wrong.

I hesitated and Damon began to grizzle again while Colleen's face crumpled. 'We're hungry,' they complained.

I picked up the phone. What else was I to do?

It pleased me to see the room so orderly and calm, the children at the dining table, their faces clean, quietly eating the hamburgers I'd ordered. For a moment I let myself forget the real reason I was there. Then I heard footsteps sounding on marble, the rattle of a key in a lock. The door of the Cupola Suite was flung open and there he was filling its frame, the great Mario Lanza.

I could only stare. To be there in the same room, to be so very near and almost a part of his world … it was unbelievable. I barely managed to breathe, never mind speak. Still as a lampstand, I stood in the corner, quietly watching the scene unfold.

The smile he'd worn for his fans had gone, his hair was rumpled and the tie was pulled loose from his throat. Striding across the room, he reached for a decanter from the sideboard, pouring a glass half full with amber liquid and drinking it down. Then he turned to his wife, still collapsed on the couch, and scowled at her.

'Goddamit, what's wrong now, Betty?' he asked.

48

Holding her hands over her face, she refused to answer.

'Didn't I tell you we have to go to this reception Bob Edwards has organised? Welch will be there, Rowland, Stoll and a whole bunch of reporters. We can't miss it.' He poured himself another drink. 'Look at you ... shouldn't you be at the hairdresser or something? You're not going to let me down, are you? Come on, get up.'

'The governess quit,' she told him, her voice muffled as her hands were still pressed to her face. 'We had a fight and she walked out. It wasn't my fault. The foolish girl wouldn't listen to what I was telling her.'

His eyes swept over me before returning to his wife. 'If the governess has quit then who the hell is that?' he asked, gesturing towards me, glass in hand.

Uncurling herself unsteadily from the sofa, she gave me a glance. 'I have no idea. She just walked in and started tidying up, then ordered some lunch for the children and made them stop crying, thank God, because they've been on and on for hours.'

'Did the hotel send her up?' Draining his glass, he tossed it back on the counter so carelessly I was amazed it didn't shatter.

'I told you, I don't have a clue who she is. I suppose they must have sent her because the kids were making such a terrible racket. Perhaps some other guest complained again. Where have you been all this time, anyway? Downstairs in the bar, I guess?'

Damon must have sensed his parents were set for a fight. Winding himself round his father's legs, rubbing his head against him, he tried to divert his attention. 'Poppa, Poppa,' he keened.

Softening a little, Mario asked the child, 'What's happening, eh? What's going wrong around here today?' He reached down and ruffled his son's hair.

49

'The spaghetti was bad. I couldn't eat it. That lady got me a hamburger instead.' Damon pointed at me.

'I showed her how to call for it on the telephone,' Colleen added proudly. 'I told her what to do.'

His eyes met mine for the first time and he stared at me for a moment. I felt as though he'd taken in every detail from the scuffmarks on my shoes to the strands of hair escaping my ponytail. Never had a man looked at me with such intensity before and I dropped my own gaze to the floor.

'Did the agency send you?' he asked me in Italian.

'I'm sorry, Signore Lanza, so sorry,' was all I managed to stammer.

'Sorry? Why?'

'I am not a governess,' I admitted.

'Who are you then?' His tone was brisk. 'Do you work for the hotel?'

'No, Signore. I was downstairs by the entrance earlier and my sister sang for you. Do you remember? She has a lovely voice. She gave you "Be My Love".'

He frowned. 'Yes, yes, I remember. But it doesn't explain why you are here in my suite.'

'I came up to ask if you would please listen to her again. She wants to be a singer so much.'

'And you just walked right on in?'

'The door was open ... your little boy was in the corridor ... I brought him in.'

He glanced down at Damon. 'Is that so?' he said. 'You decided to run away, did you?'

The child nodded. 'The spaghetti ... I didn't like it.'

'You naughty boy.' He smiled indulgently at his son and looked back at me. 'Thank you for taking care of him.'

'You're very welcome, Signore. I will go now. I'm sorry to have intruded.'

As I moved towards the door, I saw his wife clutch at his arm. 'Don't let the girl leave,' she pleaded. 'There's no one else to look after them. How am I supposed to come out to this reception with you? I can't leave them on their own.'

'Heck, Betty, this girl is a stranger who's walked in off the street.' He was speaking English again but slowly enough for me to understand well enough. 'She could be anybody at all. Of course we can't leave our children with her. She shouldn't have been here in the first place. Why don't you talk to someone on the desk downstairs? I'm sure they'll find help for today. Tomorrow you can get the agency to send over another governess.'

'But she's so good with them. Better than all the women the agency have offered us. Please, Mario darling, can't she stay?'

Sensing my chance, I spoke up. 'I would be pleased to help,' I said tentatively. 'I am very good with children and I'm a hard worker.'

'Sure.' He sounded wearied by this domestic trivia. 'If you want to apply for the job then we will need the usual references. Give them to my wife, she can decide.'

'References?' I asked, confused.

'Yes, character references ... from your doctor, your priest, a previous employer ... anyone like that would do.'

'I can't,' I said, floundering.

'No references, no job. That's how it is.'

He reached for the door and I knew it would be the last time I ever had an opportunity like this one.

'There is nobody who could give me a reference. It's impossible for me.'

He sighed, his fingers already on the door handle. 'What's so difficult? There must be a family lawyer or a teacher who could vouch for you.'

'There is no one.' Hot desperate tears began to leak from the corners of my eyes and I scrubbed them away with my knuckles. 'I left school when I was fourteen to care for my little sisters. The teachers won't remember me.'

'Then I'm sorry. It was kind of you to help my wife this morning but we would never take a governess without references. No one with an ounce of sense would.'

He opened the door and I glimpsed the corridor beyond it and the elevator that would take me straight back down to Carmela's disappointment.

'Signore, my mother is a prostitute.' My hands flew to my mouth. I'd never used the word before, barely even thought it. I couldn't believe it had rushed from me now.

Mario Lanza took a step back and then he actually laughed. 'Your mother is a Roman prostitute and you want me to let you care for my children? Do you think I'm *pazzo*?'

'But, Signore, I don't want the same life for me and my sisters.' I was crying properly now, had given up trying to hide it. 'I want something better. I'll do anything; work all the hours, clean, cook, whatever you need. Please help me, let me prove myself. Help my little sisters.'

His expression was stern but I kept talking, as if by words and sheer will I could make him understand the good person I was. 'If you were to trust me with your children I'd look after them as though they were my own family,' I promised. 'I care about my family, Signore. I love them. They are the most important thing in the world to me.'

He moved towards the telephone and I feared he was going to call the concierge, have me removed, thrown on the street, taken away by the police even.

For a second time it was Damon who helped to set my life on course. Breaking free of his father, he slipped his hand into mine, whispering at me not to cry any more. Even then another man might have had me leave but, as I would come to learn, Mario Lanza had a bigger heart than most and that must have been why he decided to take pity on me that day.

'What is your name?' he asked. 'How old are you?'

'I am Serafina Maggio and I'm nearly twenty,' I told him, my voice still ragged with tears.

He took a crisp linen handkerchief from his pocket and passed it to me. 'What you've told me today, it is the whole truth?'

'Yes, it is completely the truth, I swear.' Holding the handkerchief against my face, I breathed the scent of him, of musk, soap and cigar smoke. 'My mother is a good woman, please believe that. I do respect her. But I want a different future for myself and my sisters. And I don't know how I'm going to manage it unless someone takes pity and helps me.'

For a moment he only looked at me. Then he shook his head quickly as though he had lost an argument with himself and came close enough for me to find the whisky on his breath. Mario Lanza wasn't an especially tall man but he was broad and barrel-chested, he had presence. As he squared up I stepped back until my shoulder touched the open door and I could go no further.

'If I give you a chance,' he said, his voice low and steady, 'if I trust you … if I decide to … then I don't expect to be disappointed. Do you understand?'

'*Si*, Signore.'

'It's a promise, then? You will keep your word?'

'Oh yes, Signore.' I was fervent.

Turning back to his wife, he spoke to her again in English. 'So you like this girl? You want to keep her on?'

'That's what I said, isn't it?'

He didn't tell her the truth right then; I wonder if she ever knew. 'Very well,' he said, letting the door swing shut. 'She's not qualified to be a governess. But what if we hire her to help you, to be your personal assistant?'

'What would she do?' She sounded doubtful.

'Translate for you, fetch, carry, make appointments. Whatever you asked.'

'My own assistant,' she said wonderingly. 'To do anything I wanted? To help me every day?'

For the first time she managed a faint smile and I saw it

reflected in his face. 'Would it make you happy?' he asked.

'Oh, yes,' she told him. 'Very happy.'

'Well then, we'll take her on.'

Mario Lanza's handkerchief was still balled in my fist and without thinking I slipped it in my pocket for my tears had stopped and now I couldn't stop smiling. I had a job, a special one working for famous people – an opportunity beyond my dreams. This would be a way to make a life of my own. Who knew where it might take me? I could barely believe my good fortune.

'Oh, thank you, Signore,' I repeated feverishly. 'I won't let you down, I promise.'

In all my excitement I had forgotten about my sister Carmela waiting downstairs in the lobby, hoping for her chance to sing.

And Here You Are

I never really grew accustomed to the grandeur of their lives. Even though the doorman at the Excelsior soon recognised me and the dark-suited men merely nodded when they saw me cross the lobby, not once did it feel as though I belonged.

In the Cupola Suite it was a constant battle to stop the children running wild. There were so many precious things that might get broken, so much space for adults to live in, so little of it suited to a family. And I never knew who would greet me when I got there – the stylish, sparkling Betty Lanza wife of a great star, or the woman in a stained hotel bathrobe that could barely bring herself to get out of bed.

To begin with I was only trusted with the little things. I picked up and put away, wiped and tidied, did jobs that were beneath the two new governesses. It seemed as though everywhere the children moved they left a mess behind them, Betty too quite often. She spilt her face powder over the dressing table and never thought to wipe it up, left clothes on the floor, lipstick stains on towels, dripped her coffee and red wine from cups and glasses. If I hadn't followed them around, neatening and cleaning what they touched, the Cupola Suite would have been destroyed, I'm sure.

It was a relief when she told me they were moving to a villa where the children could be freer. 'A proper household for us in Rome,' she said brightly. 'Somewhere we can be at home, where the children will be safer and where Signore Lanza can be himself instead of always feeling so on show.'

To me the Villa Badoglio in Parioli seemed more a castle

than a home. Five storeys high and made of white marble with a long staircase sweeping to the entrance, it was hung with Venetian glass chandeliers, decorated richly in deep purple and gold, with mirrored walls and marble floors. The Lanza family had taken only two floors of the building but still they had fifteen rooms in all – one reserved for Mario's television set and radiogram, another for his grand piano with shelves to stack his musical scores and film scripts bound in leather and stamped in gold. There were so many bathrooms, a ball-room, grounds as big as a park filled with magnolia trees, a swimming pool, terraces, tennis courts, even a gymnasium where Signore Lanza went to lift heavy weights each day.

Straight away Betty set about hiring more staff: people to clean and cook, serve at the table – a whole household to surround her. And I was a part of it.

Every morning I woke early, keen for the adventure of the day ahead. On the tram as it jolted and bumped its way to the city, I felt marked out from the other passengers. *I work for Betty Lanza, the wife of the famous Mario*, I longed to blurt to strangers. This might be the day I heard him singing at last, listened to his voice vibrating through the marble halls of the great Villa he lived in. I might glimpse him in a corridor, tugging at his tie to loosen it or kissing his children goodbye. Perhaps he would even speak to me: '*Buongiorno*, Serafina.' Each day was rich with possibility.

Very quickly I could see how Betty needed me. She was lonely living in a strange country with no friends or fam-ily near. I grew used to gauging her mood each morning as I took in her breakfast tray. If she were feeling heavy and dull then it was a struggle to make her drink some tea. On those days she was hungry only for the pills that made her so drowsy she would spend hours in bed, her door firmly shut, refusing meals and company.

But if I could coax her with a softly boiled egg and a few bites of buttered toast then she might let me open the door for the children to pile in and climb beneath the covers for cuddles.

It was my job to keep Betty moving through her day if I was able. We'd start by choosing the clothes she'd wear. Her closets were deep in luxury – fine furs, smart suits, shoes and matching handbags. She had boxes of jewels and wrist-watches, drawers full of make-up and perfumes, so much of everything. Sorting through it all, selecting what was right for the weather and her mood could take half the morning.

Only once her hair and make-up were flawless would she consent to drive through the iron gates of the Villa Badoglio. 'There may be photographers following us,' she explained once, although I never saw any.

If the day was fine and she was feeling sunny too, she would put on a hat and dark glasses and we would take the children to the Villa Borghese gardens, buy them balloons or go boating on the lake. There were always the governesses and a driver accompanying us. It seemed astonishing to move everywhere in such a swarm of people.

But when her nerves were troubling her, the children with their noise and fuss were not what she needed. Instead, the driver would take us to the Via Condotti where I would dis-tract her with shops and pretty things. I had never seen any-one spend cash as freely as Betty Lanza, anything she liked she bought. 'As my husband always says, it's only money,' she often repeated as she considered a new hat or a pair of shoes. 'And I have to look good, don't I?'

I never disagreed with her. It wasn't my job to offer an opinion but to keep her mood smooth so that when he came home after a long day in the recording studio the great tenor would find the wife he wanted: loving and supportive, not filled with the mysterious sadness she seemed to feel so fre-quently.

Often there was company at the Villa in the evenings. The long marble table in the dining room seated twenty guests and some nights every chair was taken. I never dined with them, of course, but I stayed to listen to the parties, the popping of champagne corks and the surge of conversation as the doors opened and the staff carried in another platter of seafood or a tray of clean glasses so they could properly taste a different vintage of wine. This was how I had expected a movie star to live. Mario Lanza didn't disappoint me.

Then the parties stopped and Signore Lanza disappeared altogether, although where he had gone nobody at the Villa seemed able to tell me. Without him the gloss went from life there and from Betty's mood. She slept for longer in the mornings, ate less food, swallowed more of her medication. She relied on me even more.

There were times she gossiped as though to a friend and I liked the confidences, encouraged them whenever I judged her mood was right. I loved to hear about her family, the famous people she had met and the parties she'd attended. Most of all I enjoyed listening to her speak about Mario.

'Has Signore Lanza gone away on a trip?' I asked while pouring her tea one morning. 'I don't think I've seen him at home for days.'

'No, he's gone, he's gone to … well, actually he's in hospital,' Betty confided. 'Oh, don't worry, he's not unwell. He's there to take a weight-loss cure. They say he must be much thinner for this picture he's making and so that's why he's left us for a while.'

'How long do you expect him to be gone, Signora?' I felt heartsick, for there had been no chance for me to mention Carmela. I had bided my time, hopeful of managing it sooner or later, but wary of pushing too hard and risking my own position.

'Not long, perhaps no more than a couple of weeks,' she told me. 'He can shed weight very quickly and the doctors have him on a strict regime. They're even injecting him with the urine of pregnant women. Can you imagine that, Serafina?'

I shook my head. It sounded disgusting and I had no idea why anyone would consent to such a thing. 'Urine? Nor really, Signora?'

'Yes, yes, it is the latest treatment, apparently. His doctor is one of the top dieticians in Europe. He says it will help burn up the fat faster.'

I was tempted to ask about Signore Lanza's voice. The rumours he had lost it seemed to have quietened and certainly when I glimpsed him on his return from the recording studio each day his mood appeared merry enough. But still I hadn't heard him sing a note myself.

Betty pulled herself a little higher in the bed as I arranged the pillows at her back. 'It's so difficult – this business with his weight.' She sighed. 'Mario sings well when he's a little heavier but looks better on film when he's thin. That's why he refused to take this cure until most of the recordings for the movie were completed.'

'Oh, are they finished?' I was delighted. 'Have you heard any of the songs?'

'No, not yet. He sang them in the Vatican Auditorium, you know.' She sounded proud. 'The first commercial recordings ever made in the Pope's own theatre. Even the great conductor Arturo Toscanini was denied permission but they said yes to my Mario.'

'I can't wait to hear them.'

'Well, I expect it will be a while yet as there's work to be finished. They're still to record a very funny scene where he imitates famous singers. Oh, and the song with the girl, the little street singer. The trouble is she seems to have disappeared and no one knows how to find her.'

That was when I learned about Luisa Di Meo, the girl who had serenaded Mario Lanza while my sister was stuck at home in Trastevere with Mamma still so angry at her.

She was a street singer, and we had come across her many times in the Piazza Navona or near the Spanish Steps. She performed in the Neapolitan style that was popular with the tourists back then. When Mario arrived in Rome she must have moved to a new spot in the piazza below his hotel, for Betty told me they had heard her singing from six floors up and both been charmed by her voice. They sent down a huge tip and so naturally she returned to sing beneath his window the next day and the next, eager for more of his generosity. Finally she was asked up to his suite so she could meet Mario Lanza in person.

'She's nine years old and Mario thinks she's a slice of the real Italy,' Betty explained. 'He says she sings with such expression in her voice and he's determined to perform a duet with her.'

'But there are lots of girls in Rome who can sing, Signora,' I said carefully. 'My sister Carmela has a wonderful voice. Perhaps she might audition for the duet instead if they can't find this Luisa Di Meo?'

'No, no, I'm afraid Mario only wants the little street singer.' Betty sighed and closed her eyes. 'Do you think you could draw the curtains, Serafina? The sun is so bright and my head is aching. If I feel a little better later then have Liliana and Anna-Maria bring in the children. But keep them away in the meantime. And fetch my pills …'

It was never easy to go home after a day spent at the Villa Badoglio. Our rooms in Trastevere seemed shabbier than ever and I noticed things I'd missed before: dirt in corners, paint peeling from the walls, the clutter. To move from one life to the other was disorienting. I'd taken to staying the night in the Lanza household whenever I could, using my early mornings and late nights at work as an excuse when really it was the lure of a soft bed all to myself and thick curtains that didn't let in light or noise. I knew I didn't belong there but still it was so lovely to pretend. Lying awake, too full of the day to fall asleep, I thought of how so many girls would have changed places with me. Yes the hours were long, but my life was cushioned by the same luxuries the Lanza family enjoyed. I ate their food, slept in their home, listened to Betty's stories. Surely no one in Rome was closer to her?

My mother couldn't understand it. To her being a servant was the lowliest thing. From that very first afternoon when I returned from the Excelsior Hotel, flushed with triumph and excitement, she was never anything but chilly about my job. It was as if I had disappointed her.

'You're at their beck and call all day,' she complained. 'Is that really what you want?'

'I'm working for Mario Lanza, the great star,' I argued.

'You're working for his wife,' Mamma pointed out, 'and serving her is the same as serving anybody else.'

'They're famous Hollywood people.'

Mamma was unimpressed. 'People are people, famous or not.'

'But it's such a good opportunity. I never expected to have a chance like this.'

'If you say so.' Mamma shrugged. 'I suppose you can always leave if you grow tired of being ordered around …'

'I won't.' I was fierce and sure. 'I love this job and I like them, too. I'll stay as long as they need me.'

Carmela, too, was disappointed, and a little envious, I think. There was an entire week when the only time she spoke was to call me selfish and uncaring. I had gone up to the Cupola Suite tasked with helping her and managed only to help myself. But then she saw the possibilities and came to share my joy, outdid it even. On the nights I was at home, she whispered for hours in bed, planning and plotting, certain I could win her the chance to sing again for Mario Lanza.

'I'm trying but I can't promise anything,' I kept insisting.

'I'm caring for his wife and he's out all day and busy working. I hardly ever see him.'

'Don't be stupid.' Beneath the covers she kicked my leg. 'You're there all the time. You have so many chances.'

'I'm trying ...' I repeated guiltily.

'He must listen to me properly next time,' Carmela decreed. 'No autograph hunters bothering him or people screaming his name. It has to be just him and me, you understand? Some day I want to sing on stage, to make a recording, be in a movie. You're the only one who can help me, Serafina.'

By then it was too late, of course. Luisa Di Meo had sung for Mario and he had chosen her to be in his movie. But poor Carmela was still dreaming, believing in her a chance. How would I ever tell her?

Come Dance With Me

Mario Lanza's hands moved when he talked, expressed his meaning and his mood – in that way he was more like an Italian. His accent might have been American, but he looked like he belonged to us. He had a quick temper, too, his mood could shift in an instant and then the marble halls of the Villa Badoglio would echo with his raised voice. I longed to hear him sing rather than shout but the grand piano remained untouched and the only music we ever heard came from the opera records he played on his radiogram almost every evening.

He returned from the hospital after only nine days looking pale but noticeably thinner. At first he seemed subdued and Betty anxious. She was making such an effort, rising from her bed every morning, trying to turn herself into the wife he wanted.

My mother had shown me how to paint a face and finger-nails so, once Betty had managed a little breakfast, she took her place at the dressing table and I used these skills to help her. Hers was a beauty that needed to be re-made each day. She had strong features: teeth that protruded very slightly and wavy brunette hair that I had to discipline with curlers. Often she barely spoke as I made her ready for the world, only nodding to show her approval once I'd finished. But when she broke from her trance, she filled the silence with words, sharing confidences no one else among the household staff ever heard. On those days I could prod her with questions and she seemed pleased enough to answer.

What Betty liked most was revisiting the early days: her and Mario's romance, their first years together. Those were her favourite stories and I enjoyed them, too.

'When did Signore Lanza fall in love with you?' I asked once as I brushed the kinks from her hair.

'He always says he fell for me the moment my brother Bert showed him my photograph,' she told me, delighted with the memory.

'So how did the two of them meet?' I was eager for the story.

'Bert is an actor too, you see,' Betty explained. 'They were in a show together during the war. When they came to Los Angeles, Bert brought Mario home for dinner. I still remember what I was wearing that night – new red slacks and a little off-the-shoulder blouse. I so wanted to impress him …'

The thought held her and her voice tailed off so I nudged the story onwards with another question. 'What did you think when you first laid eyes on him? Did you like him straight away?'

Betty smiled. 'Oh, I thought he was handsome, of course. He was such a big man with a huge smile and the liveliest pair of eyes I'd ever seen. When the two of them came in Bert announced: "Family, this is Mario Lanza" and the whole room lit up.'

'Were you nervous?' I wondered, rolling the curlers in her hair and clipping them in place. 'I would have been, I think.'

'Yes, of course I was. My throat felt dry and I could feel myself blushing. Like an idiot I mumbled how do you do. But Mario wasn't at all shy. I remember he put his arm around my shoulders and said he felt like he'd known me for ever. All the way through dinner I couldn't take my eyes off him. He was so mischievous. He kept saying to my mother, "Mrs Hicks, make your daughter stop looking at me." He made me laugh so much.'

'And you fell in love with him right there and then?' I

prompted, picturing myself in her place, sure I would have been drawn in just as quickly.

'All of us in that room did,' Betty said softly. 'I was in love with him before I ever heard him sing.'

I plucked a few stray hairs from her eyebrows and began smoothing a sheer layer of pancake make-up over her face. Betty had good skin, quite pale but clear. She prided herself on it.

'When did he first sing for you? What did he sound like?' I asked.

'The first time he sang was for my brother Bert, not me at all. The war was still on, you see, and Bert was being shipped overseas, poor thing. Mario threw a party for him at Romeo Chianti's place, a wonderful dinner. Afterwards he took us all downtown to an opera performance. It was very late when we got back to the restaurant. Try to imagine it, Serafina. We are eating supper and everyone is begging Mario to sing for us but at first he refuses. Then Romeo puts on a recording of "Vesti la Giubba" and Mario cannot help himself. He stands, he sings, and my heart bursts. I'd been told so many times what an amazing voice he had but I couldn't possibly have imagined how powerful it was. I swear the glasses on the shelves tinkled when he hit the high notes. I threw my arms around him and from that moment on I was his girl.'

'And then he proposed to you?' I was working on her eyes by then, carefully blackening the lashes with mascara. I had to go slowly now because once I reached her lipstick we would be almost finished and there'd be no excuse to hear more.

'Yes. We went back to Romeo's place for dinner – just the two of us – it was very romantic. When he asked I agreed straight away, of course, but we couldn't get married because of the war. In fact, Mario was transferred to Washington and it was months before we saw each other again.'

'Did he write you lots of letters?'

'Oh no, Mario is a terrible letter writer, although I guess he did telephone almost every day. When he came back to Los Angeles he was in such a rush for us to get married. There was no time to arrange a proper wedding or get a dress made. He didn't even tell his parents. You see this ring?' Holding out her hand she displayed the plain silver band she always wore. 'He paid $6.95 for it. It was the best he could afford at the time and I've never let him replace it, even though he's longing to. So yes, it was a very plain affair and only in City Hall, not a church. But I had flowers in my hair, a little veil and a bouquet, Mario looked handsome. It was a good day, so happy.'

I paused, lipstick in hand. 'What did his family say when they found out? Were they very angry?'

'Mario was scared they would be; he was so nervous.' Betty smiled as she spoke. 'The first time he tried to tell them about us, he couldn't get the words out. His idea was for us to break the news together but I knew it would only make things worse. So we came up with a clever plan. I went out to the movies by myself to give him the chance to do it. I told him all he had to say was he'd married a girl who loved him and wanted them to love her too. As soon as the movie was finished I telephoned and was so relieved when he said everything was fine and they couldn't wait to meet me.'

'So they were happy?'

'Oh yes. Such beautiful people. His father embraced me; his mother kissed me and called me her daughter. It was as if I'd belonged to them for ever.' Betty's eyes misted over and I hoped she wouldn't smudge her mascara. 'Later that day we all went to the cathedral to pray together for a long and happy marriage.'

I wanted so badly to know the rest. What had changed, where had things gone wrong? To hear her tell it, the beginning was a fairy tale. Perhaps it really had been that way.

But what came after? Why was she so often unhappy when her life was forever braided with his and all a woman could dream of? Tracing her mouth with red lipstick, I wondered if I would ever know.

With her make-up finished, Betty checked her reflection, saying, 'I can't see how I ever managed without you, Serafina.' Then leaving her hair in curlers to set for a while longer, we turned over her closets, searching for an outfit to suit the day.

And so I got to know Mario Lanza through Betty's eyes and words, and it felt such a privilege. To others he was a famous star, a face on a record sleeve; for me now he was real. In every story Betty shared he was tender and kind, sweet with sick children and small animals, generous to friends and strangers. He was all I had imagined and more.

At the Villa Badoglio I lived on the edges of their lives and there were times they barely remembered I was there. But I noticed them, drank in every detail. I listened and watched, felt how a room changed when he came into it, hoped for his smile and the sound of his voice, saw all the many reasons Betty had fallen in love with him. Perhaps it's true I stayed behind doorways for longer than I needed to, pretended to be tidying the flowers in a vase or picking up toys the children had left behind, heard conversations meant only for the two of them. To me it didn't seem so wrong.

Some of their habits grew as familiar as my own. I came to expect Mario to arrive home after a day's filming, tugging the tie free from his neck and dropping it to the ground, loosening his shirt buttons and calling Betty to pour him a damn drink quickly.

Often as he finished his first glass of wine or whisky he sloughed off the frustrations of the day with harsh words. I didn't understand much of what he said. He mentioned people I hadn't heard of, situations that were strange to me.

He used slang and spoke quickly. But it was easy enough to tell how much he hated shooting *Arrivederci Roma*.

'The thing is a piece of junk,' I heard him complain one evening. 'The script is a mess and the idiots at the Studio don't know what they're doing.'

'Surely it can't be that bad?' Betty murmured.

'Yes it is. The sets aren't finished, they're rewriting every day, the equipment is falling apart. I don't see how it could be much worse.'

'But, Mario darling—'

'The poor Allasio kid barely speaks English, which doesn't help. We have to run through new dialogue before we start shooting every scene. And the heat in there, you wouldn't believe it. I don't think I can stand any more. I've given them my voice and this is the best they can do with it. It's going to be a lousy picture.'

'You told me everything would be different this time; you said that we could make it work.' Usually soft-spoken, Betty grew shrill. 'That's why we came here, isn't it?'

'I just want to make a decent picture. Is that too much to ask?'

'Can't you speak to Rowland? Surely he knows what he's doing? You told me he's been directing for ever.'

'Rowland's putting on a brave face but the truth is he's in as much trouble as I am. This isn't how they do things in Hollywood. They're breaking all the rules.'

There was a clink of glass and the sound of more wine pouring, then Mario sighed. 'I don't know, Betty; I need some luck for once. Both of us do.'

She seemed to soften then. 'Darling, what do you say me and the children come with you tomorrow?' Her voice sounded brighter. 'Spend the day on set? I can keep you company and help you learn your lines.'

'I guess so.' He didn't seem particularly enthusiastic.

'Will the Studio mind?'

'Who cares if they mind? They don't have a movie without me. If I want you there, you're coming.'

'OK then.' Betty seemed pleased. 'That's what we'll do. It will be fun … a nice distraction.'

It was such a fuss to get them ready the next morning, with Betty making the governesses, Liliana and Anna-Maria, change the children's clothes two or three times and Mario roaring with impatience. I tried to smooth things over: lacing Damon into his shoes, brushing Ellisa's hair. Even with my help they were running more than an hour late by the time they got into the car.

'Serafina, you had better come too.' Betty had a nervy catch in her voice that I recognised as a sign she was struggling to cope. 'Move over quickly, children, and let her in.'

I didn't wait to be asked a second time. With Damon on my knee, I drove in the Lanza family's Volkswagen to Titanus Studios, thinking how poor Carmela would have done almost anything to be in my place instead of still at home, waiting and hoping. I felt guilty not to have changed things for her and wondered if today I might find my chance at last.

I'm not sure how I expected making a movie would be. Glamorous, I suppose, exciting. In fact, it seemed to involve a lot of sitting and waiting. We were in a large, high-ceilinged room with cables running across the floor and lots of bright lights on metal rods hanging from the ceiling. At one end cameras surrounded a small area where they had recreated what looked like a cluttered artist's studio with mismatched chairs, an old table, paintings propped up on easels and an upright piano with sheet music on it.

'Mario says they're shooting a party scene today,' Betty explained. 'When we see the boy with the clapperboard and hear them shout "action" we must keep the children very quiet or Rowland the director will be angry.'

'Yes, of course.' I nodded, still taking it all in. I had watched so many movies and to me they had seemed real. I believed in the love stories and mysteries, was fascinated by the lives of the characters and cried even at the happy endings. It was disappointing to be faced with the truth – that my favourite films came from places like these filled with bright lights, heavy equipment and workers bustling about with clipboards or trailing wires behind them.

Signore Lanza had a canvas chair with his name stencilled on the back and so did Marisa Allasio who was sitting beside him. She could only have been a year or two older than me but already she had made seven movies and become a big star in Italy. I thought she was very pretty, with fair hair cut in a feathery fringe and pulled back into a swingy ponytail, but it was her curves that were celebrated, her tiny waist and generous bust. She giggled with Mario, leaning closer so she could point out something in the script. He was smiling back while an older woman, standing a few steps away, kept careful watch over both of them.

'That must be Marisa Allasio's mother,' Betty whispered, following my eyes. 'Apparently she won't let the girl out of her sight. Perhaps she's worried her daughter will fall in love with my Mario in real life as well as in the movie.'

The words were said lightly enough but when I glanced up I thought her expression looked strained. It wouldn't have been easy for any woman to watch such a pretty young girl flirting with her husband and for Betty everything in life seemed doubly hard.

'Stay here with the children for a moment,' she told me, fluffing her hair with her fingers and pressing her lips together. 'Don't let them bother anyone.'

The girls were happy enough to keep quiet but Damon and Marc weren't used to sitting still. They had so much energy to burn and I worried that if I let them run round as they wanted they might stumble over a cable and break an important piece of equipment. I kept busy, trying to distract them with lollipops and colouring books.

Gradually the noise level in the studio was creeping up. People were gathering beside the set, a make-up artist dusting their faces with powder and pinning their hair in place. Mario had changed into a smart blue suit and Marisa Allasio had changed her outfit too. There was an older man with them and I guessed he was the film's director. He seemed to be explaining something and Betty, now sitting in the middle of the group, was nodding and pointing. No one seemed in any rush and I wondered if they would ever get on with filming their scene. Who could blame the children for becoming fractious? I was bored with the waiting myself.

When Damon broke from my side and went racing towards his father, I jumped up to follow, certain I'd be in trouble. But Signore Lanza only laughed, pulling his son on his knee and pinching his cheek affectionately. 'Does my boy want to be in the movie? What do you think, Rowland?' He looked over at the older man. 'A mini Mario for you to direct. A new star, perhaps?'

'No, Papa.' Damon looked solemn. 'I want to go and look at the planes again.'

Both boys were fascinated with aeroplanes and, whenever hc had a free day, their father drove them out to the airport at Fiumicino. I never went along but the chauffeur told me they stayed for hours, watching the aircraft take off and land.

'We'll see the planes some other time,' Mario promised. 'Today I have to stay here and work.'

'It's boring,' Damon declared, scrambling down from his father's lap and jutting out his lower lip sulkily. 'Too boring.'

They all laughed then, even Marisa Allasio. 'He is so sweet; all of your children are,' she said in her slow, careful English. 'You must be very proud of them.'

She showed no sign of having noticed me, although I was standing right there beside Damon. By then I was used to being invisible to people like her. They all looked straight through me, Mario's guests, the important men that came to the Villa Badoglio. Often I wondered what it was that told people I didn't count for much. The way I dressed or held myself? My shoes? The style of my hair?

'I'm sorry, Signore Lanza. I'll take Damon back to sit with the others.' I bent to pick up the little boy. 'We will keep him very quiet from now on, I promise.'

Mario smiled affably. 'I guess this must be the first time you've visited a movie set, Serafina.' He gestured round. 'So what do you think?'

I paused; aware everyone's eyes were watching now he had drawn attention to me. 'It's interesting,' I said. 'I've seen all of your movies so far and never dreamed I'd see you act in person.'

'All of them?'

'So many times,' I admitted.

He smiled again, seeming genuinely pleased. 'I had no idea you were such a fan.'

'Oh yes, and my sisters, too. All of us love your films, especially Carmela. You remember her, Signore? She is the one with the beautiful voice. Her dream is to—'

Before I could plead my sister's case, I was interrupted. 'Perhaps we might find Serafina a little part in the movie?' Betty suggested, sounding excited by the possibility. 'Would you like that, dear? Would it be fun for you?'

Mario laughed. 'Hey, Rowland, how about it? We could put Serafina in the party scene. She can be one of the girls dancing in the background. She's pretty enough, isn't she?'

'Come on, Mario, don't do this again.' The older man sounded irritated. 'We don't need any more extras. Every waiter or taxi driver you meet ends up with a walk-on part. Now you're telling me you want your governess in the film.'

'She's not a governess, she's my personal assistant.' Betty surprised me with her steel. 'Mario and I both think it's a

72

wonderful idea. Wouldn't you like to have a try, Serafina? You can dance, can't you?'

I was certain I saw Marisa Allasio raise her eyebrows and a scowl cross the director's face.

'It's my sister that—' I began, then stopped myself. Why shouldn't I have a chance like this? Wasn't I as good as anyone else? It wasn't as if I would be singing, only dancing somewhere in the background and perhaps hardly seen at all.

'What would I have to do?' I asked.

They took me to a room filled with racks of clothes and dressed me in something prettier than my old skirt and blouse; they tidied up my face and backcombed my hair. I was given a tambourine to shake as I danced.

'Just act naturally, OK,' they said. 'Laugh, have a good time, like you would at a party.' I couldn't bring myself to admit that never in my life had I been to one.

Waiting with the other extras, I listened to them chatter on about the films they had appeared in and the stars they had seen. Every now and then I waved at the children and hoped they weren't causing Betty too much trouble. It was difficult not to let the nerves creep up. I didn't know what to expect at all. I wasn't sure I could do it.

'OK, let's have you on set now,' a male voice called. 'We're ready for the first scene. Quickly, everyone, places please.'

It was very hot beneath the lights. Standing at the back of the crowd holding my tambourine above my head, I waited for the director to call 'Action' as Betty had said he would. I recognised the Italian actor Renato Rascel sitting at the piano surrounded by musicians but from where I was positioned I couldn't see Signore Lanza at all. Shielding my eyes, I tried to find Betty and the children but beyond the cameras it was too dark to make out anything much.

'OK,' the director's assistant called. 'We're starting with a close-up of a tambourine and then pulling back to show the party in full swing so try to look like you're having the time of your lives.'

The set was crowded, with barely space to move, but when the music began I did my best, waving my tambourine in the air and letting myself be pulled into a few dance steps by the boy who had been picked as my partner. At the end of the scene I was breathless.

'Try it again. More energy this time, more chaos. Remember this is the best impromptu all-night party you've ever been to.'

We repeated the same dance over again until it had been filmed from every possible angle and the director judged they had it right. By then all of us were dripping but there was barely time to towel ourselves dry and fix our hair before we had to take our places for the next scene.

The music changed to a slower tempo then and we were made to dance more quietly in the background as Mario and Renato Rascel acted out a conversation beside the piano. I couldn't believe how many times they had to repeat their lines, Signore Rascel struggling with his accent and the English words and Mario clapping him on the back when he managed a whole scene without a stumble.

'OK, we'll have Signore Lanza's song next and then we'll break for lunch,' the voice called out from the darkness beyond the cameras.

'What song is it?' I whispered to my dance partner eagerly.

'"Come Dance With Me",' he replied.

'And will he really sing it? Will we get to listen?'

'I guess so.' The boy shrugged, as though the idea of Mario Lanza singing didn't interest him at all.

For the last scene we gathered round the piano, sitting on the floor beneath Signore Lanza's feet, crushed together elbow-to-elbow. When the cry of 'action' came I noticed how serious he seemed and how he stood a little taller. And then he opened his mouth and sang. It wasn't a great aria, only a ballad, and yet with my body swaying to the music and my eyes half closed, I sensed the strength in his voice, heard how easily he conquered each note, felt the joy and sweetness in it.

When Mario took one of the extras by the hand and pulled her up to dance I wished it had been me. When he sang to an old woman and kissed her forehead at the finish, I felt the envy rise. I forgot there were cameras pointed at us, I wasn't trying to act any more, I was there at a party in an artist's attic in Rome listening to the voice of the greatest tenor in the world.

I am certain Mario Lanza didn't need to sing so well that day. Surely they would already have recorded 'Come Dance With Me' at the Vatican Studios and would use that version for the movie. But he was a performer and we were an audience. He was thrilling, magical, and our applause was real even if the rest was only acting. I wished we could have shot the scene a thousand times, swayed and listened and clapped loudly for him all day long.

I believed I truly knew him when I heard him sing that very first time. He sounded so pure and strong, so perfect. I hadn't yet learned a voice can't tell you all that matters about a man. Not even Mario Lanza's voice.

Drink, Drink, Drink

Staff seemed to come and go at the Villa Badoglio, maids most especially. It wasn't the children's fault, not really. All their lives there had been people to fetch and carry for them – they'd been raised to expect it. If Colleen dropped her napkin on the floor she'd signal a servant to pick it up. If Damon left his comic book at the other end of the Villa he thought nothing of calling a maid to bring it for him. They had been treated like royalty and anyone who thought it was their job to instil a little discipline was in for a difficult time.

Then there was Betty wanting things done one way one moment and another the next, depending on how her mood was swinging. Her temper was unpredictable and our responsibilities grew and changed with each passing week. Soon it wasn't only the children who had us at their beck and call. Two dogs, one cat and several canaries joined the household and we were meant to serve them, too. Often I'd hear muttered complaints on the back stairs or in the servants' quarters and then, not long afterwards, see a packed suitcase waiting and find an unhappy maid saying a stiff goodbye.

Judging by the racket coming from the kitchen it seemed clear who would be the next to go. All of us had heard the cook shouting that morning, surely even Betty, although she hadn't said a word about it.

'Boiled shrimps,' he had cried. 'Salad with no vinaigrette. A single *grissino*. A plain steak. And that's it, day after day. Is this what I trained for? I make the lightest most beautiful gnocchi, a ragu that could break your heart. Caruso would

76

have loved to taste my *risotto alle vongole*. And what does this one ask me for? Fat-free cheese. *Porca miseria.*'

When the housekeeper tried to quieten him he crashed his saucepans together so violently she backed out of the kitchen. 'Whoever heard of fat-free cheese?' he cried after her as she fled his kitchen.

The cook's name was Filippo Pepe, although he was always just Pepe to me. None of us wanted to see him leave. He had a striking face with intense dark eyes, a slightly hooked nose and jet-black ringlets escaping from beneath the white cap he always wore. The staff meals he served up were the highlights of our days.

Pepe fed us sturdy food to fuel the long hours of work ahead: risotto so creamy it rippled into the bowls, *spaghetti alla carbonara* smoky with pancetta, fat tubes of macaroni in a thick broth of braised osso buco. Each morning we were teased by the smell of his cooking and when we gathered round the table in the kitchen there was always a moment of tense silence while we waited to see what lay beneath the lids of the pans steaming on the stovetop.

He had some secret to bringing out the flavours of everyday ingredients, I've no idea how he managed it. A plain sauce of tomatoes, a few flakes of Parmesan, a little spaghetti cooked al dente, a tangle of rocket leaves – the taste sang in our mouths and we soaked up every last smear of sauce with the crusty bread he pulled from the oven. I ate things I'd never tried before, sweet morsels of shellfish in a golden saffron soup, bread folded and flavoured with garlic and sage. It must have been torture for Signore Lanza to know his servants were eating so well when he himself was rationed to such bland meals. For the chef, too, it seemed it was an agony.

I found myself drawn to Pepe's basement kitchen, making excuses to visit, fetching cold drinks and trays of snacks for Betty, or just a glass of water for myself. This large room felt like the warm heart of the house. One wall was hung with saucepans, another with utensils, things to press and squeeze the flavours from food, to push ingredients together, reduce them, transform.

I liked what I'd seen of Pepe. He took his work seriously. At times I saw him look at food the way other men like to stare at women.

But that morning I found him sitting in his kitchen, head in hands. 'Steamed fish and green beans, espresso without a single grain of sugar,' he was muttering. 'Why would a man live like that? How can he stand it?'

'Signore Lanza is taking a weight-loss cure,' I reminded him. 'I'm sure once he's finished filming he will begin to eat properly again.'

'Go away. You don't know what you're talking about.' He sounded angry.

'But it's true,' I insisted. 'Betty told me so.'

'Let me ask you something.' Pepe's dark eyes met mine. 'I have been here for how long now? Three weeks? Maybe four?'

'Four, I think.'

'And in that time has Signore Lanza eaten one single thing for pleasure?'

'No, but he is limited to only five hundred calories a day. That is what Dr Simons ordered. He eats for nourishment only, not for pleasure.'

'This Dr Simons, who is he?'

I repeated what Betty had told me. 'He's one of the top dieticians in the whole of Europe. Very well respected. He is supervising Signore Lanza's weight loss.'

Pepe stood. He was much taller than me and when he leaned his broad hands on the table I heard the old pine creak beneath him. 'This Dr Simons, does he understand food? Tell me that.'

'I don't know. But I think—'

'Does he realise there are so few opportunities for pleasure in life and food is the only one we can rely on?' Pepe interrupted. 'Three times a day we are able to take some joy for ourselves – breakfast, lunch, dinner. Why would anyone waste that chance, throw it away on unsweetened coffee and dry breadsticks if he could afford to eat anything he chose?'

'It's only for a short while.'

'Beh,' he said in disgust. 'This morning I would have liked to serve Signore Lanza a strong espresso with the perfect *crema* on top, a crisp pastry dusted with powdered chocolate. For lunch I could have given him a plate of baked pasta wrapped in foil to take to the film studio, perhaps a couple of juicy meatballs seasoned with oregano, a few peppers tossed with olive oil and anchovies. And for dinner a ravioli of wild mushrooms, then a fleshy white fish with a paste of walnuts and a sauce of capers and vinegar. Imagine the pleasure of such food: enjoying it with your eyes, smelling it, eating your fill. Instead, I prepare a steak very rare and arrange some lettuce leaves and a tomato sliced on a plate. There is no joy in that at all.'

I wanted to remind him that Mario had many other pleasures in his life – his music, his children, his fans – and perhaps what Pepe served him was less important. But the chef seemed so unhappy I kept the thought to myself.

'The staff enjoy your cooking, all of us do,' I offered instead. 'The *pasta al forno* with the purée of basil you made for us the other night, and the *caponata*, too. I have never eaten anything like it.'

Pepe nodded but his expression didn't change. 'It was OK, I suppose. Not too bad. But he didn't so much as taste it. How can a man sing if he doesn't eat? His voice will slip away with all the weight he loses and then where will he be?'

I shook my head. 'No, no, I have heard Signore Lanza sing. He is still in good voice despite what they say. The power is still there.'

'On a film set? That is not real singing.' Pepe glowered. 'He shouldn't be wasting his talent on ballads. God made Mario Lanza's voice for opera just like he did the great Caruso's. If I could sing like that I would be performing on stage at La Scala in Milan or at the Teatro dell'Opera, not wasting my time as a film singer.'

'Do you know much about opera?' I asked, intrigued. 'Have you been to those places to hear it?'

'I know enough,' he said. 'And yes, I've been to the Roman Opera, of course I have.'

'Why doesn't Signore Lanza sing there?' I wondered.

Pepe frowned. 'You would have to ask him that question. I don't understand why he chooses to debase his voice any more than I know why he refuses to eat. None of it makes sense.'

The lid of a saucepan rattled and Pepe moved to stir the contents and turn down the heat beneath it. He strode round the kitchen as though certain of both the room and himself. At home when I was cooking for my sisters I had only a couple of saucepans, a wooden spoon and sieve at my command. I couldn't imagine an empire such as this. Yet although Pepe was young, still in his mid-twenties, he never seemed daunted.

'You know what will happen next,' he said, lifting the spoon to his mouth to taste the sauce. 'Signore Lanza will grow tired of all this self-denial.'

'And then what?' I asked.

'Disaster,' Pepe said shortly.

I failed to stop my mouth from lifting into a smile.

'No, no, I am serious.' He offered me the spoon that had been at his own lips. 'I will explain why. But first try this. Tell me what you think.'

Obediently I tasted the sauce. 'It is very nice.'

'Is that all you can say about it ... very nice?'

After thinking for a moment, I added tentatively. 'I would like to eat more of it.'

'Yes, but why?' he asked.

I tried to explain. 'Because it coated my mouth with a flavour I like. It felt silky on my tongue. When I swallowed I felt a tiny bite of chilli I hadn't noticed at first. What is the herb you put in it? Fennel? My mother showed me a dish with *salsicce* that has a similar taste.'

Pepe gave the sauce one last stir then balanced the lid on the pan, leaving a gap for the steam to escape and sweetly scent the kitchen. 'So you like this sauce because it reminds you of your mother's cooking?'

'I suppose so.'

'Of course you do, because food is one of our strongest memories,' Pepe told me. 'When I look back on my life what I recall best are the meals I ate. I grew up in a village in Campania and we didn't have much but in the winter there was always soup to warm us, heavy with beans and pasta, usually flavoured with a hock of ham. In the cellar my papa cured prosciutto and in summer we ate it with the sweet juicy melons he grew in the garden. I remember the cake my nonna made for my twelfth birthday, honeyed and dense with almonds. And the feasts she cooked on Sundays. She would blister red peppers over hot charcoal and serve them with a *scallopine* of veal. At springtime she fried courgette flowers in the lightest batter and then when the weather was cold she made stews of oxtail and celery. In my family eating was love and comfort, it was how we made each day different from the last. I expect your family was just the same?'

I could have told Pepe the truth – it was years since my mother had cooked a meal at home. She preferred to eat in restaurants, the smarter the better. Mamma liked crystal glasses, fine linen tablecloths and hovering waiters, she liked to feel herself part of the beauty of a room. She had been taught to cook by her own mother, passed the skills on to me and then done her best to forget them. But I thought

Pepe would think less of me if he knew all that. 'Yes, just the same,' I lied.

'Signore Lanza may have grown up in America but he had Italian parents so why should his childhood have been any different to ours?' Pepe asked. 'He was raised to eat well. It is his instinct. Now everyday he denies it.'

'You said there will be a disaster,' I reminded him.

'Yes, because a man can only go against his natural instincts for so long. Eventually he won't be able to control his hunger. It will overwhelm him.'

'But it's only a weight-loss diet. Lots of people try them if they are a little on the heavy side.'

'You don't know anything, Serafina.' Pepe looked so solemn. 'There will be a disaster, wait and see.'

I forgot about Pepe's strange warning. The day was busy and I let it slip to the back of my mind. What he had said about food stayed with me, though, and his childhood memories of flavours and family. I remembered the mouth-watering aroma coming from the sauce simmering on the stove and a sort of longing started in me, a sense I had missed out on something important in my own life. I pushed all his talk of disaster away. I suppose I didn't want to think of it.

Two days later Signore Lanza came home early and in a bad way. Calling for Betty, he searched the rooms of the Villa, slamming doors when he couldn't find her.

'Where the hell is she?' he thundered, catching sight of me. His face was ruddy and his brow thickly sheened with sweat. 'Where's my damn wife?'

'The Signora is resting. She has a headache,' I told him uneasily.

Mario stumbled slightly as he moved to leave the room and his knuckles whitened as he gripped the back of a chair for balance. There had been times I had seen him soften the hard edges of his day with whisky, times when his voice had grown louder and his laugh bigger, but I had never seen him like this. On quiet feet, I followed him down the hallway, determined to discover what had fouled his mood.

He left the bedroom door ajar so I didn't have to try too hard to catch the conversation within. Silently I stood outside, leaning and listening.

'Those lousy bastards have cancelled the production. They say I'm too drunk to work.'

'What? Who says so?' Betty sounded confused and groggy.

'That idiot Lombardo for one.'

'The president of the Studio?' Betty was more alert now. 'But he sent you a telegram, didn't he? He said this would be the greatest Lanza film yet and he was proud to be producing it. Isn't that right?'

'Sure and now he's changed his mind. He says he's going to sue me for ruining his goddam picture.'

'Sue you?'

'So I have a sip of wine now and then between takes. How else am I supposed to get through the day?'

'You shouldn't have let them see you with it.' She raised her voice. 'Why didn't you keep it hidden?'

'I did. The damn stuff was in a Coca-Cola bottle but still they knew. Someone must have ratted on me.'

'It's your drinking that's the problem,' Betty cried. 'Always your drinking.' The torrent of words that rushed from her then was like nothing I'd heard. There was a crash of glass as something was thrown across the room and a louder one as another item followed it.

'You don't love me,' she screamed. 'You don't care about any of us. How could you do this? You've ruined everything.'

'It's not my fault. Lombardo has got it in for me.'

'What are we going to do?' Betty was crying now. 'People will hear about it, the press, everyone back home ... this is a nightmare.'

'They're all against me.' Mario's voice was ragged. 'It's the usual story. People are plotting: Allasio perhaps, Rowland, too … they want to take me down. It's no different here than it was at home.'

'You have to make them change their minds and take you back. Mario, you have to.'

'What do you want me to do? Beg for my job?'

'Yes … oh, I don't know. If you can't do it then call Al Teitelbaum. Get him to talk to them. He's supposed to be your manager, isn't he?'

Mario replied in a lower voice, muttering words I couldn't quite catch even when I moved closer to the gap in the doorway.

'Yes, why not have another drink?' Betty was vicious. 'Drink yourself to death if you like. Just get out of my sight, for God's sake.'

The sound of Mario's footsteps hastened me back down the hallway and into the shadow of a doorway. I watched him weaving from the room, tugging his tie loose, most likely in search of his Chivas Regal. This wasn't the Mario Lanza I knew and it shook me to see him come so badly undone. His anger, the sting of his self-pity, the way the drink had overtaken him, his and Betty's raised voices; all of it was unexpected and shocking. I was worried, too, for if his movie was cancelled then it meant the future was uncertain for all of us.

That's when all Pepe's talk of disaster came back to me.

Cosi Cosa

Home felt a safer place for a short while that night. I lay in bed between my sisters, too cramped to move or sleep properly, and I was glad. There was so much to be sure of in that apartment. For as long as I could remember it had looked the same. Perhaps it wasn't quite as ordered without me there to tidy the tangle of jewellery and perfume bottles on Mamma's dressing table and line her shoes in neat rows beneath the bed. There were dishes on the draining board waiting to be washed and the laundry basket was overflowing with things Carmela needed to take to the *lavanderia*. But otherwise nothing had changed and I lulled myself into thinking it never would. I couldn't imagine those two rooms without us in them.

Mamma had been surprised to see me coming through the door, for I hadn't been home in days. She and Rosalina embraced me, covering me in kisses, but Carmela only stared. I think she was expecting me to conjure up yet another excuse for not arranging her chance to sing in front of Signore Lanza. For weeks I'd been struggling to find new reasons: he was too busy, indisposed, I had hardly seen him, his mood was sour and the time simply wasn't right. Today, for the first time, I didn't need to find a lie.

'It's all over. The movie has been cancelled,' I announced before she could overwhelm me with her resentment. 'Apparently the Studio is going to sue Signore Lanza.'

'What?'

'How do you know this, Serafina?' Concern furrowed my

mother's brow. 'Have you been gossiping ... or snooping?'

'They had a big argument. Anybody could have heard it,' I said defensively. 'They were shouting so loud.'

'What will happen now?' Carmela wondered, her forehead creased into a frown.

'I don't really know. Perhaps they'll leave, go back to America. It's too soon to say.'

Carmela clearly blamed me for ending her dream. She sulked over a magazine for most of the evening, refusing to be coaxed into a conversation. Nearing bedtime, she thawed a little.

'What will you do?' she asked. 'Will you go back to the Villa Badoglio tomorrow morning?'

'Yes, of course. I still have a job there, don't I?'

'Who knows how long it will last?' she said breezily. 'Still, I suppose if they let you go you can come home again. Rosalina will be pleased. She misses your *pasta e fagioli*.'

I tried to imagine myself back in the old life and wondered if I could settle for the way things used to be. Unaccountably I felt angry with Carmela.

'You never had a chance of singing in that film anyway,' I snapped. 'They'd already decided who they wanted. Luisa Di Meo, the little street singer. She's the only girl in Rome that Mario Lanza will perform a duet with.'

Carmela knew exactly who Luisa Di Meo was. 'You're lying.' She was shocked. 'Why ask for her when he could have me?'

'And yet he did. So you see why I could do nothing to help you?'

As soon as the words were out I felt sorry, for there had been no need for Carmela to hear them. *Arrivederci Roma* was cancelled and Luisa wouldn't be singing her duet after all. There would be no more filming, the party scene I had appeared in would be forgotten, no one would see me sway as Mario crooned 'Come Dance With Me'. It might as well not have happened.

'I don't believe it.' My sister looked shattered. 'Why didn't you say? You just allowed me to keep on hoping, even though it was pointless.'

'You wanted it so much. I knew you'd be upset and I didn't know how to tell you. And it seemed there might still be a chance,' I admitted. 'Luisa went missing and I thought if they couldn't find her ...'

'Don't you see what you've done? I've been wasting all this time when I could have been thinking up another plan. I want to be a singer and if Mario Lanza can't help me then I'll have to find someone who can.'

'But who?'

'Perhaps Mamma knows the right person. All those men ... one of them must have connections.'

'But, Carmela ...' I started to object for her words brought back all my old worries.

'If you're going to tell me I'm too young then don't bother. I can look much older if I have to. I'll do anything it takes but I'm not going to waste any more time.'

Usually when we were in bed she whispered to me beneath the covers until we fell asleep. But that night Carmela was too angry. She turned her face from mine, burying it in the pillow, and I lay awake with only my own thoughts for company.

I was dreading my return to the Villa Badoglio for I wondered how I would find things: Betty locked in her room refusing to respond to my knocking, Mario with a bottle of whisky still at his side, the children impossible to control, the governesses not knowing where to turn. I didn't want to go back but it came to me that I couldn't stay here – the green polka-dot dress was a vivid reminder of the life I'd risk if I did. It was there, hanging on the clothes rail waiting for me to need it. Waiting until the night I decided to follow in my mother's footsteps.

The next morning I picked my way through the back streets of Trastevere and waited at the tram stop. Carmela had barely been able to bring herself to say goodbye, my mother had been sleeping heavily after a late night and I felt utterly alone, unsure of where I belonged and, unlike my sister, with no idea where I wanted to be.

Only Pepe's kitchen drew me with its promise of comfort and breakfast smells: strong black coffee and browning bread. I found him there, more energised than ever, busy cooking a great feast. It seemed that with the movie abandoned so was Signore Lanza's diet and his hunger was urgent and demanding. He had requested an American breakfast: omelette oozing with soft cheese and spiked with caramelised onions, potatoes scalloped and fried until they crisped at the edges, meaty field mushrooms roasted in the oven, a pile of crisp toast and a platter of sweet pastries. It took two of us to carry the loaded trays up the stairs.

There was no sign of Betty. She had retreated from her own life just as I had known she would. At first she wouldn't open her bedroom door even to me and although I left food outside, nothing was touched. Cups of milky coffee grew cold; bread got hard and stale; pasta sauce congealed. Some mornings I stood knocking and calling her name for ten minutes or more, hoping she'd relent. Even when she did open the door and let me in at last, she would take only the tiniest amount of whatever I had brought. 'Just my Seconal and a glass of water, Serafina. That's all I want right now,' she would say, her voice barely more than a whisper.

The less Betty managed to eat the more Mario needed, numbing himself with food and wine, dazed by it in the end. They both seemed set on self-destruction. It was unbearable. As the days went by and nothing changed, I kept recalling that first moment when I had glimpsed them waving from the train. What would the crowd on the station platform think to see them now? Surely no one would believe it … I hardly believed it myself.

Down in the kitchen I discussed the situation with Pepe endlessly in a bid to understand it.

'I've never seen anything like it either,' he admitted. 'First the man refuses to eat and now he's trying to kill himself with food. He wants pizza, pasta, endless little fried things and huge slabs of roasted meat, bread slathered with butter, bottles of wine to wash it all down. This isn't eating. He's filling up without caring for the flavours, barely even noticing what he chews and swallows. All that matters to him is that there's plenty, and when he's finished he sleeps and no one can wake him.'

'But why? And what makes him drink so much?' I asked, worriedly. 'Wine, beer, champagne, whisky. The housemaid tells me every morning she finds empty bottles rolling beneath the furniture.'

By then both of us had seen what could happen when Mario Lanza drank. After several glasses he became quarrelsome, banging on Betty's door and demanding she let him in. When she refused to answer, he would go to the telephone and call people in America – his lawyers, his manager – complaining to them about what had gone wrong, drinking and drinking the whole time.

I found excuses for him. 'It's ever since they cancelled the picture,' I said to Pepe. 'That's what started this. It's entirely the Studio's fault – a disaster, just as you said it would be.'

I waited for the real Mario to return, the man in the photograph: the father I had longed for, the matinee idol. Instead, the situation grew worse until, unshaven and bloated, there was nothing handsome about him any more. It dismayed me to see him shuffling round the Villa in the grip of a hangover, finishing bottles of beer with breakfast then turning to his decanter of whisky. Aside from the children, alcohol seemed all he cared about. One afternoon I saw him crashing his fists to his knees. 'Why can't I stop?' he cried out angrily. 'Why? I hate the stuff. What am I doing to myself?' Yet still he kept on drinking.

I cursed the people at Titanus Studios who had him brought so low, and cried myself to sleep over it more than once. But while it was heartbreaking, there seemed no way to help so instead I stayed behind the doors, watching and listening, frightened both for him and for Betty.

Perhaps things would have got even worse if the American hadn't come. His name was Albert Teitelbaum and he arrived, thin-lipped and stern, carrying a coat with a deep fur collar that I longed to reach out and stroke. For hours they talked and, while I couldn't hear all of it, he seemed to be reassuring Mario, which made me feel a little better. If this wealthy-looking man believed there was a chance both the singer and his film could be saved then surely it must be true.

'The Italians don't know what they're doing,' Mario kept repeating. 'What's the point of making this picture if it's junk? Haven't I been in enough bad ones already?'

'These guys have been making movies for years,' Mr Teitelbaum told him. 'They do things a little differently here, that's all. Trust me, Mario, the picture will be fine, it's you I'm worried about. You look terrible and God knows what you sound like. How are we going to get you back into shape?'

Mario mumbled something and I heard the clink of glassware and knew he had reached for his decanter.

'No, leave the whisky,' Mr Teitelbaum ordered him. 'That's what got you into this trouble.'

'Just one drink, that's all ...'

'Look, I'll make a deal with you. I'm prepared to sort things out with the Studio if you promise to stay away from the booze until the shoot is over.'

There was more indistinct mumbling.

'The way I see it, this is your only option. It's the end of the line for you. I'll stay in Rome to help but if you touch a drop I'm going straight home and that'll be the last you see of me, do you understand? I mean it, really I do.'

I was shocked that anyone would dare speak to Signore Lanza in such a way but he surprised me by not reacting with anger. Instead, he sounded grateful.

'You know I appreciate it, Al,' he said thickly. 'Betty does, too. I'll get myself together and work hard to finish this picture, I promise you that. No more rich food. I'll go on the straight and narrow. Just good simple meals for me from now on.'

'And the booze?'

'I'll try not to touch it. I'll do my best.'

When she heard the news, Betty opened her door at last. The bedroom smelt stale and the pill bottles littering her nightstand were far emptier than they'd been the last time I'd laid eyes on them.

She'd barely eaten for so long, she was too weak to wash herself properly. I had to wipe her clean with a soapy flannel as if she were a child.

'I can't have Al see me like this,' she said, touching her ruined skin and hair. 'Serafina, you have to fix me up. Please make me look like myself again.'

And so I helped her to the dressing table and tried to restore her. It took a long time and for most of it she sat limp and silent.

'Al's going to make things better,' was all she said. 'He must … he absolutely has to.'

Day In, Day Out

There was a familiar din coming from the basement, a crashing of steel and shouting. Pepe was furious again and he didn't care who knew it.

'All this food and who is going to eat it now? It is ridiculous. How is any cook supposed to work like this?'

The housekeeper begged me to quieten him somehow. She seemed half afraid of Pepe herself but was convinced he had a soft spot for me. And so I braved the heat of his kitchen and his rage.

I found him staring at the loaded shelves of the refrigerator, his cheeks flushed from one outburst, his whole body rigidly awaiting the next.

'Please, you must be quiet,' I hushed him. 'This will reach the ears of Signore Lanza. You will get yourself fired if you carry on.'

Pepe gestured towards the forest of wilting celery, the fishy tentacles of octopus, the voluptuous loaves of bread. 'But, Serafina, look at this. It would have fed my whole village during the war and now I must watch it spoil.'

'Some of it will be eaten by the staff, surely?'

'So much will go to waste. I ordered it to feed the fire of his appetite and now he has found restraint again. Either this crazy man has to eat too much or he'll touch nothing at all. Why can't he enjoy a normal meal like any other person? I'll never understand it. Meanwhile, look ... all going rotten ...'

It was as if Mr Teitelbaum had hit a switch and life in the Villa Badoglio had changed overnight. He had managed all

I had been hoping for. The whisky had been tipped from the decanters lining the sideboard and they'd been washed and put away. A barber had been summoned to shave Signore Lanza and tidy his hair so he looked more like a movie star. The feasting was finished and it was back to the monotony of the weight-loss cure. Only the cigarette sometimes held between his fingers was a reminder of the way he'd lived before.

Mr Teitelbaum was always at his side, accompanying him everywhere, policing what he ate and drank. There was something about that man, an expression he wore when he wasn't aware he was being watched. It was as though he were constantly summing up what people were worth. Betty had told me he was a furrier as well as being Mario's manager, the beautiful white stole in her closet had come from him and he'd been a friend for a long time. She called him 'darling Al' and often held his arm. I couldn't see what she found in him to like so much.

Still, Betty was eating properly and seemed stronger already. Mario was sober and the film had been saved thanks to Mr Teitelbaum, that's what everyone said. Each day he and Signore Lanza left together for the set, with us often accompanying them. I might have preferred to stay at the Villa, but where Betty went I was called to follow.

The time we spent on the set of *Arrivederci Roma* was often very dreary. Mario looked bored and Mr Teitelbaum paced or scribbled in a notebook he pulled from his pocket. Only Betty seemed to brighten when she was there. I think she enjoyed being a part of things, offering her opinion on the way a scene should be set up or acted. She had a blustery sort of confidence when she was at the Studio that was missing at most other times.

I was hoping she might be able to influence things in my sister Carmela's favour. Once or twice I'd dropped her name into a conversation, for there was still no sign of Luisa Di

Meo. The Studio had even asked the police to trace the girl but they'd had no luck, much to Mario's frustration.

'How difficult is it to locate a beggar anyway?' he kept asking. 'Surely she has regular routes?'

'It's impossible,' Mr Teitelbaum insisted. 'The Studio says she's nowhere to be found. You'll have to pick another singer.'

'I don't want another singer. I want the little Neapolitan. She's my good-luck girl.'

'Stoll is worried her voice is too limited anyway.'

'So I'll cue her in and out and sing in her key if necessary. Stoll just has to find her.'

Betty tried to talk him round. 'But, darling, there are plenty of pretty girls with sweet voices. Hundreds of them. Why don't you audition a few?'

'You think they're all the same, then you sing with them,' was Mario's reply.

If his wife and his manager were struggling to change his mind, then what chance did I have? Instead, I tried approaching Mr Teitelbaum one afternoon when the timing seemed good. He'd bought the children liquorice sweets and was laughing at the black mess of their teeth and faces, and at my fruitless attempts to clean them up. For once his warmth seemed genuine.

'Signore, have they found the little Neapolitan street singer yet?' I asked.

'No such luck,' he replied.

'Perhaps I might be able to help.'

'You know where she is?' He sounded keen. 'How to find her?'

'I think she goes to the beach to sing for the tourists in the summer months. But there are many beaches. She could be on any of them.'

He shrugged. 'I guess Mario will just have to accept another girl then. He has no choice.'

'There is my sister Carmela? She is a street singer too and very pretty. What about her?'

'Sure. Get her to audition for George Stoll. He's the music director and he's seeing other girls so I don't see why he shouldn't listen to your sister.'

I hesitated. 'But shouldn't it be Signore Lanza who hears her?'

'No, Stoll is definitely your man. Talk to the casting people. They'll organise it for you.'

I wished I'd known it was that easy. But I hadn't realised there was such a thing as 'casting people'; or imagined they might be happy to listen to Carmela, especially when I told them she'd been singing on the streets for years.

'She is the genuine article? A slice of the real Italy?' a brisk middle-aged woman asked me. 'Because that's what Signore Lanza is asking for.'

'Yes, I know that. And she is, most definitely,' I promised.

'We'll see her on Friday, then. Tell her there's no need to bring music – we want to hear her voice without any accompaniment.'

'Will she have the chance to sing for Signore Lanza?' I asked hopefully.

'If Mr Stoll likes her, then I expect so,' the woman replied. 'This is the most important number in the film. We're only going to cast someone he approves of.'

All day I nursed the knowledge, wondering how Carmela would react when she heard it. I imagined her rehearsing for hours until Rosalina put her fingers in her ears and begged her to stop singing. So long as she was in good voice on the day of the audition, surely the duet was Carmela's? If Luisa Di Meo stayed out of sight who else could compete with her?

Excited and proud, I was keen to share the news with someone. I managed to hold on until we'd returned to the Villa and then, while Betty went for her rest, I hurried down to the kitchen.

Pepe was there as I had hoped. He was shaping meatballs for the children's supper, rolling and cupping them in his broad hands.

'I missed out on lunch,' I told him. 'Is there anything? Just a little prosciutto or some cheese?'

'Yes, yes, of course.' Suddenly Pepe was animated. 'Sit down and let me bring it to you.'

Wiping the raw meat from his fingers, he began pulling dishes from the refrigerator and laying them on the table – a plate of grilled courgettes slippery with olive oil and fragrant with rosemary needles, tiny onions simmered to softness with brown sugar and balsamic. And a mound of pearly-white buffalo mozzarella, so fresh it bled with its own milk. I felt my eyes droop with pleasure as I took the first piece into my mouth.

Pepe watched me eat. 'I always think mozzarella is the nearest food to kissing someone,' he said softly.

I was taken aback. 'How can eating be like kissing?'

'It's to do with the way it feels in your mouth, soft and delicate, yielding almost. Mozzarella makes whoever eats it feel happy.' He laughed. 'But only if it's young and fresh, of course.'

I finished every bite of the delicate cheese and my fork roved around the edges of the other dishes he'd set before me.

'I have some news,' I told Pepe as I tasted the food. 'A good thing happened today.'

'It did? Well, tell me then.'

'My sister is to audition for a duet with Signore Lanza. In three days' time she will see the musical director Mr Stoll himself. Isn't that wonderful? I arranged it for her.'

'Your sister is a singer?' Pepe seemed interested. 'What kind of music does she like to perform?'

'Carmela can sing anything she chooses. Her voice is very special.'

96

'All voices are different,' he pointed out. 'Some are low and sound like whisky and they are good for jazz, others have the clarity of water or the depth and creaminess of chocolate ... and then, of course, there are the real singers and for them there's only opera.'

I dabbed at my mouth with the paper napkin he'd passed me. 'How do you know so much about singing?'

'In my family everybody loves it. My nonno, my father, my mother, too. I grew up listening to opera. Even today if I hear Verdi I think of Mamma kneading the bread dough, her kitchen filled with music.'

'My mother prefers American singers,' I admitted. 'She loves rock 'n' roll.'

'It's fun to dance to,' Pepe agreed. 'But if you want to listen to music and really hear it then it can only be opera. That's why I don't understand Signore Lanza. His talent is huge, his diction and breath control are peerless. I listen to his recordings and feel the hairs on the back of my neck stand up. And yet he chooses to sing for Hollywood.'

Pepe seemed so certain about everything it was difficult to argue with him. But still I found myself defending Signore Lanza. 'What's wrong with Hollywood?' I asked.

'He's throwing his talent away,' Pepe said shortly.

'But so many more people hear him this way,' I pointed out. 'Hollywood brings Signore Lanza's voice to places where there are no opera houses and to people who can't afford to visit them.'

'Yes, I suppose that's true and yet by choosing to be a film star he's harmed himself. He's missed out on being one of the great tenors of his age. I think it's a shame he wasn't born ugly, for then Hollywood wouldn't have wanted him in the first place.'

'I'm very glad Signore Lanza wasn't born ugly,' I said, laughing at Pepe. 'And I don't understand this fuss about opera anyway. Why is it so much better than listening to a voice on the radio or in a movie?'

'If you'd seen an opera you would understand.'

'I've never had the chance. Some day I would like to see one.'

'I will take you then,' Pepe offered. 'We'll go to the Teatro dell'Opera and listen to Puccini together.'

'Really?' The idea was exciting. 'You would do that?'

He smiled. 'It would be wonderful to watch you listening to a whole opera for the first time. You will love everything about the theatre – the spectacle onstage, the people dressed in their finery and dripping with diamonds. It is a beautiful experience.'

'Finery and diamonds?' My heart sank. 'I have nothing like that, only one good dress and perhaps that isn't smart enough.'

'No one will notice,' Pepe told me. 'They won't care about you; only about the opera.'

All I could think about that evening was Pepe's promise. For the first time I wondered if the housekeeper was right and he really did have a soft spot for me. As Betty rested and I went about my work, hanging up her clothes, tidying away her face creams and cosmetics, I couldn't help singing to myself, softly and almost beneath my breath but still clearly enough for her to open her eyes and smile.

'"Golden Days". Such a pretty song. You sound happy, Serafina,' she murmured drowsily.

'Yes, yes, I am.'

'That's nice, dear. Keep singing. I like it. It makes me feel happy too.'

If

Betty loved to find a reason to celebrate. When her mood was light she was so much fun and the prospect of a party brought a smile to her face. If there were no special occasion on the horizon, she would try to invent one.

'Things have been so dull. Let's have a birthday party,' she would announce.

If no one had a birthday coming up, she would simply laugh and say. 'Well, we'll have an un-birthday party instead.'

'Will there be candy?' Ellisa was always eager for she had a sweet tooth.

'Candy, cake and ice cream too,' Betty promised one afternoon. 'Whatever you like because it's your un-birthday.'

The whole household was pulled into the preparations. Pepe set to baking and whisking cream while I helped the governesses dress the girls in tulle and little shoes with kitten heels. We blew up balloons and wrapped comic books in coloured paper.

And Mario played his part, singing 'Happy Birthday' in Italian to the children, giggling at the joke of it all. He teased Ellisa by pretending to eat her ice cream and tried to convince Damon that the comic books were really meant for him. He let Marc ride him like a horse and covered Colleen in kisses.

Mario always seemed at his happiest at those silly parties, with his children so excited. Watching them together, I realised these were the moments my sisters and I had missed. This was how it was for other people but never for us. And I envied those lucky children their proud papa, found myself wondering how it must feel to be so certain where you belonged.

Those were the best times at the Villa Badoglio. Still, we knew by then how fleeting they could be. Once the gifts were unwrapped and the cake eaten, Betty's mood might fall flat and Mario's grin could fade. And then I would remember how fortunate I was, for I had the promise of many golden days to come. Carmela was to audition for the movie; Pepe was to take me to an opera. As I took down the party streamers and cleared away the creamy cakes, I almost felt sorry for Betty having to try so hard to make up reasons to be happy.

On the day of Carmela's audition I was more nervous than her, fussing as I helped her to get ready. For once she held back from glamour – her nails were left unpainted, her hair pulled back loosely and her face was bare of make-up. But she had borrowed my polka-dot dress once again and it seemed as though her curves now filled it out and there was less need for extra padding.

'Even if I'm to seem like a poor street singer I refuse to wear an ugly old dress the first time I visit a film studio,' she told me, examining her reflection.

'Do you know the song? Are you sure?' I fretted. 'Have you practised enough?'

'Stop worrying. When did I ever not know a song well enough?'

I straightened the straps of her dress and pushed a few stray wisps of hair from her eyes. 'You don't mind that you won't be singing for Mario today, only Signore Stoll and the casting people?'

'I don't see why you couldn't fix it for him to be there. Surely he's the one with the influence.'

'If it goes well, you'll be singing with him soon,' I promised. 'Just do your very best for Signore Stoll because I don't know if I'll ever be able to get you another chance like this one.'

I had taken the morning off work so I could accompany her to the Studio. Together we took the tram, barely speaking as it pulled away from Trastevere. Mamma had dabbed a little of her fragrance on Carmela's wrists just before we left and every now and then I scented it on the air. It felt strange – as though my sister was changing, growing up right then and there.

'What if they've found Luisa Di Meo? Will they turn us away?' she asked, her nerves beginning to fray.

'I'd have heard about it if they had,' I reassured her. 'Don't worry, she's probably gone home to Napoli and we'll never see her again.'

The doorman at the Studio gave me a friendly nod and tipped his cap as he waved us through. I led my sister through the maze of corridors. 'The casting director's office is down this way, I think. We're early, though, so we may have to wait a while.'

For thirty minutes we sat on the wooden bench outside the office door, Carmela rising every few minutes to pace back and forth, no longer trying to disguise how anxious she was.

'Will it be much longer? Where do you think they are?'

'It's always like this,' I told her. 'So much sitting and waiting.'

Finally the casting director appeared along with a slightly rumpled man with greying hair and a strong nose. Carmela stood but neither of them glanced her way. Opening the door, they disappeared inside, closing it firmly behind them.

For another ten minutes we waited in the airless corridor, Carmela pale and me wishing it were over.

Then the door opened again and Carmela's name was called. I rose to follow her but the casting director shook her head. 'Just your sister, please,' she said. 'We're ready for her now.'

For a long time there was nothing but silence. Later Carmela told me they'd asked so many questions she'd begun to wonder if she'd ever get a chance to sing. Then I heard the familiar sound of her voice raised in song but so muffled through the closed door that it was impossible to tell how well she was doing. I crossed my fingers and hoped they were impressed.

When the singing had finished there was yet more silence. At long last Carmela reappeared. 'I think they liked me,' she said breathlessly. 'They listened to two songs.'

'What next?' I was excited. 'When will they let you know?'

'I'm not sure. First they have to speak to Signore Lanza. It all depends on him now.' Carmela grabbed my hands and pulled me round to face her. 'Serafina, you must make sure he says yes.'

'But how?'

'You're there, working in his house, and he trusts you, doesn't he? Just talk to him.'

'It's not as easy as that. You don't understand.'

'How can it hurt for you to put in a good word for me?'

'I'll try ... but I'm only a servant. I don't want to seem like I'm taking advantage and risk my place with them.'

Carmela hissed impatiently. 'You keep saying that. But you'd never have got that job if it weren't for me. I'm the reason we were at the Excelsior Hotel in the first place. It was me that got you up to Signore Lanza's suite, remember?'

'Yes, I know, but—'

'Then this seems the least you could do.'

'I've told you I'll try. I can't promise anything more than that.'

Carmela pulled a powder compact and lipstick from her bag, both items I recognised as belonging to my mother. 'I'm leaving school,' she told me, as she tended to her face. 'Mamma thinks it's best.'

'What will you do? Mind the house and care for Rosalina?' I asked.

'For a while, I guess. But Rosalina is growing up and there's not so much that needs doing in such a small apartment.' Carmela's eyes met mine. 'Sooner or later I'll have to work, earn money. Mamma can't support me for ever.'

Staring back, I understood what she was trying to tell me. I knew the kind of work that waited for my sister. She was a pretty girl and most likely she'd do well at it.

'I'll talk to Signore Lanza,' I promised, more determined. 'I'll make sure he says yes.'

There was no opportunity to speak with him that day, for I arrived to find the Villa Badoglio bristling with people. Mario was busy with a costume fitting that had been hastily called by the wardrobe staff. By then his weight loss was obvious and waistbands had to be tightened and seams taken in before any more scenes of *Arrivederci Roma* could be shot.

In the next room Mr Teitelbaum was on the phone, his voice raised, as he argued his point with someone.

'It seems an unnecessary interruption,' I heard him saying. 'Yeah, sure, the publicity would be nice but is it worth delaying filming? ... Well, I'll talk to him but contractually we don't have to. Yes ... OK ... OK ... So you're saying we don't have much choice? Fine ... I said fine, didn't I?'

He threw down the receiver and I heard him mutter 'Goddammit,' and then call out, 'Hey, Mario, tell Betty to pack a suitcase, we're going to Naples.'

'I thought you were going to get us out of that?'

'I tried but the Studio is insisting. Apparently they want to make you an honorary citizen of the city and Caruso's son is going to present you with an award. They've organised some sort of charity ball. It's a bore but the publicity will be good for the picture so we have to do it. And Betty won't mind a jaunt to Naples, will she?'

'I guess not.' Mario sounded resigned.

Betty seemed jittery at the thought of the trip. We spent the afternoon pulling apart her wardrobe and planning what she would wear. Her prettiest dresses still hung loose on her but finally we settled on a plain, dark frock that fitted well enough and would look smart with her hair pinned up and some pretty diamond drop earrings.

'You'll come with me, won't you, Serafina? I'll want you to do my hair and make-up. And you'll accompany me to the ceremony, of course.'

'Oh yes, if you'd like me to,' I said, surprised. This would be my first chance to travel beyond Rome and she must have sensed my eagerness.

'These things can be very dull,' she warned. 'Still, it's sweet that they want to honour Mario.'

Betty was at her dressing table. She looked washed out and was holding one hand against her stomach, her face creasing into a frown.

'Are you all right, Signora?' I asked. 'Can I get you any-thing?'

She tried to smile but the effort seemed to cost her. 'Just my pills, please, Serafina. They're the only thing that can help me when I feel this way.'

'Are you unwell?'

'I have a little pain. It's nothing too serious.'

'Was it something that you ate?' I wondered. 'Surely not from Pepe's kitchen?'

She pressed her hand flat against her stomach again. 'No, just women's troubles, I think. It gets this way from time to time. The doctors didn't want me to have more babies after Ellisa, but I had my boys and now I'm paying the price, I guess.'

I fetched the pills and a glass of water, not really appreci-ating what she meant. I was too young to understand all the things that can go wrong with a woman's body: the cramps and cysts, the days of the month when it feels like life is draining from you. Later I knew how Betty must have felt but that afternoon, handing her the pills she relied on, I only pitied her.

'At least it's not too long a journey to Naples,' she said when she had swallowed them. 'I'll be glad to have you there, though, Serafina. At these big parties everyone wants to speak to Mario, to have their moment with him. He's a star so naturally they do. And yet for me ... Well, as I said, it will be good to have you there.'

Thrilled by the prospect, I began to plan my own outfit. The polka-dot dress, of course, although it might be a wrench getting Carmela to part with it. I'd wear my hair down and fluffed around my face, put on a little make-up. If I was to be beside Betty for the evening I didn't want to let her down by looking drab.

The trip was little more than week away and there was more than the thought of the party to excite me. We were to travel by train, all in the same carriage. It would be my chance at last talk to Mario, to steer him towards my sister and help her away from the other life that was tempting her. I held high hopes now, as I knew how kind his heart could be when his mood was good. Betty had told me so many stories but the one that stayed with me was about a little American girl called Raphaela Fasano who was dying of cancer and whose greatest wish was to hear him sing. It brought tears to my eyes when I learned of all the good things Signore Lanza had done for that child: flying her to Hollywood, throwing a party and showering her with gifts then telephoning to speak to her every Friday afternoon, regular as clockwork, for almost a year until the day she died. If he could do so much for a stranger then surely he would help my sister who sang like an angel?

The person I most wanted to share my news with was Pepe, for I was certain he would be happy for me. But at that hour his kitchen was a busy place. He would be cooking spaghetti for the girls to eat when they arrived home from school, making a nourishing dish for Betty's dinner, trying to add flavour to Signore Lanza's plain food. There would be no moment for him to pause and listen to me talk about the trip to Napoli.

I missed Pepe on days when there was no time for us to spend together. I had never met anyone who spoke the way he did and our conversations always left me with so much to wonder about. During mealtimes with the other staff he was different: not as feisty or free with his opinions. He didn't talk about music to the housekeeper or maids, didn't ask the governesses to taste new dishes he was trying out, certainly never mentioned kissing when they were eating mozzarella.

I knew it must mean he liked me best and hugged the knowledge to myself along with all the other things I was so excited about that summer.

The Loveliest Night Of The Year

Madama Butterfly was the opera Pepe had tickets for. He spent a quiet half-hour explaining the story and describing the music to me. There was bread baking in the oven that morning and the warm air smelt sweet. Upstairs Signore Lanza was rehearsing and we could hear his voice bouncing from the marble floors and walls, filling the whole of the Villa Badoglio.

'If only he were going to perform in *Madama Butterfly*. That would make it completely perfect,' I said.

'He is in good voice,' Pepe agreed. 'Do you hear how every word he sings is fully formed? Can you sense the darkness in his voice and the emotion?'

'Yes, it's beautiful. I still find it difficult to believe it's really him and not just a recording I'm listening to.'

That week he had sung for an hour every morning, first warming up his voice by humming or making an odd siren-like noise, then unleashing it on an aria. Pepe knew what each song was called and which opera they came from. When the music started he stopped whatever noisy work he was doing – pummelling veal into thin escalopes with his rolling pin, or hacking up a chicken – so he could listen more closely. All of us paused when Mario Lanza began to sing. His voice worked its magic on everyone in the household.

'Before he came to Rome I read that the Signore had strained his throat,' I told Pepe as the aria reached its ending. 'But that must have been a lie because each time I hear him he sounds perfect to me.'

'Where did you read this?'

'In gossip magazines like *Confidenze*,' I admitted, expecting him to disapprove.

Pepe only nodded. 'Perhaps it's inevitable there would be rumours. He never sings live, hasn't for a long time. That might have given rise to the idea he no longer has a voice.'

'But he's singing live now. We just heard him, didn't we?'

'It's one thing to sing when you're alone in a room and quite another to stand up before a theatre audience. If Signore Lanza wants to put an end to the gossip that's what he must do – and very soon.'

'Perhaps he'll sing at the charity ball in Napoli this weekend,' I suggested. 'Wouldn't it be wonderful if he did and I was right there to hear him?'

Pepe had lifted his rolling pin to continue tenderising the beef but now he paused, arm in air. 'But you're not going to Napoli with them, are you?'

'Oh yes, I'm to accompany Betty to the ball. I meant to tell you the other day but you were busy.'

'No, you can't go,' Pepe told me. '*Madama Butterfly*, remember? Our night at the opera is happening this weekend.'

Unbalanced by all the many excitements in my life, I hadn't realised the two dates clashed. 'Oh, no. What shall I do?'

'You must speak with Signora Lanza. Tell her you won't be going.'

'But I can't let her down. I promised.'

'What difference will it make whether you're there or not?' Pepe sounded snippy. 'I have the tickets. They were expensive.'

'I know ... I'm sorry.'

'So you will talk to her?'

I remembered Betty's face as she'd described those big parties. I knew she would be lonely, pushed to one side by the crowds eager to reach Mario, for I had seen it happen on the set of *Arrivederci Roma* and once or twice out on the street. Always she held herself proudly, kept the smile fixed to her face, but it must have been dispiriting seeing people's backs turned, knowing she wasn't the important one.

'I promised her ...' I repeated weakly.

'You promised me, too.'

'It's my job to go. I'm her assistant.'

'But I want you to come to the opera with me, Scrafina,' he insisted. 'I've been planning this. Surely the woman can manage without you this one time?'

'I don't think so,' I said apologetically. 'She needs me and I need this job; I can't risk losing it. Is there no one else you could take instead?'

Pepe grunted and, throwing down the rolling pin, turned his back on me. I couldn't bear to think I had made him angry, souring our beautiful piece of the morning. Watching him pull the golden-topped breads from the oven and tipping them onto a wire rack to cool, I wanted back the light mood we had just a few moments before.

'Pepe, I'm so sorry,' I began.

He refused to face me. 'Mario Lanza is not the only tenor in Italy, you know,' he said, dusting flour over the hard crusts of the loaves. 'There are others who are great – Di Stefano, Tagliavini, Raimondi, many more. They have timbre, passionate delivery, everything he has. You think Lanza is the best but only because you've heard none of the others.'

Deflated, I left him to his ruined mood, sorry to have caused it but not knowing what else I might have done. Betty needed me; of that I was sure. And I needed her and Mario so what choice did I have?

All week Pepe seemed determined to sulk. At staff meals he sat as far down the table from me as he could. There were no special tastes of food offered, no shared glances. I was starved of his company and his conversation.

Of course I regretted what I would be missing – myself in an audience and at Pepe's side, the strings of the orchestra warming up, the stage lit, the sound of magnificent voices. And the discussion afterwards when he asked me what I thought and explained the things I might have missed. None of it would happen now and I was sorry. But I was sadder still to have lost his friendship.

I grew tired of seeing his shoulders set against me, his face turned away, and tried several times to coax him into conversation. Late one morning as I was waiting for Betty's tray of soft-boiled eggs, toast and tea, I dared to ask him, 'Did you find someone to take the spare ticket for the opera?'

Pepe laid a starched napkin on the tray and next to it put shining cutlery. 'Why would I do that? You are coming with me,' he said stubbornly.

'But I told you—'

'I don't want to hear it.' The teapot clattered onto the tray followed by a toast plate and eggcups.

'You're being impossible, Pepe. You know I'd love to come.'

'There's no one stopping you, as far as I can see. Now run along and take the woman's breakfast to her before it goes cold.'

Carrying the tray upstairs, I heard him shouting at the housekeeper, complaining about a mistake in a food order and some missing flour. His voice echoed from the marble just as loudly as Signore Lanza's singing had earlier that morning.

For once even Betty commented on the noise he was making. She was awake when I took in the tray and sitting up in bed. 'That cook,' she said, as I poured out her tea. 'His food is delicious but he's so terribly temperamental. So much shouting all the time. I'm beginning to wonder if we'll have to let him go.'

'Oh no, please don't do that,' I said, feeling a flush creep over my face.

Betty's lips twitched. 'Do you have a little crush on him? He's very handsome, isn't he?'

'No, no,' I tried to insist. 'Today his bad mood is all my fault, that's all.'

'Whatever did you do?' Betty took the fine bone-china teacup from my hands and set it on her side table. 'Did you complain about his cooking?'

'Of course not.' I hesitated for a moment. 'He wanted to take me to see *Madama Butterfly* because I've never been to the opera. And then after he'd bought the tickets I told him I couldn't go after all.'

'But why did you do that?'

'The date clashes with our trip to Napoli. Both are happening this weekend.'

'Oh, I see.' Betty gave me a shrewd look. 'I think you'd prefer to go to the opera with the handsome chef, wouldn't you? You say you're not sweet on him ... but I'm not sure I believe you.'

Embarrassed, I felt my cheeks begin to warm again.

'You do like him, don't you?' Betty teased, laughing. 'Admit it, you do.'

'Perhaps a little,' I conceded.

'How romantic.' Ignoring her breakfast tray, Betty pushed back the covers. 'We must choose something for you to wear. I'm sure you'll fit into some of my gowns even though you're taller than me. Let's try one straight away. Now what would be nice for a night at the opera, I wonder ...'

'But, Signora, I'm coming to Napoli with you.'

'That thing in Naples isn't so important. Al is coming with us so he'll look after me when Mario is busy. You know, I think with your dark skin you'd look pretty in paler colours. I've got a silk dress I wore for *The Chrysler Shower of Stars* a few years ago that would be perfect on you. It's a little out-dated but has a lovely décolletage, rather low cut.'

I tried to object but Betty was too bright-eyed to listen. Zipping me into her clothes, she hung pearls around my neck, hunted for a matching clutch bag, even draped a stole around my shoulders, although the weather was too warm to wear it. She seemed captivated by the idea of my evening with Pepe.

'You'll look so beautiful the handsome chef won't be able to resist you,' she promised. 'You must tell me everything about the night when I get home. I remember the first time Mario took me to an opera. It was in Italian but he was so good at explaining the story to me. It's a lovely thing for a man to take a girl to. I'm so excited for you.'

I felt awkward in her clothes, fearing I'd stain or rip the gown that was surely a hundred times more expensive than anything I'd ever worn before. I tried to refuse the favour.

'Really, you don't have to … this is too much … I have a nice dress my mother made,' I stammered.

'Nonsense, this one looks so good on you I won't hear of you wearing anything else.'

Examining my reflection in the mirror, I realised in a gown like this no one would stare through me as though I didn't exist. I looked older and classier, like I belonged in Betty's world.

'Thank you, you're very kind. Both you and Signore Lanza have done so much for me. I'm grateful.'

'Well, you're welcome, I'm sure. Now let's change you back into your own clothes and you can run down and tell the temperamental cook you're going to the opera with him after all.'

Pepe must have looked at me differently after he saw me in Betty's evening dress. It certainly changed the way he treated me. He touched me lightly, his fingers in the small of my back, guiding me into the theatre. Twice he told me I looked beautiful.

All my glimpses of the person Pepe was had come through our conversations about music. In those he was forceful and opinionated. Now I saw another side of him, gentle and attentive, rather romantic even. I realised Betty had been right. Truly it was a lovely thing for a man to take a girl to the opera.

And sitting in that theatre felt so grand. Above us glittered a vast chandelier made from thousands of crystal drops, around us soared tiers of boxes filled with rich people. I saw older women with heavy strings of pearls and diamonds round their necks; men in velvet capes and bow ties, holding silver-tipped canes.

When the music began I thrilled at how those voices swelled to fill every corner of the auditorium. It was so powerful, yet beautiful too. I wanted to pay attention to every single note, to feel and live it the way I did Signore Lanza's singing. But I was aware of Pepe sitting close, his leg resting against mine, his hand brushing my bare arm. I knew he was watching my face as much as he was watching the people on the stage. While the opera was glorious, it felt as if we two were together and outside of it somehow.

Afterwards he took me to a pavement café on the Via Veneto. We had shaved ices flavoured with coffee and a dish of almond cakes and talked in a way we never had before. Pepe didn't lecture me about the opera as I'd expected. Instead, he pressed me to talk about myself.

I was careful how much I said, for there were things I preferred him not to know. But no one had ever shown such an interest in me before and I found myself opening up. I talked about my mother's beauty, how sweet but lazy Rosalina could be, how headstrong Carmela. A sympathetic ear turned out to be a most seductive thing and I couldn't stop some of the worries that filled me from leaking free.

'What does the future hold for us all?' I wondered, crumbling an almond cake on the plate. 'Perhaps I'll be able to find a job in some other household if the Lanza family leaves Rome, but what about the others? Carmela believes she'll make her living as a singer but few people are so lucky. And

Rosalina ... right now all she thinks about is sweet food and pretty dresses. What will become of her?'

'Must you be the one to care about all this?' Pepe asked.

'I'm the eldest. I've always been the one to look after them. I can't help it.'

'You can't plot out their lives, though,' he pointed out. 'They'll choose their own way in the end – especially your sister Carmela if she's so strong-willed. All you can do is try to make the life you want.'

'I'm not sure what that is, though,' I admitted. 'You have your talent for cooking and Carmela her voice. But there's nothing very special about me.'

Pepe smiled. 'I think you're wrong about that.'

And I smiled back at him, suddenly feeling shy.

We strolled up and down the Via Veneto until late that night, past the glass-walled pavement cafés full of couples sharing supper, sipping cocktails or coffee. It seemed strange to think all this vibrant life went on after dark on the streets of Rome long past the hour when I had gone to bed.

Pepe pulled my arm through his and we fell in step together, him in his borrowed evening suit, me transformed by Betty's gown, looking as though we belonged among the well-dressed crowds.

'I don't want tonight to end,' I told him. 'It's been so perfect.'

'Don't worry, Serafina.' Gently he squeezed my arm. 'There will be other perfect nights. I'm sure of it.'

All The Things You Are

I had imagined Mario and Betty would be buoyed by the celebrations in Napoli, pleased at the adoring crowds and being honoured by the city. Their return seemed a good time to raise the subject of Carmela. All I had to do was remind them of her audition and how wonderful she would be for Signore Lanza's duet. I was sure I could help her win the part in *Arrivederci Roma*.

But the moment they walked through the door it was obvious the whole thing had been a disaster. I had never seen Mario so taut with temper. His raised voice could be heard all over the Villa.

'How could you put us in a position like that?' he kept yelling at Mr Teitelbaum. 'What were you and the Studio thinking?'

'I've told you I had no idea what was going on,' he tried to defend himself. 'How could I have known? They tricked me, too.'

'You're my manager. You're meant to know.'

Too exhausted for their sparring, Betty went straight to bed. I took up a hot drink made from fresh lemons. She was oddly distracted and silent as I washed her face clean of make-up and brushed the knots from her hair. I had been looking forward to telling her about my night at the opera but she seemed to have forgotten all about it. Her mind was some other place entirely.

As she climbed beneath the covers, I busied myself shaking out the dress she had worn for the concert and hanging it near the open window where it could air, hoping she might tell me what had happened.

Only once her head was on her pillow, did Betty find her voice. 'Thank God we're home,' she said with a sigh.

'Did something go wrong in Napoli, Signora?'

'Oh, it was awful.'

'But why? Did they not honour Signore Lanza as they'd promised?'

'Oh yes, they honoured him. But it wasn't what we thought.'

I stayed in the room, fussing with jars and brushes on her dressing table, rearranging and tidying, waiting for the rest of it.

'Did Signore Lanza sing?' I prompted her.

'Yes, because they begged and begged him. He wasn't prepared but how could he refuse?'

'Is that why he's so angry?'

'No, of course not.' Betty pulled herself up in bed again. 'He's cross because it wasn't a concert; that was just a ruse. It was really a political rally and we were being used. Behind it was some scoundrel called Lucky Luciano. He's notorious, apparently, perhaps you've heard of him?'

'No, I don't think so.'

'Al found out he's a mobster, a proper Mafia Don. And poor Mario had to shake his hand – he had no choice. Now we're so worried. If these people latch on to us, who knows what will happen? Will we ever be rid of them? I'm afraid they may blackmail us, threaten the children. You hear about all these terrible kidnappings, don't you?'

Betty was agitated, her face flushed. Hoping to calm her, I offered a few sips of the lemon drink. 'You need to eat, Signora. Can I fetch you something from the kitchen?'

'No, I couldn't face food right now. But I'm glad to be safe in my own bed, I can tell you.'

The mood in the Villa Badoglio was sombre that day and

Lucky Luciano all anyone could talk of. It turned out Pepe had heard of him since his home village wasn't far from Napoli and the man was infamous even there.

'Is he very dangerous?' I asked.

Pepe shrugged. 'Men like that usually are. I expect he skimmed most of the profits from that charity concert. Whether he would threaten us here I don't know. I hope not.'

Later, one of the governesses told me Betty had asked her to watch over the children extra carefully and report any suspicious people they saw hanging around. They were to stay away from busy places like the Borghese Gardens for the time being. The driver was to take them everywhere and the children were not to be left alone for a moment.

If the sudden spectre of the Mafia wasn't enough, the next day there was an even worse crisis. The morning had begun with the usual routine: Mario woke early and warmed up his voice with singing practice before leaving for the Studio with Mr Teitelbaum; the driver and one of the governesses took the little girls to school; the boys stayed at home to be amused with crayons and comic books.

Betty still felt low but sat with her sons for a while and I convinced her to eat a little pasta at lunchtime. Not long afterwards we heard the front door slam, and there was Mr Teitelbaum trying to help Mario, who was sloppy drunk and reeking of whisky, into the hallway.

For a few seconds there was a terrible silence and then a scene broke out unlike any I had witnessed so far, Betty gathering every shred of energy to fuel her fury, hurling bitter words at Mr Teitelbaum and refusing to be calmed. Standing quietly in a corner of the room, I watched and listened without being noticed.

'How could you allow him to drink? You're supposed to be taking care of him. I trusted you and now you've let this happen,' Betty cried.

'Don't blame me,' Mr Teitelbaum told her. 'I can't watch him every minute. He's a grown man and if he wants a drink no one can stop him.'

'How did he get hold of the stuff in the first place?'

'I don't know. I left him in the make-up room while I went to make a few calls. I suppose he must have sent the chauffeur to buy a bottle. By the time I found him he'd drunk the whole thing.'

'I'm sick of this,' Betty declared. 'I can't take it any more.'

'Neither can I.' Mr Teitelbaum's voice was cold and his expression fixed. 'I told Mario when I arrived that I would only stick around if he stayed off the liquor and I meant it.'

'But you can't leave him.'

'Yes I can. I'm not just *leaving* him, Betty … I'm washing my hands of him. He can find someone else to follow him round because I'm finished here.'

I'm not certain if Mario heard any of the fight, loud as it was, since he was passed out cold on the couch. The next day he was still in bed nursing his hangover when Mr Teitelbaum left, his plush fur-collared coat over his arm and all his other belongings packed in a large suitcase. He carried it out of the Villa Badoglio and that was pretty much the last we ever saw of him.

Betty was left to deal with the mess left behind. Again the situation was dire with filming postponed a second time and Signore Lanza declared unfit to work. Pacing the halls of the Villa in despair, she struggled to know what best to do.

'He has to go some place where he can't get his hands on a bottle. If he dries out for a couple of days maybe things will be OK.'

'What about the hospital?' I suggested, keen to help. 'Like when he went for his weight-loss cure? There wouldn't be any alcohol there. He would be safe from it, surely?'

Betty stared at me, weighing up the merits of the plan. 'Perhaps you're right. I guess people don't need to know why he's there. I can say he's been working too hard and is getting some rest. It may really be all he needs.'

That afternoon I overheard another big fight between the two of them, and the very next day Mario was admitted to hospital suffering from stress and exhaustion.

Everyone in the household knew the truth but none of us mentioned it, not even to each other, for fear our words would reach Betty. She was brittle and quick to tears. There was no consoling her, although all of us tried: Pepe baking sugary treats and the governesses teaching the children Italian songs to entertain her. Colleen especially had a pretty voice and Betty cheered a little while listening to her but soon the bleakness would settle again.

'She's so sad,' I told Pepe one afternoon as I helped him shell fava beans. 'She and Signore Lanza love each other but it doesn't seem to do them any good. If only he'd give up drinking then perhaps they could be happy.'

The kitchen had become my place away from the sadness that filled the rest of the Villa. There was comfort to be found in the reliability of mealtimes and a joy in the flavours and smells. And there was Pepe, too, always happy to worry at a puzzle with me, to talk it round and share his thoughts.

Once the fava beans had been blanched, I peeled away the skeins of grey that hid their vibrant green hearts and watched him preparing dinner. He was quick and inexact in the kitchen, never measuring ingredients or following a recipe, cooking almost by sleight of hand. I wondered if I would ever be able to reproduce the dishes he made and have them taste the same.

'How long do you fry the onions for?' I asked as he started a sauce.

'Until you put a dent in them,' was all he said.

'How do you make those little *orecchiette*?'

'It's nothing, flour and water.'

Despite his nonchalance there seemed no limit to the

trouble Pepe would take with food. A crunchy, bitter salad of puntarella was a work of careful devotion, of separating leaves and slicing spears then soaking them in water to curl prettily. An anchovy dressing meant energetic work with the pestle and mortar. Watching him free a pouch of creamy burrata cheese from its wrapping of green leaves or knead bread dough with strong fingers; tasting how the flavours changed and deepened as a sauce simmered; hearing the snap of spaghetti as he broke it into a pan of foaming water ... I was warmed through by the life of his kitchen.

Often he let me help with the simpler things: hold the wooden spoon and nudge frying onions through hot oil, pop tender pods of fresh peas and fill a colander, grate a block of Parmesan – so it felt as if I was cooking with him. It was a good way of being together.

Both of us had grown used to starting each day with the sound of Signore Lanza's singing practice. It became how we measured other things: whether it was time for me to wake Betty and take the temperature of her mood, for Pepe to warm the oven to bake bread or rub a paste of garlic and rosemary into a side of meat, for the governesses to dress the girls in their school uniforms and run a brush over their hair. Always I thrilled at the sound of his voice and was sure the others did too. But now, with Mario in hospital, the house was silent and subdued.

The loss of his voice had affected us all. Antonio the janitor stopped whistling as he worked, the chauffeur didn't bother winking flirtatiously at the prettier maids, the housekeeper seemed grim. Gradually even Pepe's mood started to grey and the joy seemed to leak from his kitchen, as day after day we heard no news of Mario.

Betty had taken to waking early and wandering the empty rooms dressed only in her light wrap. Often I'd come across her sitting alone in one of the reception rooms, curled into an armchair, her face pale and eyes bleak.

One morning I arrived to find everything especially off kilter. There was no smell of coffee rising from the kitchen, no sign of the housekeeper who most days had straightened up the cushions and drawn back the curtains by then. Even the governesses were late hustling Colleen and Ellisa out of the door for school.

I went downstairs to see if Pepe was there and boil water for Betty's morning pot of tea, but found the kitchen empty. It was a lonely place without him, bare and ordered, smelling only of detergent. The pans had been scrubbed and hung away, the clean knives slid into their blocks, glassware polished, plates stacked on shelves where they belonged. Usually there was noise and colour here, the sound of chopping, the smell of something being simmered or heated in oil; and in the centre of it all Pepe, with his energy and unpredictable moods.

When he did appear that morning he was more abrupt than usual and in a hurry to catch up with his chores. He seemed to have no patience for my chatter. I tried to help him by making coffee for the staff, setting up Betty's morning tray and boiling eggs to mash on toast for Damon and Marc. Once I'd delivered the breakfasts I went back to help some more.

All night I'd been thinking about Mario, wondering how things had gone so wrong in a life that held such promise. I had hoped to talk it through with Pepe as I so often did, but that day he couldn't be roused at all.

'Life is complicated,' was all he said when I spoke of Mario's drinking and Betty's heavy sorrow. 'Nothing is as simple as it seems.'

'Surely they ought to be happy,' I argued. 'Look at all they have – money, fame, talent, a beautiful home, four sweet children. If I had those things I would be content, I'm sure.'

'You would find a reason to be unhappy, people always do. There'd be some loose thread in your life you'd niggle at until it unravelled.'

I had never seen Pepe like this, never heard his tone so flat or his words so pessimistic.

'What's the matter with you today?' I asked. 'You don't seem yourself.'

'I am myself. This is who I am,' he said shortly.

'But you're unhappy? Something must be wrong,' I insisted. 'Tell me, please.'

'Nothing is wrong. Perhaps I'm just not in the mood to be happy right now.' Pepe busied himself slicing potatoes thinly on a mandolin, lost in his task, as brooding and silent as the house had been all morning.

I gave up on him and went in search of some lightness elsewhere. Wandering upstairs, hoping to tempt Betty with an outing to the Via Condotti, I found her on the telephone, her face more animated and her voice elated.

'Of course, I'll tell him as soon as possible,' she was saying. 'He'll be so pleased. Thank you so much for calling and letting us know.'

'Such good news,' she told me as she put down the receiver. 'That was the Studio. They have found the little street singer at last and she'll be able to sing the duet just as soon as Mario is well enough to start work again. Isn't it wonderful? Exactly what he needed to hear.'

I tried to smile but my face refused to move. 'He's been calling the child his good-luck girl,' Betty continued happily. 'He'll see this as a good omen, I'm sure.'

She was keen to go to the hospital directly so I ran her a bath and laid out an outfit, readied the curlers and make-up, went through the usual motions of smoothing her way into the day. But all the time I was thinking only of my sister and how disappointed she would be. More than once I cursed Luisa Di Meo, but mostly I blamed myself for failing to get everything settled. By fearing being thought pushy, by being distracted by Pepe, even by choosing to go to the opera instead of to Napoli – I had ruined Carmela's chance of singing in *Arrivederci Roma*. How would she ever forgive me? She had needed my help and I had failed her.

Now I understood how Pepe felt, for I was no longer in the mood to be happy either.

More Than You Know

For a while it seemed there might be a chance for my sister after all, for Luisa Di Meo's brother was demanding crazy money for her to appear in the film. He was convinced Signore Lanza wanted the girl so much he'd fight for her no matter what. I wasn't so sure.

'He's full of bravura and keeps saying what they've offered is peanuts for a piece of the real Rome,' Betty confided as I tided her hair early that evening. 'But it's tens of thousands of lire – surely that's more than she could earn in a month singing on the streets?'

'I should think so, Signora,' I agreed. 'So what will happen now? Will they pay what he's asking?'

'No, of course not. Apparently they have another girl who has auditioned and is very good. Perhaps Mario will offer her the role now.'

Hoping she might mean Carmela, I fumbled with her hair and tried to decide what best to do. I might have sought Pepe's advice but for some reason his mood remained muted and his kitchen not as welcoming as it had once been.

Instead, I resolved to speak with Signore Lanza as soon as possible. He had been released from hospital, contrite but cheered, and ready to continue filming. Since his return I hadn't seen him unsteady on his feet or heard his voice thicken and slur, but I knew he was still in the habit of slowly sipping a glass of whisky to unwind from the day's filming, and decided it would be the best time of all to approach him.

In truth, I was nervous, for Betty always complained about

people taking advantage of Mario's big heart, and I didn't want to seem yet another one among them; or have him think me a girl on the make. But if a word from me might sway him away from Luisa Di Meo then surely I had to try.

That evening he burst through the door of the Villa, calling out to Betty and the children. There was an excitable greeting; play-boxing with Damon and Marc, bending to be kissed by Colleen and Ellisa. Before long, the sideboard drew him, with its full decanter waiting beside a polished crystal glass. I gave him a few moments to sip his whisky and knocked on the door.

'Signore Lanza, if you don't mind could I have a moment?'

'Is it Betty? What's wrong?' He sounded anxious.

'No, Signore. I had a personal thing I wished to ask, if you don't mind.'

'Of course, Serafina, what is it you want?'

He smiled when he said my name and for a moment all I could think was how it was to be alone in a room with him. Mario had a way of making everyone feel important: looking us in the eye, speaking as to an equal. Even so, I was always a little shy with him.

'Serafina?'

I took a breath and, half begging half boasting, tried to make a case for my sister and her beautiful voice.

He listened and shook his head. 'I'm sorry but it's too late. The Di Meo brother has seen sense and everything is settled now. But I'd heard there was another girl with talent, a natural performer. I didn't realise she was your sister. Did I listen to her once? On the street beneath the Excelsior on the day I hired you?'

'She sang "Be My Love",' I reminded him in a small voice.

'That's right. Don't look so glum, Serafina. Things might not have worked out this time but I'm sure we'll find another opportunity. A pretty voice like that shouldn't be allowed to go to waste.'

'Really?'

'Yes, but not on this film, I'm afraid.' He seemed regretful. 'I'll be sure to keep her in mind, I promise.'

'Don't think I'm not grateful for all you've done, Signore—' I began.

But draining his glass and glancing at the gold watch on his wrist, he interrupted. 'Is Betty ready? She's remembered we're having dinner with Red Silverstein this evening, hasn't she? I don't want to be late.'

In the days that followed, Luisa Di Meo came to the house several times to play with the children. She was a pleasant enough girl and I couldn't resent her for long, even though in my opinion she sang not half as well as my sister.

Although it felt a little disloyal to Carmela, I couldn't resist going along with the others to watch her film the duet scene by the fountain in the Piazza Navona. All of us were there: Betty, the children, the governesses, the housekeeper, everyone but Pepe. It was a golden day and the crowds were gathering, eager to catch a glimpse of whatever was to happen. We were close enough to have a clear view and I thought how uncomfortable Luisa looked, dressed in a new blue sweater and skirt, balancing on a railing. As the accordion player began the first few bars of the song and Mario serenaded her, she didn't seem to know what to do with her face, first managing an unsteady smile and then mouthing the words of the song back at him.

He was so tender, taking her arm and encouraging her to stand and sing her solo, she might have been his own daughter. Arms outstretched, she belted out the tune at the top of her lungs. I never was a fan of that harsh Neapolitan way of singing and winced at the sound. Even when they finished together, him softly and easily, she was still strain-ing for volume. Carmela would have made a better job of it, certainly, but still the crowds clapped appreciatively and everyone seemed pleased enough.

Afterwards, Mario signed autographs and treated us to another song. He was in fine voice that day and I don't think I ever saw him look as handsome nor as sleek as he did dark-suited, with his coal black hair slicked smooth and his eyes, always so expressive, truly sparkling.

Filming for *Arrivederci Roma* was almost finished by then and his mood seemed to lift with each passing day. Betty, too, was gayer and there was talk of parties and trips, visits from American reporters and TV presenters, maybe even a live performance. At the Villa Badoglio life was full of excitement.

At home in Trastevere the mood was not so bright. Although I had reassured Carmela that Signore Lanza wouldn't forget his promise, she didn't want to believe me.

'The next film,' she said scathingly. 'There may not even be one. Surely they need to see what the critics say about *Arrivederci Roma* first? What if it's a flop?'

'It's sure to be a big hit,' I insisted, 'here in Italy and in America. Everyone says so.'

'Just because you listen in on other people's private conversations doesn't mean you know a thing,' she tossed back.

My sister's words stung, for it was true that often I heard talk not meant for my ears. It is amazing how quickly people stop noticing servants. They grow used to us being there, passing through the commonplace scenes of their days, they forget how much can be observed. By then Betty and Mario's lives seemed more real than my own. They were on centre stage and I was their audience, fascinated by the spectacle. I couldn't look away from it.

'I do hear lots of things,' I said to Carmela. 'It would be impossible not to.'

'If you say so,' she muttered, making sure I noticed her eyes rolling upwards.

'Don't be nasty. I did my best and, I keep telling you, your chance will come so long as you're patient.'

'It doesn't matter anyway. I have plans of my own.' And then Carmela turned away and refused to tell me more no matter how I pushed her.

The next evening I left work earlier than usual and hurried straight home to Trastevere. Mamma had a heavy cold coming on and I wanted to give her the hot lemon drink Pepe made when anyone was feeling low. I was carrying a string bag full of the waxy-skinned fruit, a little jar of honey and a cinnamon quill I had taken from the kitchen. Autumn was setting in, the warmth and light were fading from the day and I walked quickly, head down, anxious to reach our apartment and check on my mother.

It was sheer habit that made me glance up as I passed the corner bar, for I knew Mamma was far too sick to be out and sitting there. I spotted her friend Gianna, though, and a couple of the other regulars, all dressed up as always and talking to a younger woman I didn't recognise. She was sitting with her back to me, wearing a red dress much too flimsy for such a brisk evening. It wasn't until Gianna raised a hand in greeting, and the girl in red turned to look, that I realised it was Carmela. She had painted her mouth with cherry lipstick and my mother's diamante daisies glittered in her ears. I was shocked by how grown-up she seemed.

'What are you doing here?' I asked.

'Having a drink, obviously.' She tilted her glass at me insolently.

'You should be inside, looking after Mamma and Rosalina.'

'You're here now so you can take care of them.'

'I think you should come,' I insisted.

Gianna reached out a hand, the silver bracelets on her wrist tinkling as she moved. 'Don't fuss, Serafina. It's only a little drink and then she'll be home.'

'She's too young …' I began furiously.

'Too young for a glass of soda and Angostura?'

'Well …'

'And a few minutes conversation with her mother's good friends?'

'She doesn't belong here.'

Gianna patted the empty chair beside her. 'Why don't you sit down, have a Cinzano Rosso and relax for a moment? We never see you since you started working for the big Hollywood star and his family. Come and tell us all about it. Sit, sit,' she urged.

'I don't have time …'

'Yes you do. Your mother is resting and your sister Rosalina is with her. Have a little fun for once. You're always so serious.'

I wondered if that was how people saw me, as serious and rather dull. Despite myself, I took a seat and accepted the drink they ordered.

'Where did that red dress come from?' I asked Carmela. 'I've never seen it before.'

'It's a new one of Mamma's. She knows I've borrowed it.'

My sister seemed at home among these women, chatting and laughing easily. Even with a glass in my hand and my chair drawn up to their table, I felt out of place, struggling to find things to say. These were my mother's friends, women I'd known for so long they were almost like aunties, and yet seeing Carmela so comfortable among them bothered me.

When night closed over, they left the bar and picked their way in high heels over the cobbles, perhaps heading to the lighted cafés of the Via Veneto or the Spanish Steps. I was glad Carmela wasn't to follow, however much she may have preferred to.

Instead we returned to the apartment to find Mamma in bed, crumpled foil wrappers on the kitchen table and Rosalina's face and fingers smudged with the chocolate she'd been bribed to silence with. I wiped her down briskly with a damp flannel and busied myself making Mamma's drink, squeezing lemons and heating the juice, filling the apartment with the scent of sharp citrus, instantly making everything seem cleaner and fresher.

'I'm worried about Carmela,' I told my mother in a soft voice as I gave her the drink. She was full of the sickness, her eyes watery, her nose red and streaming. I knew she wouldn't have left her room that day, as she hated to be seen that way.

'She's fine,' Mamma insisted. 'She was with Gianna and the others, they were looking after her.'

'She's not fifteen yet.'

'I know how old she is, Serafina,' she said tartly.

'Dressed in your clothes she might have been my age, older even.'

'My new red dress?' Mamma sighed wearily. 'I told her she couldn't wear it but you know how she is. I was much the same at her age. Worse, I expect.'

Sitting on the bed near her feet, in the quiet of the room, with just the two of us, the question came surprisingly easily. 'How old were you when you began working, Mamma?'

'Older than Carmela but not by much,' she admitted, and then gave a wry smile. 'My parents wanted me to take a job like the one you have, as a maid in a rich family's house.'

'So why didn't you?'

'I hated the idea of serving anyone. Instead I ran away and for a while things were hard because I was young and alone so it was easy for people to take advantage of me. But all that changed and now here I am an independent woman.' She blew on the surface of the lemon drink and took a sip. 'No one gives me orders. I don't have to cook or ruin my hands washing dishes. My life is arranged the way I want it.'

Even lying in sweat-soaked linen, her hair teased to a frizz by the pillows, her nose rubbed raw by her handkerchief, there was a magnificence about my mother, a strength I never dared to push against.

'You wouldn't want my life, Serafina; you've made that clear,' she told me crisply. 'Now do you understand that I don't envy yours either?'

'But Carmela … ?'

'It's my job to keep her safe.' She took another gulp from her cup. 'Thank you. This is exactly what I needed. You are so good at looking after people, *cara*. I think it's what you were made for.'

For the second time that evening I wondered if I truly was as drab as everyone seemed to imagine.

There's Gonna Be A Party Tonight

There were so many parties thrown at the Villa Badoglio and I loved to be a part of them. Anchoring myself to a tray of canapés, I would circle the reception rooms, moving between American visitors, Italian starlets and singers, sometimes recognising faces from the magazines I'd read but more often unable to guess who any of these strangers might be. Betty seemed familiar with most of them, gracious and welcoming, in the best of party moods and Mario equally bright, for nothing pleased him more than good company and a chance to show his generosity.

Beneath us in the kitchen, Pepe, too, was in his element, revived by the challenge of cooking the extra dishes requested for the guests. For the larger parties more staff came in to help but where food was concerned Pepe alone ruled and his kitchen was a serious place where there was no laughter and little chat. He had to be everywhere: at the stove, tasting and stirring, calling instructions and inspecting every platter or dish before it was allowed to go upstairs. To me he felt like a stranger, so stern and diligent, nothing like the friend he had been before.

Everyone seemed different then, I guess: Betty more confident and Mario bursting with ideas and excitement now that filming was finished and he was free.

'I'm singing like ten tigers,' I heard him tell his guests at one party held for yet another American visitor. 'Just wait till you hear our plans. We're going to tour Europe, sing for the Queen of England, we'll perform all over the world.'

'What about the opera, though, Mario?' someone asked. 'Are you going to sing at La Scala?'

Half the room fell silent as they waited for the reply. 'La Scala?' he said breezily. 'Well, they asked me years ago to open the season but movie commitments and one thing or another prevented it.'

'Perhaps now there will be time?' the guest suggested.

'You never know; perhaps so.' Mario clapped the man on the back, roaring as he did so, 'I'd fracture 'em at La Scala!' And his guests laughed with him.

I repeated the exchange to Pepe when I went down to the kitchen to load my tray with tiny toasts spread with salmon mousse. He dismissed it as party talk but I wasn't convinced. Ever since Signore Lanza's friend Costa had arrived from New York it seemed as if they had been preparing for something important.

Costa was a soft-voiced man, quite short, who often wore heavy, dark-framed spectacles and seemed happiest when he was sitting at the piano accompanying Mario. There were times I heard them fighting, and once or twice they refused to speak to each other for days, but still they seemed to have a bond like no other.

'They've known each other for ten years,' Betty had explained as I was helping her get ready for the party thrown in Costa's honour. 'Mario always does his very best work with him.'

There came a point in any evening when the guests would beg Signore Lanza to sing and he could never refuse. That night they gathered round the piano, Costa played a few bars to introduce him, and Mario filled the room with the richest, most satisfying sound.

He sang with so much emotion it was as if he was baring his soul, and I paused, tray in hand, my eyes half-closed so I could forget about the press of well-dressed bodies all around me and care only about the miracle of the voice flowing from Mario Lanza.

First he gave us 'Santa Lucia', then 'Because You're Mine' and finally my favourite, 'Ave Maria', holding the last note long and steady, then smiling at his guests at the finish. There must have been people in the room that had never listened to him save on a recording and perhaps they believed the rumours his voice was lost or had no power without a microphone. Now they heard it for themselves and they knew.

'Bravo, Mario, bravo!' they called out, applauding.

When the singing was over the party returned to what it had been before: champagne was poured, the hum of voices rose, someone put on a record and the dancing began.

A crowd of guests remained standing round Mario but I noticed how Costa was left alone at the piano, flicking a little awkwardly through a bundle of musical scores.

'Signore, may I give you another drink?' I asked him. 'Champagne?'

'Thank you.' He smiled and nodded towards the bottle. 'Is it Dom Pérignon? How delicious.'

I let the napkin fall so he could see the label.

'Ah yes, only the finest will do for Mario.'

I poured carefully – I had seen how champagne could fizz and spill over the top of a glass.

'Is it good? I've never tasted it,' I admitted to Costa.

'Truly?' He looked amazed. 'But the stuff is flowing like water tonight, I'm sure we can spare a little.'

Finding an abandoned glass, he wiped the brim clean with a napkin and took the bottle. 'A girl shouldn't have to pour her own drink, certainly not in this house,' he told me.

The champagne was creamy and smooth in my mouth, the bubbles foaming against my tongue, the flavour reminded me of yeast, honey and lemons.

'I see that you like it.' Costa smiled. 'Best not to get a taste for it unless you earn the millions Mario does.'

Smiling, I shook my head.

Costa glanced over at the tenor who was still holding court, a bottle of wine in each hand, pouring freely for his friends. 'He's the greatest since Caruso, you know,' he said softly. 'The first time I heard him singing it felt as if the most incredible joke had been played on me. I could barely believe what I was hearing.'

'Why is it his voice is so beautiful? Where does it come from?' I wondered. It was something I'd never understood and I was glad to have the chance to ask an expert like Costa.

'I guess it's a natural God-given talent. It comes from the lungs, the diaphragm, the vocal cords, resonates through the bony cavities of the nose, throat and mouth. Mario would tell you it comes from the top of his head.'

'And will he really sing for the Queen of England like he keeps saying?'

'That's why I came to Rome. We're getting ready for a Royal Command Performance at the London Palladium. Mario is to sing on stage again at long last.'

'But what about the opera?' I asked. 'Will he perform at La Scala as well, do you think?'

'That I don't know,' Costa admitted. 'He speaks of it, and right now he's so happy to be in Italy anything seems possible. It may change ... it usually does.'

I wanted to ask more questions, to hear what arias they planned for the Queen and know when they would be leaving for England. But I had spotted Colleen and Ellisa, wrapped in tulle and wearing their pretty shoes with the princess heels. Somehow they had sneaked into the party without being noticed. Sweet-toothed Ellisa was at the stand of little cakes on the sideboard, while Colleen twirled to the music.

'We're having fun, don't make us go back to bed,' she begged when I shooed them from the room.

'It's a grown-up party,' I told them. 'You're not invited.'

'But we wanted to talk to Uncle Costa.'

'Shh, go to sleep. He is busy.'

By the time I returned Costa was indeed busy, talking to a pretty fair-haired woman. I had mislaid my half-finished glass of champagne and was tired of pouring other people's drinks and emptying ashtrays. It was very late and I knew the party would continue until dawn – Mario hated people to leave and would call for more wine, turn the music louder, sing again; anything to keep them there.

Pausing to wrap some honey cakes in a napkin for Rosalina, I slipped away without saying goodbye, not even to Pepe. Tomorrow I would see him but most likely he would be far too busy planning dinner menus and cocktail food to talk to me of Bizet and Puccini. Like the champagne I had tasted, he seemed out of reach yet I longed for more of him.

Because

The trip to sing in London was less than a month away and Costa seemed anxious that he and Mario weren't properly prepared. By then another guest had joined us, an Englishman called Mr Prichard who was in charge of planning the concert tour. He was a lively fellow, full of bonhomie, and liked to start each day at the Villa Badoglio by opening a bottle of champagne at breakfast. By mid-morning, when Costa came by to rehearse, Mario often wasn't in the mood to work. If the girls weren't at school he might take them to the Excelsior Hotel for coffee instead. Or he would put on a hat and special spectacles with no lenses, and thinking himself well disguised, take a drive or stroll through the Borghese Gardens.

Costa never tried to force him if he was unwilling to sing. Instead, he'd pack away his scores and say, 'Perhaps tomorrow then, eh, Mario?' Or he would simply wait, hoping he might change his mind.

I had decided Costa was a kind man. If we happened to pass in the corridor he always had a smile for me but a lot of the time he looked so distracted and apprehensive that I too worried London would turn out to be a disaster for Mario.

When I learned I was to accompany them there, my anxiety grew stronger but now it was mixed with excitement. Never in my life had I dreamed of leaving Italy, never thought to have the chance. It seemed a thing only others did. Now I was to take the express train to Paris, then travel on to London in the famous Golden Arrow. I was to stay in a smart hotel and eat my dinners in a restaurant, take my place in a concert hall in the company of royalty. The thought of it … the very idea; it hardly seemed real.

But as preparations were made, I grew more excited. It was truly happening.

'You must make sure all your papers are up-to-date, Serafina,' Betty urged. 'Mario and Costa will be busy working. I'll need you to keep me company.'

We would be away ten days altogether and packing for the trip took me hours. Betty was particular about everything from the shoes she would wear to the jewels, determined to look her very best at Mario's side.

'November there may be cold and wet so we'll need hats too,' she fussed. 'And warm stockings. And perhaps a fur? I don't want to be catching a chill.'

'Of course, don't worry,' I replied, trying to sound calm though in truth I was almost as jittery. 'We'll lay out everything before we pack it so you can see exactly what we're taking.'

Betty patted my shoulder. 'Where would I be without you?' she said, as always. 'You don't mind coming with me, do you? There isn't another opera in Rome the handsome chef wants to take you to?'

'No,' I said shortly, for Pepe still seemed cool towards me. There had been no more talk of evenings at the theatre. In fact, in recent weeks he had hardly spared time to stop and chat at all.

'Oh dear, is it like that? Never mind, Serafina. We'll have so much fun in London, you and I. You won't miss the chef at all,' Betty promised.

It was thrilling to travel, especially in the style the Lanzas preferred. The Golden Arrow was an elegant train, Pullman coaches with deep armchairs and soft lamplight. Mario and Betty were accustomed to such luxury and even Costa barely seemed to register it. Only I walked everywhere with my mouth hanging open, astonished at how ornate a train could be, constantly exclaiming at the elegance of it all. Already I was storing up little details I longed to share with Pepe – the meals served in the plush dining car that came hidden beneath a silver metal dome, the tea and cakes served from a linen-covered trolley that was pushed through the carriage. It was all so perfect and I might have been happy enough if it had taken us three times as long to get to London.

Betty had told me Signore Lanza was very popular in England but I never expected a scene as extraordinary as the one that greeted us on our arrival at Victoria Station. A great mob of mostly young women were pushing and shoving, keeping up a constant chant of 'We want Mario, we want Mario'. It was much like the crowd I had been caught up in on the day he had arrived in Rome but from the windows of the train it looked more daunting. I wasn't surprised when Mario needed a glass of wine to face it.

There must have been two hundred of them and when we stepped onto the platform they surged, breaking through the barriers and knocking Mario off his feet. Quickly we retreated but, unable to resist his fans for long, Mario leaned out of the carriage's open window and broke into a snatch of song that set them roaring and rushing forward again as policemen in tall hats struggled to hold them back.

When he stepped down the second time there was more screaming and a reporter's microphone was pushed towards him. Smiling, he paused to be interviewed. I was trapped in the crowd beside Costa and had to strain to hear their voices.

'How long are you going to be in England?' the reporter asked and I was astonished to hear Signore Lanza saying he hoped to come back and live there for a while with his wife and children, for it was the first I'd heard of such a thing.

Later I would find time to wonder what it might mean but right then, clinging to Costa as we fought our way towards the car waiting to take us to our hotel, I was too overwhelmed to think properly.

Mario seemed unfazed by the hysteria, enjoying it even. Struggling into the car, the smile still on his face, he called out, 'It's just like a football match with me as the ball', laughing at his own joke. He was still beaming as we were driven away. I saw him put his hand over Betty's and give it a reassuring squeeze. 'Are you OK, darling? Still in one piece?'

She leaned in closer. 'See how they love you here, Mario. Didn't I say so?'

It was a short drive to the Dorchester Hotel, past mansions and monuments and a great park that I hoped I might find time to stroll through. The hotel was very handsome, with marbled pillars and liveried staff. I stayed close to Betty as we checked in, taking my cues from her, unsettled by the strangeness of being in a foreign country where everything looked, smelt and felt so very different to home.

The Lanzas were staying in a beautiful top-floor suite with a private terrace and wide views across the London skyline. My room was much smaller, of course, but still so richly furnished, with lamps to cast a soft light in the evenings, tasselled drapes over the window and a pretty floral counterpane. The moment I entered it I opened every cupboard and bounced on both the armchairs and the bed.

A knock on the door startled me. Outside I found a waiter carrying a single glass of champagne on a silver tray. That sweet man Costa had sent it up. Raising the glass in a silent toast to him and Signore Lanza, I downed every drop and wished those people in Rome who had made me feel so solemn and dull were able to see me now.

If it hadn't been for the newspaper reporters perhaps everything might have gone more smoothly for us in London. A press reception had been arranged for the following day, to be held in the Lanzas' suite. I was there that afternoon and saw how tense Mario became as he waited for the newspapermen to file in. Betty and I had helped choose his clothes – a navy suit, white shirt and blue tie. He was a little heavier since filming had finished, his eyes looked darkly shadowed and his colour a little sallow, but still he looked handsome and I assumed he would charm everyone the way he always did.

At first he seemed pleased to pose for the photographers, smiling and fooling around, and for a time the mood was light. Then the reporters began to fire their questions. If only they hadn't brought up his weight, but they couldn't resist, of course, and it angered him so much that for a moment I thought he might punch the man who first raised the subject.

'Why doesn't somebody ask me about my singing for a change?' he railed. 'For God's sake, isn't there anything else you can ask an artist? All this stupidity about waistline and weight. Did I come here to fight for the heavyweight championship of the world? No, I'm here to sing for the people, so why do you guys keep burning hell out of me about personal things like my weight?'

Wisely they changed tack, asking him about the new movie instead but Mario's mood had frayed and he began drinking champagne dangerously and quickly.

'I don't think the new picture is so good,' he admitted, as they scribbled down his rash words in their notebooks. 'It's my own performance I'm speaking about, of course, but the public may go for it.'

Those English reporters weren't easy on him – there were some mean jibes, with one man accusing him of being temperamental and explosive. Mario chided them in return, reminding them he was still the biggest selling recording artist in the world. Then he tired completely and dismissed them all.

'I'm not meaning to be rude, gentlemen, but I don't care about reporters,' he said, getting to his feet. 'Yesterday's news is forgotten by everybody except newspapermen. It's the public applause that counts to me. They're the ones I have to satisfy, not you.'

Once they had filed back out of the suite and the door was closed against them, Mario ordered more champagne and drank on. Betty tried to stop him, so did Costa, although we had seen him like this before and knew it was hopeless.

'You have to rehearse tomorrow,' Costa reminded him. 'You don't want to have a hangover.'

Hugging the champagne glass to his chest, Mario shook his head. 'I don't know about this performance. What if I forget the words? It's making me crazy worrying about it.'

'You know the songs perfectly well. We've practised them enough times. You won't forget,' Costa reassured him.

'But I might go blank once I'm up there. What if that happens? You'd better mouth the words to me while you're conducting. Promise me you will.'

'OK, if that's what you want. But no more champagne, Mario, please.'

'Yes, listen to Costa,' Betty pleaded.

'A little wine relaxes the throat,' Mario reasoned, pouring another glass.

Once a couple of bottles had been emptied, he grew emotional and incoherent, eventually falling asleep. Wrung out by the events of the day, Betty decided to skip dinner and rest with him. So that night I ate dinner with Costa as a string quartet played to us in a great room filled with palms and mirrors. He ordered steaks drowned in a buttery sauce, a dish of crisply roasted potatoes, another of creamed spinach, and had the waiter bring me another glass of champagne. I stared at it; pale gold and fizzing benignly. I was almost reluctant to take a sip after witnessing what it had done to Mario that afternoon.

'Why does he have to drink so much?' I asked Costa.

'I've spent a lot of time wondering the same thing,' he admitted. 'I don't believe he's an alcoholic, for there are times he barely drinks at all. The problems begin when Mario wants to avoid reality. I guess it must help him find peace, if only for a short while.'

I remembered the sense of warmth spreading through me after a second glass of Campari at the corner bar in Trastevere, a sort of unclenching of everything, and thought I understood how Mario might want that same feeling.

'Will he be OK to sing tomorrow?'

'I hope so,' Costa said soberly. 'Whether he'll be fine on the night itself is another thing ... this is his first live appearance in almost seven years. Who knows how it will go? What most people don't understand about singers is how much they all dread that the voice might fail. He's no different than the rest.'

'Is it likely, though?' I asked, concerned.

'I guess it's always possible. The vocal cords are only two little muscles, after all. They can swell, become strained or stretched, lose their elasticity like any other muscle in the body. When Mario stands up and opens his mouth to sing the very first note, the fear will be there for him. What if the voice is weak, what if it cracks on the high C? What if his gift isn't with him?'

The World Is Mine Tonight

The rehearsal the next day went well enough: Mario remembered the words to the songs and his voice was true even on the higher notes. Briefly we were relieved. But then he made the mistake of reading the newspaper stories the English reporters had written about him. Most were unflattering, calling him overweight, of course, but other unfair things too, like crude, petty and volatile.

He responded by drinking with a quiet determination, emptying bottles of champagne with friends that came by, with waiters on occasion, alone if he had to – trying to kill his nervousness and disappointment. Magnums of it were delivered to Lanza's suite both day and night and no one could stop him from finishing them.

The drink only seemed to make him feel lower still. More than once I saw him raise a glass to Costa and Mr Prichard, mournfully repeating the Italian saying: *'La vita è breve, la morte vien'* – life is short, death is coming. I think there were even tears in his eyes.

No matter how much he hurt his body with alcohol, Mario never forgot to cosset his voice. In the day or two before the performance he rested his vocal cords, talking very rarely and then only in a whisper. Often he wrote in a notebook rather than speaking aloud, he gargled with aspirin and wore a scarf wrapped round his throat. His voice was the most important thing to him, to Betty, to Costa ... and to me as well. I understood how we must all play our part in caring for it.

There were other stars on the bill with him that night at the London Palladium including the American actress Judy Garland but I couldn't look forward to seeing her because it was plain how nervous Mario was becoming. We were counting down the hours and minutes until he took the stage, praying he would be a success and receive the reception he deserved.

At last the big night arrived. In a borrowed dress, with Betty's jewels round my neck, I sat beside her on the short car ride to the Palladium. Neither of us spoke but our thoughts must have been the same. If it went badly, what would that mean for Mario?

There must have been thousands of people seated in the theatre's wide banks of red velvet chairs: all waiting to see the great Mario Lanza, to listen and judge him. Standing on that immense stage in his tuxedo, he cut a lonely figure. His face looked a little bloated and the shadows beneath his eyes had darkened noticeably. As he waited for the music to begin, he fidgeted, brushing at his forehead as if wiping away a heavy dew of perspiration, shifting from foot to foot uncomfortably.

Costa tapped his baton and the orchestra began the introduction to 'Because You're Mine'. Mario nodded to the Royal Box and blew a kiss to the audience. They applauded in response and the clapping went on until he held up his hands to quieten them.

In the darkness, Betty gripped my arm. 'Oh dear God, I hope he's going to be all right,' she whispered.

As Mario stepped forward, the microphone dropped away – he didn't need its help to project his voice and fill that vast theatre with its beauty.

The first song received rapturous applause. Next he began an aria that Betty whispered was from *Tosca*. She was clutching my hand by then, squeezing it hard, as both of us prayed Mario's voice would be robust enough to see the song through.

Only once the last note of the aria was sung did I let myself relax a little. His voice hadn't seemed close to cracking, I was certain of that. It was strong as a pillar from top to bottom. There was only a simple love song to finish so surely we were on safe ground now.

The final number was 'The Loveliest Night of The Year'. Mario stumbled over his words a little while introducing it and I gripped Betty's hand again, fearing he was losing his nerve. Then he settled himself, loosening his collar and tie, pushing a hand quickly over his sweat-drenched forehead, and began to sing. His gestures were sparing, his face solemn, he seemed overawed, and yet when he'd finished there was no one in the audience who wasn't roaring. I had never heard a sound like it. Relieved and proud, I joined in, clapping until my hands were sore.

The applause continued as he took a bow, as he gestured to Costa in the conductor's pit, and for a long time after he'd left the stage. Glancing at Betty, I saw tears in her eyes. 'Wasn't he terrific?' she said. 'And they love him ... listen to them.'

Afterwards, all the performers lined up to shake hands with the Queen and later there was to be a party. To my eyes Betty looked worn out but she refused to return to the hotel, for she thought Mario needed her. 'His job is to sing, mine is to provide support,' she insisted. 'I'll stay and I'll be fine.'

When at last we caught up with him, Mario seemed jubilant. Only I sensed the uncertainty, recognised the strain in his expression and heard him whispering to Betty: 'I was pouring with sweat up there; could you see? Was it obvious? How did I sound? Tell me the truth.'

'You brought the house down,' she assured him. 'I'm so proud of you, Mario darling, so happy. I knew you could do it.'

Once there was a drink in his hand, his tension seemed to ease and then he grew more buoyant, regaling us with all the details of being presented to the Queen. 'She told me she never knew human lungs could produce such volume,' he confided, grinning boyishly. 'I'll bet she thought I was going to tear off the roof when I sang the top notes.'

It was a long but happy night, and I was delighted to be a part of it. Betty looked radiant even if perilously thin, Costa laughed a lot and Mr Prichard told the same joke endlessly – that he'd been sure to stand right behind Mario in case he got carried away and tried to give Her Majesty a kiss on the cheek. The mood was light enough that, no matter how many times he repeated it, it still seemed funny.

After the party we tried to manage a late supper, although it was difficult to eat with Signore Lanza besieged by fans and signing autographs. He didn't seem to mind the interruptions. For every fan he had a few kind words. I think he must have won a lot of hearts in England that night.

The whole evening long my thoughts kept returning to Pepe. Surely now he couldn't accuse Signore Lanza of throwing away his talent. Once I had described the triumph I had witnessed, made him understand how perfect it had been, then he would have to agree nothing could surpass it – not even an opera.

There was so much ahead now, so many exciting plans: a return to the Palladium to perform a second concert, a long tour of Europe, more audiences, more songs. I imagined Mario on all those stages, just a man and his voice, no tricks and nothing clever, but so dazzling that those who heard him clapped until their hands grew sore.

In the Lanza household trouble nearly always followed a triumph. Now it was Betty's turn to be sickly. On our return to Rome she began complaining of a stomach ache. I found her bent double one morning, breathing in short, pained bursts and begging me not to let the children glimpse her like that.

'What if there's something seriously wrong?' she fretted. 'I feel so weak and exhausted all the time; and these pains are tearing at my insides. I've never known anything like it.'

To the doctor her condition was a mystery. No pill he prescribed seemed to help, the stomach pains kept coming and Betty was helpless in the grip of them.

Then she took a bad fall in the hallway, hitting her head against the marble floor. Hating to see her so weak and unwell, fearful she might injure herself seriously, Mario was edgy. It seemed better for everyone if she were admitted to hospital for tests and recuperation. Still it felt awful to see her wheeled out of the Villa Badoglio, her face as pale as paper above the blanket they'd drawn up to her chin.

When it was discovered Betty was suffering from malnutrition we were dismayed.

'I make such good food for her,' Pepe said angrily. 'It's crazy to be under-nourished in a house where there is so much to eat. I don't understand it.'

'When she's struggling with her nerves she can't swallow, no matter how good your cooking is,' I reminded him. 'And she's anxious right now. London was hard on her and they're planning this huge concert tour, which means months on the road and travelling to so many countries. That's why she isn't eating because she fears it will be too much for him.'

'When she comes home from hospital I'll make soups from beef bones and root vegetables,' he decided. 'Food that's light and nourishing, easy to swallow. Surely she will manage that?'

Caring for Betty was something for Pepe and I to do together. We sat at the kitchen table and listed dishes to tempt her: lemony risotto with delicate flakes of white fish, soft ravioli filled with puréed beetroot and butter, velvety *ribollita* soup, food full of nourishment, meals to bring her back to us.

I favoured the quieter flavours but Pepe disagreed. He wanted to surprise Betty's palate with bolder tastes, to keep her eating even when she didn't think she felt hungry.

'I'll make her a broth of lobster like they do in Sicily, spiced with cinnamon and fennel, sizzling with chilli,' he told me. 'Or a soup of salt cod and garlic. What about fat anchovies pressed into polenta and fried until they're crisp. And calf liver with lots of sage and sweet red onions. Might you get her to eat that?'

'I could try,' I said doubtfully.

It felt like a long time since Pepe and I had talked this way, although it was only a matter of months. So much had happened to keep us apart: Mario's drinking, the parties and travelling, the unpredictable lurches of everyone's moods. Now it seemed Betty's illness was helping bring us together.

Despite my good care, Betty was still so weak she had another bad fall only days after leaving hospital. Mario began talking seriously about carpeting the marble floors to protect her if she fell again. It was nearing Christmas and they'd both been so excited about celebrating it in Italy for the first time. Nothing was to be allowed to spoil the holiday.

Over the next week Betty rallied a little, gaining some colour in her cheeks thanks to spoon after spoon of Pepe's rich broth. She was determined not to miss out on any of the fun and was delighted by the Christmas tree that had been delivered to the Villa Badoglio. It was the largest I had ever seen; its tip touched the ceiling and its branches spread magnificently. Betty had it decorated with shining tinsel, coloured baubles and foiled chocolates. Presents were piled beneath, so many of them and gorgeously wrapped in gold paper and silver ribbons. There was something for every single one of us. Most of the tags, though, bore the children's names. Already there was an entire room in the Villa filled with their toys: pedal cars, scooters, tricycles and dozens of dolls. Now we must find space for even more.

On Christmas Day we gathered round the tree, the staff, the Lanza family, and Costa, too, for Mario had insisted the whole household should celebrate together. It was my first time away from home and I missed our small traditions: the sweet treats eaten as we shared our gifts, the one proper meal of the year my mother wanted to cook. Still I was dazzled by Christmas at the Villa Badoglio. The rooms looked pretty strung with tinselled garlands and lit by church candles dripping wax into saucers. There were platters of cold meats and good cheese, champagne in silver buckets filled with ice. Betty was made comfortable in a chair, a warm shawl round her shoulders and a paper hat on her head, and she watched happily as we unwrapped our parcels.

Mine held a scarf made of fine wool in a shade of blue she knew would suit me. There were books for the governesses, rock 'n' roll records for Antonio the janitor, embroidered handkerchiefs for the maids and housekeeper, and for Pepe a box of cigars since Betty must have noticed how he liked to sit beneath the magnolia trees and enjoy a smoke whenever he took a break from the kitchen.

The children were allowed to stay up much later than usual that evening. Once they'd tired of their new toys, Mario got down on his hands and knees and let them take pony rides on his back. When they grew drowsy he sang them lullabies until Betty insisted it was bedtime.

He was his best self that day, as relaxed as I'd seen him, chatting to Pepe and Antonio as though they were old friends, telling jokes and taking pleasure in their laughter. I tried to overhear, but judging by the way he dropped his voice and turned his back on the women in the room, he didn't think the jokes fit for our ears.

Before our little party was over he sang carols for us, his voice warm and full of love. Softly we joined in, with Costa at his place at the piano and Betty pretending to conduct from her armchair.

Later I was given a second gift, something entirely unexpected. I had put on my coat and slipped a scarf over my head for it was wet outside, and just as I was about to leave Pepe slipped an envelope in my hand.

'*Buon Natale*,' he said.

'What's this?'

'Open it and see.'

Inside were tickets to an opera. I stared at them, surprised.

'There is a gala performance of *Norma* next week,' Pepe explained. 'Signore Lanza procured the tickets weeks ago and I've been saving them to surprise you. I thought you would be pleased. Are you not?'

'I didn't expect it, that's all.'

'But you will come?'

I hesitated, wanting so much to spend another evening with Pepe and yet unbalanced by this new shift in his mood.

'It is the great Maria Callas who will be singing. You mustn't miss her,' he urged me.

'If you really want me to ...'

'Of course I do.' He smiled. 'Maria Callas! I can't wait.'

All the way home I tried to make sense of what had happened. How could Pepe seem friendly to me one moment and indifferent the next? I searched my mind for reasons but found none that were convincing. Pepe, it seemed, was impossible to understand.

You Are Love

Later I heard stories about Signore Lanza, that he was a womaniser, unfaithful to Betty, that he paid whores and treated them badly. I can only say that in all the time I spent with him I never saw a sign of it. To me they seemed to adore each other. He touched her often: a hand on her arm, a kiss on her cheek. And while both had tempers that were easily fired, I saw them tender more than they were angry.

Over that Christmas and New Year they were together all the time. Costa was staying at a *pensione* in the Via Veneto but often he would come to share meals and conversation, for Mario preferred to have people around. He liked chatter and music, cigar smoke and reasons to laugh. I think he had a dread of empty days and empty rooms.

The concert tour was to begin early in January and I heard them discussing the plans. So many cities: Sheffield, Glasgow, Newcastle, Leicester, London's Albert Hall and then on to Germany. I wondered how Mario would find the energy for it. Betty certainly wasn't strong enough to accompany him and they seemed unhappy at the prospect of such long stretches apart.

'I'll be terribly lonely,' Betty complained, 'and the children will miss him too. If only he could come home every night the way he does when he's making a movie.'

'It will be very quiet here without him,' I remarked, for I would miss his presence too.

'Quiet and dull,' Betty agreed. 'We'll have to make some

fun for ourselves – have little tea parties, plan some treats to cheer ourselves up. Let's make a list.'

I fetched some paper and a pen, and we sat together in her room dreaming up ways to make the long weeks of Mario's absence pass more quickly. I loved these moments with Betty – when she let me into her life, asked for my help, seemed more friend than employer.

It was her I turned to when I was struggling to understand the puzzle of Pepe. She had experienced much more of life than me, and I hoped she might guess what lay behind his behaviour.

'One moment he's friendly and the next distant,' I confided while the two of us were out shopping on the Via Condotti. 'I never know quite how I'll find him. Often I'll be left wondering if I've done something wrong but I can't think what it might be.'

'Men do blow hot and cold at times,' Betty told me, gazing at a lemon-shaded silk dress in a store window.

'But why?' I pressed her. 'There seems no reason for it.'

'I think they're quite different to us. Work to them is almost everything and if it's not going well that's when they can seem moody or distracted.'

'But Pepe's work is not like Signore Lanza's. He's just a cook, after all.'

'To him it's still important, perhaps the most vital thing in the world. Men can be so single-minded.' She turned away from the dress in the window, and we walked on past the shops together.

'He's asked me to accompany him to another opera,' I told her.

'Well, that's good, isn't it? Are you pleased?'

'I don't know ... Should I be careful not to seem too keen? Would it be better to refuse—'

'Do you care for him?' Betty interrupted.

'Yes, I think so.'

'Well, don't play games – men hate that.' She seemed thoughtful. 'Don't expect him ever to be easy, though, Serafina. He won't change. What you get now is what you will always have.'

And then we went for tea and cakes at the café near the Spanish Steps and the conversation turned back to the lemon-coloured dress and whether it would suit her.

Maria Callas' performance that night in the Rome Opera House has gone down in history. I was there in the audience and it was clear from the very first note that the great diva's voice was in ruins. Both Pepe and I tensed, unable to believe she could continue straining to sing. We sat in shocked silence while around us the audience jeered. It was a fiasco, particularly when she tried to reach the higher notes and her voice blurred and wobbled, slipping away from her.

When she refused to return after the first act, Pepe said he wasn't surprised. Amongst the rest of the audience, though, there was pandemonium, a near riot at her walkout and so much anger – people shouting for refunds and demanding she leave Rome – that it seemed the singer's life would be in danger were she to appear again.

'This is what Signore Lanza fears,' I said as Pepe helped me through the crowds and away from the theatre. 'Exactly this.'

The next day all sorts of rumours were published. The reporters wrote that Callas had been up late drinking champagne at a nightclub and when she woke on the day of the performance her voice was reduced to a whisper. They said she begged to be replaced but the artistic director refused because there was no understudy to be found. Pepe and I spread the newspaper over the kitchen table and pored over it, certain that upstairs Mario must be doing the same.

'In a few days he must stand up onstage in England and sing,' I said. 'What if he opens his mouth and there's no voice there, if it fades and shakes like hers did last night?'

Pepe frowned. 'Then his career will be over just like hers surely soon will be.'

'It seems so cruel.'

'She failed,' Pepe said simply. 'People don't forgive failure.'

I had expected Mario to be subdued but instead the opposite was true. Fuelled by beer and refusing to submit to another of Costa's rehearsals, he demanded a celebration, unexpectedly appearing in the kitchen and causing Pepe and I to fold away the newspaper hastily.

'Tomorrow I must begin serious work, so today is for feasting and drinking,' Mario announced. 'Hey, Pepe, what do you say we cook a ton of fettuccine and some chicken cacciatore? You and me, eh?'

Pepe looked astonished at the idea of sharing his kitchen with the great tenor but Mario didn't appear to notice, pouring more beer and rolling up his sleeves enthusiastically. 'You have an assistant so tell me what to do,' he urged.

Side by side they chopped onions, then started a cacciatore sauce and were noisily jointing a couple of chickens when Betty came down and put her head round the door. 'Are we having a party?'

'You bet we are,' Mario replied.

None of us mentioned the business with Callas nor did we talk of the concert tour, not even when Costa joined us. It was food Mario wanted to discuss, the dishes he had eaten and the ones still left to try.

'In England it will be roast beef and potatoes day after day,' he sighed to Pepe. 'I wish you were coming with us to cook up a decent plate of pasta for me.'

We ate at the kitchen table, with Betty and the children, the staff too, even the driver. More beer was poured; then glasses of Chianti, and Mario gave us sticky-sweet liqueurs to finish; until all of us were flushed and talking loudly in wine-soaked voices, the room ringing with the sound.

As the light faded, people began to leave: first the governesses took the children up for their baths, then Betty followed them to bed, the housekeeper returned home to her husband, the maids, the driver and the janitor left, until finally there were only three of us around the table. By then the empty wine bottles were lined up next to the kitchen sink. While Mario was busy opening yet another, Pepe brought more food to the table, a wedge of Parmesan cheese, a finely sliced ripe pear, a bowl of walnuts. He offered Mario a cigar from the box he had been given for Christmas and the pair chatted like old friends while I sat by quietly and listened.

'So, Pepe, tell me, how did you end up becoming a cook?' Mario asked.

'Mamma taught me when I was a boy. She said anyone who knows how to cook will always make a decent living and she must have been right because so far I have.'

'Our mothers are wise women, surely. Mine knew it was only ever going to be about the music for me. She worked hard to pay for my lessons and it was Papa who ended up in the kitchen.' Mario smiled at the memory. 'Usually my mother wasn't very satisfied with what he did there and she wasn't afraid to let him know it. I didn't care so much about food then. Music was what mattered to me.'

'You always had a voice, even as a boy?' Pepe asked.

'I guess so.'

Leaning his elbows on the kitchen table, Mario told us about his childhood, how he'd sung along to the records of Caruso when no one was home to hear, how he was certain of his destiny right from the beginning. 'And it all happened in a big rush exactly as I'd dreamed it would. There was no struggle,' he told us. 'Success came so fast for me. Maybe I had it too easy.'

'There must have been hard times, surely?' Pepe asked.

'Yes, but mine has been a mixed-up, back-to-front career. My heartbreaks and setbacks all came after I reached the top, not during the climb.' Mario swirled the wine in his glass and took another sip. 'Still, I have very few regrets. I've made mistakes but if I could live my life again, I'd play most of it the same way. I've got success, money, a beautiful wife and my children. I'm a lucky, lucky man.'

'You are indeed, Signore.'

The words didn't ring true. Even with all the success he had and all the luck there was often a great sadness about Mario. I felt it right then and am certain Pepe did too.

'You were at the theatre last night, weren't you?' he said suddenly, fixing Pepe with bloodshot eyes. 'You witnessed her disgrace?'

'You mean Callas?' Pepe looked uncomfortable.

Mario nodded fiercely. 'She wasn't well, you know ... They shouldn't have made her do it. She sang against the orders of her doctors and how could that have been anything but a disaster?'

'Why did she appear?' Pepe wondered.

Mario shrugged. 'There's always someone who wants to turn a profit from you, who benefits from forcing you on stage. Did you see how she looks? They say she's lost sixty-five pounds. It's not good enough to have a voice; a singer must also be a fashion plate ... a matinee idol ...'

Mario's mood had shifted and it was clear he wasn't speaking of Callas any more but of himself. He began to rant against his managers, the press reporters, people in Hollywood he believed had mistreated him, and most of all the critics.

'They talk about my waistline, demand to know how much I weigh.' He slammed his fist down on the kitchen table. 'Don't these fools see how it is? We need the weight to keep the ribs open, to give us the power to control the breath. Without it you can't get your phrase, your voice thins, you crack the high notes. In Hollywood they care about none of that. They give you a script that's a piece of junk, there's no respect for your voice … '

Neither of us tried to interrupt for he was in full flow, the words rushing from him. 'The rubbish they print about me,' he complained. 'If I cough, if I have a red throat, they say I'm losing my voice. It's as if they want it to happen. They don't understand … hardly anyone does … how it is to have a voice … how it takes over your entire life … my wife is married to a voice … my children raised by it …'

His speech was slurred by then, his eyelids heavy. 'Thank God I'm in Italy now,' he told us. 'Hollywood is six thousand miles away – little more than an unpleasant dream.'

Together Pepe and I helped him upstairs. Mario was a wide-shouldered man and very heavy to manoeuvre but somehow we managed it. We laid him on the couch to sleep off the wine, hoping he would be himself again by morning.

Turning off the light, I heard him mutter, 'A man must be free or there is no will to sing.' And soon the only sound was his snoring.

When the concert tour began, Pepe was keen for me to carry any snippets of news down to the kitchen. He drew me there with savoury delicacies he knew I would enjoy – pastes of artichoke heart and chopped almonds spread on crisp crostini, a wedge of ripe taleggio cheese smeared on crusty bread, a celery stick filled with creamy gorgonzola and toasted pine nuts. Suddenly he had time to listen and chat. Pepe was turning towards me again but I didn't trust the change in him entirely.

I had no time to linger anyway for I was busy with Betty who had decided she wanted to fly to London for Mario's next performance. On this occasion she was happy for me to stay behind at the Villa and help care for the children, needing assistance only to choose her outfits and fold them carefully into her case.

'It's just for a few days,' she told me. 'We'll have our same suite at the Dorchester so it will feel like home and Mario's made lots of plans to visit with friends. Lana Turner's making a picture over there. She's rented a house in a pretty part of London called Hampstead that she says would be perfect for the children if ever we do decide to shift to England.'

I had hoped the talk of leaving Rome had been no more than a story for the British reporters so was taken aback by this second mention of it. 'Do you really think you'll go to live there?' I asked. 'I thought you loved it here.'

'Oh, we do, but we'll go where Mario's career takes us as always. Don't worry, Serafina, you'd be coming with us, and Liliana and Anna-Maria, too. We couldn't be without any of you.'

I had liked London well enough but didn't want to leave Rome. My life was here, my family, everything that was familiar and belonged to me. And Betty hadn't mentioned Pepe's name amongst the staff she would take with her. Exasperating as he could be, I didn't want to leave him either.

The whole time Betty was in England I dreaded her return, convinced she would bring home the news that they had found the dearest little place and we were to pack up the Villa Badoglio immediately. I didn't share my fears with any of the staff, because I didn't want to worry them. But when I woke in the night and sleep was hard to find, it was all I could think about.

Happily, nothing about London pleased Betty this time. She came home complaining about the Dorchester and about Costa who she claimed was being unreasonable and greedy. She didn't have a good word to say about a single person. 'Everyone is cheating us,' she said querulously. 'All of them, dipping their hands in our pockets. It has to stop.'

Even the much-anticipated visit to the movie star Lana Turner's house hadn't gone well, for Mario had stumbled on some steps leading down to the garden and bruised his ribs.

After that I was relieved to hear no more talk from Betty about moving to England.

While Mario was away she was subdued and I am certain she worried about him every single day. Her nerves were bad for most of the time and it was a struggle to coax her to eat even the most delicious meals Pepe conjured up. The plates stayed full but the pill bottles she kept in her room were emptying as quickly as ever.

'I'm worried Mario is pushing himself too hard,' she confided. 'He didn't seem at all well when I saw him in London.'

'Was it his voice?' I asked, alarmed. 'Did it sound strained?'

'No, his performance was fine. But he was very tired and I thought his leg looked rather swollen. He's promised to see a doctor about it. I hope he doesn't put it off for too long in case it's something serious.'

Betty seemed distressed but not at all surprised when the news came that all Signore Lanza's engagements had been cancelled and he was returning to Rome. 'I told him this tour was too much, but he wouldn't listen,' she said. 'He's pushed himself too hard.'

Next we learned he had been diagnosed with phlebitis, a mysterious condition to me but the housekeeper knew about it because her mother had suffered the same thing. It was a clot, she told me, deep in the veins of his leg, and if it moved then it could cause a blockage so severe it might kill him.

I refused to believe such a thing at first. How could a man so full of life be felled by a tiny clot of blood? But then we saw him and it was clear poor Mario was in a great deal of pain. His face was washed pale and the shadows beneath his eyes had deepened to bruises. All his sparkle had gone.

As soon as he arrived in Rome, his own doctor examined him and he was rushed directly to the hospital. For thirteen days he remained there, everyone so worried, Betty most of all.

'Can they heal him, Signora?' I asked, knowing the rest of the staff was wondering the same. 'Will he be all right?'

'I hope so.' She looked stricken and her voice was hushed. 'But it's much more serious than people realise. In Munich they told him if he didn't take care he could be dead within a year. His health is terribly fragile and he must have complete rest until this crisis is past. There will be no more touring, that's for sure.'

'Is there anything we can do to help?' I asked.

She shook her head. 'It's up to the doctors now. They're treating him with blood thinners and he must wear special stockings. I'm told he's in very good hands. The Valle Giulia is one of the top clinics in Rome and everyone speaks well of Dr Moricca. Let's just pray to God he will be better soon.'

For much of that time Betty kept her door closed and only I was allowed to pass in and out with trays of food she refused to touch and glasses of water to wash down her medication. There was so little flesh on her now; she seemed frailer than ever. Not for the first time, I felt afraid for her.

I tried to talk to my family about it on one of the few afternoons I dared leave the Villa Badoglio. Carmela had found me searching for the box I had left beneath the bed and tried to peer inside as I pulled out the photograph of the Lanza family I cut from *Confidenze*, the one of the six of them walking hand-in-hand on the studio lot.

'Don't you see enough of those people when you're at work?' she asked scathingly. 'Must you stare at pictures while you're here as well?'

'I wanted to see if they looked the way I remembered,' I explained. 'They all seem so happy in this picture. See the smile on Mario's face.'

'He is world-famous and worth millions, why wouldn't he be happy?'

'It's more complicated than that. You don't understand.'

My mother was at the dressing table, brushing tangles from

her hair before she set it into rollers. 'You seem worried, *cara*. What's wrong?'

'It's awful there right now,' I told her. 'Everyone is concerned about Signore Lanza's health, but Betty is far from well too. The only people she agrees to see are me and Dr Silvestre. He says she needs rest but it doesn't seem to be helping. If I can't get her to eat then surely she will waste away?'

'Serafina, this woman is not your responsibility,' my mother told me, sounding concerned. 'You shouldn't be the one who has to worry about her. Does she not have family ... friends?'

'They're all in America. Here in Rome there is no one but me.'

'You are employed by these people, they are not your family,' my mother insisted. 'I'm angry that you've been put in such a position. It should never have happened.'

'I don't mind ... I'm happy to do anything I can.'

'But, Serafina ...'

'If you had heard him, Mamma, if you listened to his voice in the mornings when he practises ... It's glorious, so unique; it fills you up. If I can help him, support that voice in any way, then surely I'm doing God's work.'

Both my sister and mother were staring at me, wearing odd expressions. 'You really are in love with him, aren't you?' Carmela said wonderingly.

I shrugged off her words, for surely anyone who knew him would feel as I did? Yes, I loved him, but it wasn't the kind of love my sister meant. How could it be? Mario Lanza wasn't mine; he belonged to Betty and the children. I loved him for his talent, for his sweetness and sadness, and most of all for the moments when it seemed he needed the help of a little Roman servant girl no matter how very great and famous he was.

'This is serious,' I told my family. 'You think I'm

exaggerating, I know, but neither of you have seen them.' I stared down at the photograph in my hand. 'When I look at him like this, I can't believe it's all gone so wrong. When was this picture taken? Two years ago, three maybe. How can life change so quickly?'

Gently my mother took the photograph from me, slipping it back into the box. 'Forget about him for now. Come and help me with my hair. And you must listen to your sister's news. She has a job, lots of work; she is earning almost as much as you. You're surprised? Well, perhaps that's because you're so concerned about the Lanza family these days, you forget to ask about your own.'

Guiltily I realised she was right. I had no idea Carmela had found work singing in the local cafés and bars, sometimes even at private parties. She showed me the evening dress Mamma had sewed for her – midnight blue in sheerest silk – and told me proudly of the tips she collected every time she wore it. 'So you see, it doesn't matter that I didn't get to be in that silly film. I'm going to be a star anyway, I just know it.'

The thought of her in that flimsy dress, standing up and performing in front of strangers, made me uneasy. Still, she was singing, I reminded myself, it was her dream and it needn't lead to anything else even if she was too young for those sorts of clothes and parties. In truth, there wasn't a space in my head for more worries, even if they were about my sister. It was full as could be with Betty and Mario's problems.

With A Song In My Heart

Mario was home again. He had shrugged off the warnings from his doctors, blaming his phlebitis on too many antibiotics and insisting he was on the mend. Although still walking with a cane, he seemed restless and was bravely determined to continue with his concert tour as soon as he was able.

In private, Pepe and I wondered if he were running short of cash. We saw how freely money was spent in that household, heard Betty complaining of steep medical bills and the size of Costa's accompanist's fee.

'Perhaps Signore Lanza has no choice but to continue singing,' I suggested late one morning as I watched Pepe preparing a lunch.

'Caruso kept going when he was unwell and it didn't do him much good,' he replied grimly.

It was cold outside and the kitchen windows were fogged with steam from a chicken stock that had been simmering on the stove for hours. Pepe was planning a hearty soup, bolstered with barley and flavoured with lemon.

'But Signore Lanza only has a bad leg,' I said. 'Surely it shouldn't stop him performing.'

'Remember what he told us that night when we were sitting round this table together? With a voice so much depends on the physical. He needs his strength to sing,' Pepe reminded me as he strained the mess of rendered chicken bones and pulpy vegetables from the broth.

Pepe was the only one I felt able to talk to about what went on within the walls of the Villa Badoglio. While he never got to see or hear as much as me, still he understood and I think he worried too.

'Have you heard how his speaking voice seems to have deepened?' he asked. 'I wonder what that means for his singing.'

Neither of us had heard Mario practise since his return from hospital, as Costa had forbidden him from even trying to warm his voice until he had fully recuperated. Every morning we waited, hoping to hear the silence broken by his vocal exercises and then listen to him sing his lucky aria, 'Vesti la Giubba'. Such quiet was an unhappy thing for those of us who knew how gloriously the silence might have been filled.

'He has only just turned thirty-seven,' Pepe observed. 'Most voices grow in power and weight. Perhaps that's why his is changing. It's darkening, becoming even richer.'

Tasting the chicken broth, he frowned and added a pinch of white pepper and salt. There were slices of onion sizzling in warm olive oil, cut lemons waiting to be squeezed, a pack of barley open; but the soup was still an hour away, Betty was taking a rest and we had plenty of time to talk.

I can't recall where our conversation went that afternoon. Perhaps we chatted some more about music or the Lanza family. The children had been running wild of late, causing their governesses no end of trouble, with Mario too indulgent and Betty too drained to do very much about it. A maid had left and the housekeeper seemed unhappy. We might have discussed that or Mario's health; talked about the meals Pepe was planning or the very best way to make a chicken stock. We were easy in one another's company again. Despite all the problems that beset the household, this one thing made me feel happy.

As always, Pepe took great care with Betty's food, warming a roll of bread and spreading it with butter, grating Parmesan to carpet the soup, tasting it carefully and adjusting the seasoning again before ladling it into the bowl. If the tray returned to him later with the food barely touched he would be crushed but still make the same effort next time.

'It smells very good. I'll try to make her eat some,' I promised, taking the tray from him.

'Good luck,' he called after me.

Upstairs in Betty's room the curtains were closed and she was lying still and silent in her bed.

'Signora, it's time to wake up,' I said briskly.

'Serafina?' she murmured. 'Is it you?'

'Yes, I've brought some soup.'

'Where's Mario?'

'He went to the Excelsior to have lunch with Mr Costa.' Putting the tray on the bedside table, I went to draw back the curtains.

Betty rubbed at her eyes as the light flooded in. 'I expect he'll be nagging at Costa to let him sing,' she said. 'He's so impatient to go on the road again, especially now his new picture has been scrapped.'

'What new picture?' I asked, helping her sit up to eat.

'Oh, I don't know, it had a silly sort of name, something about love,' she said vaguely, leaning back into the pillows and half-closing her eyes. 'Mario liked the script and he was meant to start shooting in England next month but they cancelled the whole thing when they heard he was sick.'

'Perhaps he can make another movie here in Rome instead,' I suggested hopefully.

Betty yawned. 'I don't think so. They've booked more tour dates for him, all over England, back to the Albert Hall and on through Europe. So many performances.'

'Is he well enough?'

'He says so. But I'll have to go with him, at least for part of the time. Someone has to make sure he looks after himself and I can't rely on Costa any more.'

'Then you must build up your strength. Pepe says this soup is tasty and very nourishing. Will you try a little?'

She looked at the bowl. 'I'm not hungry.'

'He put so much love into making it. Just a taste … I'm sure you'll like it.'

There was the ghost of a smile then. 'Do I take it things with the chef have taken a turn for the better?' she teased.

'He's my friend, that's all.'

Betty took the spoon from my hand, raised it to her lips and took the tiniest sip. 'Ah well, perhaps that's for the best.'

'It is?'

She took a more generous taste of the golden broth, swallowed it down and nodded. 'Well, if I'm to go on some God-awful trip round Europe then you'll be coming with me. And I'll feel better if I know you won't be pining for him.'

Despite Betty's plans, the tour began without her. Clutching his cane, his leg tightly wrapped in a rubber bandage, Mario left for England with only Costa for company. No one was happy about it but it couldn't be helped because Colleen had caught mumps and wanted her mamma close by.

Our journey was postponed a second time so both girls could make their First Communion. They were sweet that day in their white dresses and veils, serious-faced throughout the ceremony. Mario insisted on travelling all the way back from England, so determined was he not to miss the occasion, and there were lots of pictures taken outside the church to make sure the girls would always remember their special day.

To me Mario seemed rather weak and sickly. Wrapped warmly in a velvet-collared coat and woollen scarf, he leaned heavily on his cane and his eyes were tired. Yet he smiled whenever the camera lens was pointed his way, stooping to wrap his arms round his girls, so loving and proud that, looking on from the edge of it all, I was reminded of being

167

younger and dreaming he was my father. So much had happened since then. I had met new people, visited new places. My life had changed completely and I was no longer that same girl. But still I longed to have a tiny piece of him to keep for ever.

Once the family photographs were finished, I took my chance. 'Signore Lanza, may I have my picture taken with you too?' I begged.

Fatigued as he was, he couldn't refuse. 'Of course, of course. Come and stand beside me, Serafina. That's right, just there is perfect. One, two, three, smile … and there we have it. One more to be sure, do you think?'

Putting an arm round my shoulders, he pulled me close enough that I could breathe his cologne and sense the warmth of his body. The camera shutter clicked, the photographer wound on his film and I stood in the nook his shoulder made as if I belonged there.

'Got it?' he called to the photographer, dropping his arm. 'That should be a nice shot. Make sure we remember to get you a print of it, Serafina.'

'Thank you, Signore Lanza. I will treasure it always,' I promised.

What I remember most about that tour of England was the bone-tiredness at the end of every day. We moved from place to place, never staying anywhere long. For me that meant packing and unpacking Betty's suitcase, ordering hotel food and making sure she managed to eat some, listening to the litany of her complaints about everyone who surrounded Mario. There were so many people that came and went — in favour one minute, their names unmentionable the next. The latest was an actor called Alex Revides. I never really understood what his job might be, only that Mario fell into his old ways of staying up late and drinking too much, and it made Costa crazy.

Fortunately, Signore Lanza's health troubles hadn't affected his voice at all; in fact, with each performance it seemed bolder. Yet there were little things I noticed and Betty remarked upon too. Often while he stood on stage he'd shift from foot to foot or kick his legs about as though he felt uncomfortable. The critics tore into him for it, declaring him too casual. They censured his choice of lounge suit over evening dress, hated the way he pulled his tie loose and crooked when he grew hot, even condemned him for drinking water onstage. One called it 'pure American slovenliness'; another said he was 'a badly behaved boy'. We were so angry but there was nothing we could do. Mario didn't want any fuss about his health, or for the audience to know exactly what it took each night for him to stand on that stage before them.

The moment he began to sing he held them every time, his voice free-flowing, soaring, elastic. Each time I listened I remembered the doctors' warnings – if he didn't take care his life was in danger. I tried to imagine the world without him and thought what a cold, empty place it would be.

The pace of our life took its toll on Betty and she wasn't able to sustain it. Before the month was over we had returned to Rome for her to rest. Mario must have been concerned, for no matter where he was he telephoned her every day. Often the connection was bad and I would hear Betty's voice ringing through the hallways of the Villa Badoglio as she struggled to make herself heard.

She liked to repeat the conversations after she had put down the receiver, and so I heard how Signore Lanza had triumphed in France and in Belgium, how next he was to return to Germany. How everywhere they loved him. The tour was going like a dream. Then in Hamburg, Mario stumbled.

I never got to the bottom of the whole business but it had something to do with Alex Revides and involved drinking and singing all night at the top of his lungs until he had used up enough voice for three concerts and the hotel's guests were sleepless and complaining. The next morning there were medical examinations and injections, Mario's throat was sprayed but still he wasn't well enough to sing and at the final moment the audience was told the concert was cancelled. We heard it was like that night with Callas all over again: the audience storming the stage and police called to help Mario and Costa out of the theatre, an angry mob following them to their hotel, jeering and booing.

'This is a disaster. He won't sing again for months,' Pepe predicted.

I didn't want to believe it. Nor did I want to hear what Betty whispered to me tearfully later that afternoon, that it hadn't been Signore Lanza's throat that most concerned the German doctor.

'He says Mario's in terrible shape.' Her head was in her hands. 'Thinks his health is lousy and his life most certainly in danger again. I'm so scared, Serafina. How can we make him well? I want it all to go back to the way things used to be.'

And I reached out to stroke her hair, in sympathy and sadness, because it was all I wanted too.

When the rest of the tour was cancelled, Mario flew back to us. It was early afternoon when his plane landed, a warm spring day with the lightest of breezes. We waited on the tarmac; me, the children and Betty. As we saw him step from the plane, Betty's hand covered her mouth and she fell silent. Like me she must have noticed how heavy and spent he looked and that he seemed to be dragging his right foot when he walked. He had aged, his smile looked forced, his eyes had lost their brightness.

Hugging and kissing his family, Mario tried to make light of his illness and reassure us. 'I'm fine,' he promised. 'Stop worrying so much, I'm strong as an ox, Betty, you know that. All I need is some rest and I'll be good as new again.'

A Little Love, A Little Kiss

I didn't belong to Trastevere any more. The waiters at the pavement cafés barely raised a hand when I passed; the old lady shelling peas on her front doorstep didn't pause to smile at me. I never shopped for day-old bread or wilting greens at the Testaccio market, never went to Mass with my mother on a Sunday, or wandered Rome with my sisters. I hadn't meant for all that to come to an end but now everything was different and their lives seemed to be moving on without me.

Even in the apartment things had changed. There were no cooking smells in the cramped kitchen for they preferred to eat in cafés; no damp clothes hanging over the balcony since they could afford to send their washing out to a laundress. The rail in the bedroom sagged under the weight of Carmela's new dresses – lavishly beaded and figure-hugging, hot pink in silk brocade or shiny in satin, taut at the waist. Amidst the clutter were new shoes with skinny heels, a matching handbag with a silver clasp, diamante earrings, and a velvet-covered box where she kept her red lipsticks, pancake make-up and nail lacquers. I chose to believe my sister when she told me how important it was to look well when she was singing at cafés and people's private parties. If there were other reasons for this new finery then I couldn't bear to know them.

It was Rosalina who was always happiest to see me when I went home. Often I would arrive with sweet treats from Pepe or comic books the Lanza children had finished with, and find her alone and bored, with no sign of my mother or

Carmela. 'They're out working again,' she would complain. 'They never let me go with them.'

She seemed so neglected and sad that I began taking her with me sometimes to the Villa Badoglio on days when there was no school. She was close in age to Colleen and Ellisa so they played well together, and I think Betty was pleased for her daughters to have an Italian friend. At first my Rosalina was goggle-eyed at the toys those children had: the play-house and the pedal car, the dolls with outfits the maids had stitched for them. By her third or fourth visit her shyness had worn off and watching her playing at being fairies or painting pictures, it felt as though my little sister was starting to belong at the Villa almost as much as I did now.

I wonder if she felt out of kilter when we were home again with only one doll to play with and no grand rooms with staff moving through them. I don't think so. It seemed as if Rosalina accepted both places, not finding one better than the other, ready as ever to be pleased by life.

Often we would arrive home to find Mamma and Carmela stationed at their table at the corner bar and, if the evening were warm, we might sit with them while Rosalina drank a glass of *limonata* and I toyed with a Campari. Mostly I stayed quiet, listening to the others speak, surprised how often Carmela led the conversation. Her talk was mostly of money: the tips she had earned and what she planned to buy with them, her voice loud so that all the neighbouring tables were forced to hear it. Perhaps she was envious to learn of Rosalina slotting so happily into the Lanza household, for she made several tart remarks and seized any chance she found to criticise Mario.

'I saw your boss the other night in a café not far from the Villa Badoglio,' she told me, a sly look crossing her face.

'Oh yes?'

'He was with a girl, much younger than his wife, very dark, glamorous too. They seemed to be having a good time.'

'Was she the sort of girl Mamma might know?' I couldn't help asking, uneasy at the thought of Mario frequenting the same places as her.

'Perhaps … it was dark in there and rowdy, I didn't get close enough to tell. But he was drunk, anyone could see that. When I started singing "Arrivederci Roma", he got to his feet and joined in, bellowing at the top of his voice.'

'So you finally got to sing your duet with him …' I was wry.

'Yes and I was a thousand times better than Luisa Di Meo, that's for sure. Not that he'd have been able to tell, the state he was in.'

'Signore Lanza is allowed to go to cafés and have a good time just like any other man,' I defended him. 'He always brings home flowers for Betty from the street peddlers.'

'He wasn't thinking about his wife that night,' my sister said spitefully.

Her one sighting gave Carmela so much to talk about. She held forth on how stout he had become, how red in the face, how much older than his years he looked. 'He's not the same man I saw outside the Excelsior Hotel a year ago,' she kept saying. 'I guess I understand now why you're so worried about his health.'

'He'll be fine,' I said tersely. 'His doctors are the best money can buy. They'll have him fixed soon, no problem.'

I was lying to my sister. The truth was Mario's doctors were painting a gloomy picture and each new detail I heard made me more anxious. His heart was enlarged, his liver sick, his lungs inflamed, his blood pressure soaring. He was taking some sort of medication that left him flushed and short of breath. And while he requested the kind of spartan food that helped him shed fat, when it was presented to him he changed his mind and demanded the dishes he loved – spaghetti silky with egg and fatty with pancetta; a *fritto misto* of sardines, cuttlefish and scampi tails; pork loin cooked with milk and fennel; pizza baked over a wood-fire that Pepe lit in the garden. Mario ate the way he drank champagne, as though it filled a hole in him, brought him peace when nothing else could.

Carmela was right: he was not the same man. Overweight and withdrawn, his enthusiasm for life was draining away. The weather was warm yet he wasn't interested in taking the children to the Borghese Gardens or lunching on the Via Veneto with Costa. He didn't care to listen to music or throw parties. Most of his friends stayed away from the Villa Badoglio now and he left home only to visit the nearby bars where I suppose he felt free of Betty's disappointment and his doctors' orders.

The basement kitchen had become his refuge, surrounded by cooking smells and with Pepe for company. He would escape there for hours at a time, sitting at the long pine table, a glass of Campari and a dish of fat, green Sicilian olives before him, resting his bad leg over the side of a chair, drinking and talking.

'What is it you speak about together for all that time?' I asked Pepe once.

'I listen to him complaining,' he replied. 'He is under pressure to make another movie, to give concerts in South Africa. They're throwing money at him but I don't see how he can manage any of it. He has no energy. All he wants is to sleep, eat, drink and forget about everything else.'

It was awkward for me with Mario so often in the kitchen. It felt as though I were intruding if I stayed around for any length of time. The two men were talking and their words weren't meant for my ears. But if I pushed open the kitchen door and heard their voices, I was sure to pause and listen. That is how I learned about so many of Mario's worries: the Mafia men still hanging around him, the threats to sue for the cancelled concert tour, his fears for the future. And it was how I knew Pepe was trying to convince him to take a whole year off and study seriously for an opera role.

'I've listened to you again and again.' Pepe was fired up with his passion. 'I never cease to marvel at your power and control. There's nothing you couldn't tackle. If I had your voice—'

'If you had my voice, my friend, you'd realise as I do that it's a gift from God,' Mario said evasively.

'But surely your gift is wasted in Hollywood? It deserves to be used in one of the great opera houses.'

'There are plenty of offers,' I heard Mario reply. 'Covent Garden wants me to do *Otello*, La Scala asked me to open a season there. Some day it will happen, I'm sure. But what's the hurry? My voice isn't going anywhere.'

Mario didn't care to talk about the things he ought to do. Mostly he dwelt instead on all that made him unhappy: the broken promises, the shoddy treatment, the screaming fights he continued to have with Betty, the plots against him. He had taken to sipping beer all day then switching to Campari and cognac as the afternoon wore on. Even when his voice was syrupy with alcohol, still he found excuses to keep drinking.

If Betty tried to talk to him it ended in shouting. She was fearful and it made her harsh. She kept at him to take up exercise again, to cut down his eating and most of all to stay away from beer and whisky.

'When I'm happy I don't do these things,' he slurred to her. 'Don't be angry, don't think I'm crazy, it's just that I have to get away from all these troubles in my head.'

Despairing, she summoned a doctor who sat Mario down and warned bluntly if he kept drinking he would soon be dead. For a short time he seemed chastened by the lecture but a couple of days later Pepe found him back in the kitchen, beer in hand, stuffing down cold pasta from the pan.

'I'm strong,' he kept insisting to Betty. 'I can rally myself and lose weight. I'll start eating simple foods again. Next week I'll begin, I promise. I won't feel so low by then.'

When it was first mentioned, the twilight sleep therapy seemed a miracle. We were told Signore Lanza would be taken to a sanatorium, high in the Bavarian Alps, where the air was pure and healthy. There he would be eased into unconsciousness and for days would sleep, freed from the torture of his thoughts and worries, while his body let go of all the fat it had stored.

Betty was enthusiastic about the treatment. 'He'll be there for weeks but it's the only way for him to get in shape for this next picture,' she confided. 'It's a very exclusive place, this sanatorium. Richard Burton and Elizabeth Taylor were both treated there so they should be able to handle Mario.'

At first Signore Lanza was reluctant to go away. There were more raised voices at the Villa Badoglio with Costa brought in to help Betty convince him it was the only thing to do.

'It's in your contract, Mario,' I heard him pleading. 'You must drop forty pounds before you make this picture in September.'

'Seven weeks in Bavaria, caged like a tiger? I'll go crazy, die of boredom.'

'You don't have a choice,' Costa insisted. 'It's the sleep therapy or nothing.'

'Can we talk about this tomorrow?' Mario pleaded.

'There's nothing more to talk about.' Betty was firm. 'They've had to postpone this movie once and won't be pleased to do it again. You're going to Walchensee and Dr Fruhwein is going to help you. We won't hear of anything else.'

Mario spent most of that afternoon in the kitchen, returning there late the next morning and I know there was more beer drunk because later I saw the empty bottles. And I tasted the leftovers of the fettuccine dish Pepe had cooked for him, swimming in cream, braised leeks, Parmesan and bacon – a final feast before the diet began. I have no idea what the two of them talked about while the pasta was being eaten as Pepe refused to tell me. But three days later Mario travelled by train to a tiny village in Bavaria and checked in alone to the clinic, agreeing to submit to whatever treatment his doctors thought necessary.

Before long Betty confided that Mario wasn't doing well in Walchensee. He had been telephoning to say how much he missed her and the children, how he hated the twilight sleep therapy, even complaining he was a prisoner of his doctors. After only two weeks he was begging her to rescue him with a visit.

And so the suitcases were pulled out again and I filled them with plenty of warm clothes, for the air would be crisper up in the Alps. We were to drive in the family's big Volkswagen bus since the children and both governesses were coming along too. At the last moment Betty decided to make space for Pepe. 'We'll have to eat, even if Mario is living on canned peaches and cottage cheese,' she pointed out.

Walchensee was lovely. A tiny settlement of chalets on the shores of a deep lake and so tranquil it was like a holiday for all of us. There was little to do beyond swim in the icy lake, hike forest trails, listen to birdsong and breathe the clean air, but the place worked its spell, even on Mario. Relieved once he was finished with his sleep therapy, he spent the days exercising, playing ball games with the children, or taking Betty on shopping expeditions to the nearest town. Within days of our arrival he was declaring Walchensee, 'a bit of heaven'.

With our time so much freer, Pepe and I were able to explore together. Those were golden days indeed: delighting in the soaring mountains and the smell of sun-warmed pine, shrieking at the icy rush as we plunged into the lake, picnicking on its banks, fishing from a rented rowboat. But what I loved most was the chance it gave me to see the man Pepe really was.

He had hidden himself so well in his kitchen at the Villa Badoglio – using his job as a buffer, escaping by moving off to stir a sauce or chop an onion, fiercely frying slabs of meat in oil-spitting pans, barricading himself behind sharp knives and boiling liquids. Here in the empty landscapes he couldn't hold me at bay with his busyness. We were together all the time, walking for miles and talking for hours, squabbling and laughing, emptying our thoughts. It was the closest I had ever felt to him ... to anyone.

The day he kissed me we were sitting shaded by trees at the lakeside, eating an early lunch of breaded escalope in hunks of crusty bread. Afterwards, he dabbed my hands and face clean with the napkin he had used to wrap the sandwiches. From there it was the easiest thing in the world to take my hand and, leaning closer, touch his mouth to mine; gently at first, then more boldly until we had kissed for so long my lips were burning.

It was the first time I had allowed a man to touch me like that. After we pulled apart there were a few moments when I could only manage to breath, and then I touched his cheek and said: 'I didn't expect that ... but I never know what to expect from you, Pepe.'

He claimed to be confused so I recounted all the many ways he kept me off balance: the unaccountable silences, the barely warmed-over moods, the sense I got at times he didn't like me much.

Pepe pinned his eyes to the lake's far shore but I knew he was listening to every word. When I had finished he heaved a sigh and tried to wrong-foot me. I was too sensitive, he said, these slights were imagined; of course he liked me, wasn't that obvious? He had kissed me, hadn't he?

'Kissing is easy,' I told him. 'It doesn't prove a thing.'

I saw him frown. Curling my fingers round his hand, I squeezed it tightly. For a long time both of us stared at the light playing over the ripples of the lake. My eyes followed a sailboat tacking against the breeze; I watched a night heron stilled at the water's edge; and I waited for Pepe to speak.

'Sometimes,' he said, 'I'm afraid of my own moods. It's as if I'm not in charge of them.'

I wasn't sure I understood. Staying silent, I hoped for him to continue but the only sound was the lapping of water and the softest of breezes through the pine trees.

'All of us have bad moods,' I said finally. 'It's a normal thing.'

'Not like this, not so extreme.' Pepe's eyes stayed on the lake. 'You don't understand, because I've never let you see, not really. It's a blackness, an emptiness; and if it's with me then I'm sure I'll never feel light again. There are moments I think I'm going crazy and all I can do is try to hold myself steady and hope it will pass. I don't want you to know me like that, Serafina. I shouldn't have kissed you, or even taken you to the opera. You deserve better than me.'

'You're a good man.'

'Not always.'

'You try to be, that's the important thing.'

Pepe's eyes met mine. 'I'm sorry, Serafina ... I love you but I'd never make you happy.'

'You love me?' I repeated back at him stupidly. 'Really?'

'Surely you knew that? Don't smile at me; it's not such a happy thing.'

'But what if I loved you back again? Would it make a difference?'

'No, don't say that.'

'But if—'

'I would hurt you even if I was trying not to,' he insisted. 'In the end you'd be just as afraid of my moods as I am.'

Perhaps it was the lake or the light on his face, perhaps the fresh scent of pine on the breeze, but in Walchensee it felt as if nothing bad could happen. This time I kissed Pepe.

We were several weeks in the mountains and all of us grew sleek and tanned. Even Betty looked more robust. After a day outdoors she had an appetite for simple foods: soups filled with starchy potato dumplings, boiled white sausage and sweet mustard, vinegary braised cabbage and sour curd cheese. As for Signore Lanza, he seemed a changed man and was vowing to return to Bavaria and spend the rest of his life there. He had disciplined himself heroically, barely touching the local beer and following the sparse diet his doctor had prescribed. When Costa joined us he rehearsed every day, more than ready to get back to work. It was such a relief to hear that voice again, powerful and expressive, somehow more joyful than it had ever been before.

By the time we left Walchensee all of us seemed happier. Mario had shed his forty pounds and no longer had to balance on a cane when he walked; Betty was so relieved to see him restored to health and she in turn felt better.

And I was happier, too – for I felt surer of Pepe and my feelings for him.

When You're In Love

As soon as she suspected what was happening, Betty began furnishing me with endless reasons to visit Pepe's kitchen, requesting cups of tea or glasses of chilled Coca-Cola, little snacks at odd times of the day. She seemed delighted to have a romance flourishing beneath her roof, teasing me about it until I blushed.

'I was wondering why our chef's mood was better,' she joked. 'We should have sent the pair of you to Bavaria much earlier.'

It was awkward with the staff, though, so I tried to behave the way I always had, unless we were alone. Nor did I say a word to my mother or sisters. This thing between Pepe and me was new and untried; it seemed safer kept as a secret.

Of course, I never had a hope of hiding it from Betty. She knew from the beginning. That day when we returned from our lakeside picnic she had seen how my lips were rubbed and reddened, smiled at my attempts to find excuses for it. 'Wind burned? Chapped by the sun? I don't believe the weather has a thing to do with it.'

By then I felt very close to her. I had seen Betty curled beneath the bedcovers at her lowest ebb and shared her triumphs, too. I might have been a little sister or a friend. Often she remarked how she would hate to be without me, was always making gifts of little things: diamante hair clips, a lipstick that was the wrong shade for her. Now and then she tried to help me by sharing small wisdoms, lessons she had learned in her own life that might be useful in mine.

I didn't always find the importance in Betty's words but there was one conversation I never forgot.

We were being driven out to see her seamstress as her figure had changed so much and her clothes needed altering again. She was gazing through the window, watching Rome pass by, mostly silent and wrapped up in her own thoughts when suddenly she turned and said, 'Serafina, may I ask you something?'

'Yes, of course.'

'Are you completely sure about this chef? He seems rather a difficult man to me.'

'He's not straightforward by any means,' I agreed.

Betty looked at me thoughtfully. 'It's one thing falling for a difficult man but then you have to live with him.'

'It won't always be easy, I know—'

'No you don't, not yet,' she interrupted. 'You don't know anything at all.'

It was my turn to stare out of the window. 'No one is perfect, are they?' I said.

'That's true,' agreed Betty.

'Surely there are some men who are just as wonderful as they are difficult? Aren't they worth the trouble?'

'Perhaps … if you really love each other.' Betty touched my arm lightly. 'So long as you understand the choice you're making.'

She didn't mention Pepe to me again that day. Our car had pulled up at the kerb and the next hour or two was filled with fittings and the tutting of a seamstress with pins in her mouth; with talk of the next season's fashions; and cups of espresso brought on a silver tray by a waiter from the café next door.

It was stuffy in the salon and I was hoping we were almost finished when Betty declared there was one more special thing she wanted. 'An evening dress, an exquisite one.' From her bag she pulled a handful of photographs clipped from magazines. 'My husband's new movie is to premiere in Rome at long last and I want to look beautiful for him on the red carpet. Something totally exclusive, full length and shimmering, to wear with long white gloves and the new diamond necklace he gave me.'

'A dress like that will be very costly, Signora,' the seamstress muttered as she leafed through the cuttings.

'I expect it will be,' Betty replied smoothly.

'And we would be most delighted to create it for you,' the seamstress hurried to add.

On the way back to the Villa, I peppered Betty with excited questions about the premiere of *Arrivederci Roma*. Where would it be held? Was there to be a big party? What famous people did she expect to see there?

'And does that mean the film will soon be showing in all the theatres?' I wondered. 'I will have to see it the moment it opens.'

'Oh, but of course you'll be coming to the premiere, Serafina,' Betty told me, smiling at the treat in store. 'All of the household is; Mario wouldn't have it any other way.'

Later I learned Signore Lanza had invited many of the people he had got to know in Rome: waiters and porters, the man who owned his favourite café, taxi drivers as well as friends and business associates. Even Lucky Luciano the mafia man from Napoli had scored an invitation, although Betty's mood blackened whenever his name was mentioned.

As for the staff of the Villa Badoglio, all we could talk about were the gowns we would wear and the film stars we might see. I kept wondering about my own tiny role in the party scene, hoping to glimpse an image of myself dancing and swaying up there on the screen, wondering if anyone would recognise me.

Among us only Pepe seemed indifferent to the prospect of such an occasion. Talk of red carpets and starlets didn't interest him and he wore a slightly pained expression if he were forced to overhear it.

'The picture will be terrible anyway,' he reminded me whenever he had a chance, 'and not worth the fuss everyone's making.'

'Aren't you even a little bit excited?'

Pepe made a face as if tasting something bitter. 'Why be excited about seeing him selling himself short, debasing his voice in yet another foolish film?'

Wary of doing anything that might injure his mood and bring the blackness back, I didn't argue and was careful not to mention the premiere again, instead saving my enthusiasm for when he was out of earshot, chattering away to Betty and the governesses every chance I got.

I had imagined my sister Carmela would be another one who would sour at any mention of *Arrivederci Roma* but she surprised me with her enthusiasm, insisting I try on all her lovely dresses and even her favourite shoes, the ones with the slender, high heels.

'You remember how I borrowed that sweet polka-dot dress Mamma made for you?' she reminded me. 'Now I have so many lovely things. You must wear something of mine to the premiere. Really, you must.'

Her midnight-blue silk was an inch or two short and the pink satin not so flattering. But there was another gown, slim fitting and covered in thousands of pale pearlised sequins, that did look well on me.

Carmela smiled when I put it on. 'I've only worn that dress once but I had the best night of my life in it. Somewhere there are shoes to match.' Dropping down on her hands and knees, she peered beneath the bed. 'I think Mamma wore them the other night. I hope she didn't scuff them.'

I watched her rummaging about, raising mites of dust that twinkled in a shaft of sunlight before settling down to coat and dirty things again.

'I can't wear your clothes, Carmela,' I decided.

She stopped searching and sat back on her heels. 'Why? Are they not good enough for you?'

'It's not that … but I know how you came by the money to buy them.' I felt sick at the thought of it.

'What do you know precisely?'

For a moment we stared at each other and I saw how much my sister had altered. There was a new gloss to her now, but a hardness too. She had followed in my mother's footsteps and there was no denying it.

'I didn't think this was the life you wanted,' I told her. 'Your voice? Are you just going to waste it? It's a gift from God, Carmela.'

'God wouldn't want me to starve,' she pointed out. 'Besides, I sing all the time. Some day it will be the thing I'm known for. Until then I'm not too proud to earn my living.'

'I'd have given you money, helped you out if you'd only asked—'

'I don't want your money.' She sounded furious. 'What makes you think you know what's good for me? Do you believe you're better than I am? Better than Mamma, too?'

'That's not what I'm saying,' I replied quickly. 'But you're still so very young and I'm worried you're choosing all the wrong things. I care about you, Carmela …'

'I don't need your care. If you think my dress is somehow soiled because of where I've been in it then fine, don't wear it.' She flicked a glance at my reflection in the mirror. 'But it's just a dress … and you look good in it.'

I borrowed Betty's gown in the end, the same one she'd lent me to wear to Signore Lanza's performance at the London Palladium. To match it I bought some new shoes with lower heels because I didn't want to tower over Pepe. I might have looked a little plain but at the very last moment Betty insisted on clasping a silver-linked bracelet round my wrist.

'You look lovely, dear,' she said.

'So do you, Signora.' It was true. Not only was her gown a triumph, her skin was lightly tanned, her eyes clear and most importantly she seemed much happier since our time in the mountains. Beside her, fiddling with the necktie pulled tight round his throat, Mario was slimmer and handsome too, although perhaps looking a little tired and lined around the eyes.

Cars had been organised to collect us from the Villa Badoglio and I travelled in one with Pepe and the housekeeper. We heard the crowds waiting for Mario long before we reached the theatre. Hundreds of cheering people were pressing onto the pavement and spilling into the road. Our taxi had to slow to a crawl to push through them.

'Incredible,' Pepe muttered.

'It's like this every time,' I told him.

'But why are they screaming?'

'I expect they think we're famous too.'

Pepe smiled. 'Perhaps we ought to wave at them,' he suggested mischievously. 'Make them feel all their waiting has been worthwhile.'

There was so much about the premiere of *Arrivederci Roma* that I loved. Walking beside Pepe up the narrow red carpet that had been rolled from the theatre door; seeing Betty and Mario posing for photographers, the smiles painted on their faces; hearing the crowds call their names as they passed; following them through the cordon and into the theatre. Most of all I loved the movie. It was as silly a story as you can imagine, with Signore Lanza playing an American singer who ends up in Rome where he meets a pretty girl who falls for him. But it was only ever an excuse to show off the spectacle of our city and the beauty of his voice, and in that it succeeded completely.

I must have watched that film a hundred times since. It is the one I never tire of because I was a part of its making. And yes, if you look carefully enough you can see me on the screen, flashing past the camera, my skirts flying as I jive. It is only the briefest of moments and no one has ever mentioned noticing it.

After the screening, there was a very grand party thrown in the ballroom of the Excelsior with a champagne fountain and a dance band. All the stars were there: Marisa Allasio, Renato Rascel, Peggie Castle. It was strange to see the Villa Badoglio's staff there in their finery, none of us looking quite like ourselves. I felt a little awkward at first, hugging the edges of the room. But Pepe kept busy, fetching drinks and dancing, and gradually after a couple of glasses of champagne I managed to begin enjoying myself. We danced together again and again, until my cheeks were pink and the party had almost worn itself out.

I had been hoping Signore Lanza might dance with me. It was a silly thing but I couldn't help wishing he would pick me out from the crowd and I kept glancing over in case there was a chance of it. He sang, of course, and made a speech thanking Betty and all the people who had supported him, even naming his chef Pepe among them. All of it was unforgettable; but to have Mario choose me, take my hand and lead me onto the dance-floor in front of everyone would have made the night magical.

All evening he had been circled by admirers, unable to escape even if he wanted to. Betty, too, was caught up and hadn't spoken to me since we had left the Villa. I fiddled with the silver bracelet she had slipped around my wrist; it was a borrowed thing, would never be mine no matter how pretty it looked on my arm. And at that moment I realised Betty and Mario had only ever been borrowed too.

I saw them every day, had ridden the highs and lows of their lives for more than a year, knew the smell of Betty's hair, could sense a shift in her mood before anyone. I understood them far better than the other people in that ballroom. Yet I didn't belong in their world and they had never seen mine. Some day the doors between us might close and that would be the end of it. I shivered at the idea.

There was one person who could be mine, though, who could belong to me completely and for ever. He was jiving, as nimble on the dance-floor as he was in the kitchen; his dark hair slick with sweat and his face alight. I watched him twirling one of the children's governesses – Liliana, I think – although it might have been Anna-Maria. Both were pretty girls and they danced with him more than once that night. Impatiently I waited for the number to end and for them to break apart. I wanted a slow tune next so we could dance close and feel the heat of one another's bodies. I wanted the fine wool of his borrowed evening suit beneath my fingers, to feel the way his muscles worked as he moved, to let him lead me in the dance. I wanted to belong to him.

A Kiss In The Dark

Everyone realised Pepe and I were courting – he'd even held my hand in front of the housekeeper and both of the governesses. Day-to-day life was the same: we worked at our jobs, snatched time together when we could, talked about the usual things. But now it was understood we were special to one another and that made everything different.

I helped Pepe write a long letter to his mother breaking the news. As soon as the Lanzas could spare us we planned to travel to Campania so he could introduce me to his family. In turn, he was waiting for an invitation to come to Trastevere but I kept putting him off with excuses: Mamma had a summer cold, Carmela was busy working.

How could I take him there? I lay awake every night worrying about it. When he saw what I was, where I'd come from, surely he would lose all respect for me.

Pepe had told me about his family – his father cut marble and worked a smallholding, his mother laboured in the kitchen cooking for his brothers, their wives and children. These were ordinary people who found their pleasure in music and food. My mother had hurried to escape a life like theirs. It held nothing to make her happy so she had chosen her own way without ever apologising or showing regret. How could I explain that to Pepe? Never before had I been ashamed of my mother and feeling so now left me wretched.

There was no one I could confide in. Instead, I held onto the problem, kneading away at it in my mind until it swelled and grew.

It ought to have been such a happy time: the mood in the Villa Badoglio was cheerful, Signore Lanza was feeling restored to health and had been cast in a new movie. He and Costa were working hard to prepare for it. They were especially pleased to be recording the arias in the Rome Opera House and each day the household was roused by the sound of them rehearsing songs of triumph, love and death. But my spirits were so low that even the music Mario made didn't touch me, not as it should have.

'He's in good voice,' Pepe would remark as I passed him in the kitchen.

'He sounds just terrific again today, doesn't he?' Betty said as I made her ready for an outing.

'Fantastic, Mario, magnificent!' Costa kept enthusing.

Everyone was caught in the excitement: the housekeeper and the governesses, the maids, even Antonio the janitor lingering in the hallway to hear 'Vesti la Giubba' then sighing at the sound. Heartbreaking and melancholy, that song matched the bleakness of my mood. I could hardly stand listening to it.

What difference would it make to me if Mario triumphed on stage at the Teatro dell'Opera? My life would be unchanged, my problems the same shape as always.

Pepe, though, seemed excited, particularly when he learned we were to be allowed in the audience for the all-important recording session.

'It will be the closest thing to watching him in an opera,' he enthused. 'His first real performance in Italy. To be there will be a privilege.'

'Yes, I know,' I replied colourlessly.

We were sitting in the Villa gardens, beneath the magnolia trees, while he enjoyed a cigar. It was a warm evening in late August and Pepe seemed light and happy, just as he had been since we returned from Walchensee.

'This may be the best movie Signore Lanza has ever made,'

he declared, breathing out cigar smoke. 'There is so much opera in it and he'll sing complete renditions of every aria.'

'Is it a love story?' I asked.

'Yes, but aren't they always?' Pepe shrugged. 'Who cares about the plot anyway, it's the singing that's important.'

His kisses tasted fragrant and smoky that night, his fingers moving through my hair and stroking down the length of my body. Leaning into him, I tried to free my mind and enjoy it. But I couldn't escape the dread of what I had kept hidden from him or the fear of what might happen once he knew the truth about me.

For once all my worries were for myself. I didn't feel nervous for Signore Lanza as we took our seats in the Rome Opera House on the day of the recording. Day after day I had listened while his voice grew bolder and surer. I knew he was ready for the moment.

The first recording was the triumphal scene from *Aida*. Pepe and I had heard him rehearse it many times but for other people in that theatre the sheer might of Mario's voice was a surprise. They must have believed his talent was waning, that his health had failed completely. None can have expected the passion he poured into every word, nor the power and reach of his singing. When he had finished every last member of the orchestra put down their instruments to applaud while the chorus called, 'Bravo, bravo', and Pepe's mouth twitched into a satisfied smile.

'After this they will be begging him to open the next season,' he told me once the cheering had subsided. 'Every opera house in Europe will want him.'

Each aria he sang was another victory and we could feel the excitement stirring and mounting. Mario Lanza's voice was the best in the world and no one could deny it now. But sitting in that theatre I couldn't find the pleasure I knew I ought to feel. My own problems were swamping the triumph of the moment.

If Pepe noticed the drabness of my mood he didn't mention it. 'This is a fresh start,' he enthused as we left the theatre. 'After all the problems with his health, this is exactly what was needed. Things will go well from now on, you'll see.'

To me such optimism seemed unfounded. 'We felt the same after he sang at the London Palladium but it didn't turn out that way,' I pointed out.

'This is different, this is opera,' Pepe insisted. 'Now he'll be able to escape Hollywood. It's time for him to have the career he was born for.'

When word of Mario's stupendous performance spread, the offers did pour in. They wanted him all over Europe, and South America, too, tried to entice him with his choice of singing partners and roles. La Scala dangled a two-year contract, Rome wanted him in *Pagliacci* and *Tosca*. I think he enjoyed the attention, was flattered by it. Often I would hear him discussing with Betty and Costa what he might do if only he had the time.

'But there are too many other things happening right now,' he would always conclude once he had talked over the latest offer. 'I have a picture to make so La Scala will have to wait a while longer.'

His new film was about an opera singer who goes to Capri and falls in love with a beautiful young deaf girl. While not all of it was to be shot in Italy, to my relief the Villa Badoglio would remain the family's home and all the staff retained.

'There will be filming in Vienna and Berlin so we'll to have to do some travelling,' Betty warned me. 'I want Mario to have his family with him as much as possible. We have to keep him healthy this time and you must help me, Serafina. I'm relying on you.'

Knowing there were to be long periods of separation ahead, Pepe and I made sure to spend time together, snatching a few moments in the garden, a minute or two in the kitchen, often barely enough to brush a hand against an arm or exchange a quick good morning.

The evenings were ours entirely. Once dinner had been cooked and served, we were free and Rome was waiting for us. We mightn't have had the money to eat at the fine cafés in the Via Veneto but we could walk up and down it as many times as we pleased. There was no cost for sitting by the Fontana di Trevi, milling arm-in-arm through the well-dressed crowds in the Piazza Navona, walking down the Spanish Steps. In some ways those nights reminded me of all the years when my sisters and I wandered the city. Only with Pepe there was kissing instead of singing.

In Rome there are many places to kiss: on the cobbles of quiet lanes, on the terrace of the Pincio with street musicians playing and a view over the city's domes, behind the marble columns of the Pantheon, on the bridge crossing the Tiber with the Castel Sant'Angelo all dressed up in lights beyond. The best spots are the unexpected ones like the fountain you find when you round a corner you have never turned before or the scarred wall on the sheltered side of a building.

At times as we held together Pepe and I smelt coffee on the air or the richness of roasting suckling pig. We might hear the voices of people approaching and break apart for a few moments; and if we grew hungry we would stop to share a slice of pizza or eat an ice cream. But mostly we walked and when we were still, we kissed.

Trastevere was the one place I avoided. With its maze of narrow alleys and shadowy piazzas, the risk was too great. Even wandering through the heart of Rome I tensed as we passed crowded cafés or the entranceways of large hotels. Sooner or later we would see them, Mamma and Carmela dressed finely and working the city. They went wherever the business took them and I knew some of the places they favoured from the talk I had listened to while sitting with my mother and her friends. There was a piano club in one hotel, nightclubs they frequented with men who liked to dance or listen to jazz; there were lobby bars where they lingered and cafés where they ate. I couldn't avoid every one of them.

The night it happened we had left work earlier than usual and strolled down through the Borghese Gardens all the way to Piazza del Popolo. Pepe decided we should stop at the Café Rosati to buy gelato then climb back up the Pincio to watch the sun setting.

They saw me before I noticed them. They were sitting at one of the pavement tables, drinking coffee with an older, well-dressed man. My mother stared straight at me and then at Pepe with his hand holding onto mine. She smiled and said something to Carmela who glanced up and nodded a greeting. For a moment I froze and then very casually looked away as if I hadn't seen them.

'Pistachio or *limone*?' Pepe asked. 'What flavour is your choice this evening?'

'Neither,' I said, trying to hold my voice steady. 'I think I'd prefer a *fior di latte*.'

'No, at the Café Rosati we always have either the pistachio or *limone*,' he reminded me. 'The place next to the Fontana di Trevi is where they have the best *fior di latte*.'

'Let's go there then,' I said quickly.

'You really want to walk all that way right now for gelato?'

'It's a lovely evening so why not?'

'You must really adore *fior di latte*.' Pepe grinned at me.

Struggling to seem normal, I smiled back at him weakly. In truth, gelato was the very last thing on my mind. I could sense Carmela and my mother staring and imagined what might be running through their minds as they sized up Pepe. Fearing that at any moment they might rise and come over, I tugged at his hand. 'Hurry up, let's keep going.'

Just once I glanced back as we walked away, I couldn't help it. My mother made an odd gesture: a tilt of her head, a sad lopsided smile. It was as if she was saying, 'I understand, don't worry, don't give it a thought.'

Never have I felt so ashamed of myself. For a while I wasn't sure if I could speak at all. Freeing my hand, I fell a step or two behind Pepe.

The light was pinking by the time we reached the fountain. Still feeling shaky, I found a seat while Pepe went to fetch the gelato. With a flourish, he presented my *fior di latte*. 'Whatever the beautiful Signorina wants,' he said.

I managed another smile. 'Thank you.'

For a few minutes we sat in silence, watching tourists throw their coins into the water and eating our gelato. The sweet creaminess on my tongue was soothing, the fountain beautiful, the summer night a pretty one. I tried to put my mother's face out of my mind.

'They come from all over the world to visit this sight,' Pepe mused, gazing up at the Trevi. 'Do you remember the first time you saw it?'

'Not really ... I feel like I've known it for as long as I can remember.'

'Me too,' he said. 'I always thought it would be the perfect place to ask a girl to marry me.'

Forgetting the gelato, I stared at him.

He laughed. 'I've taken you by surprise? Don't worry I've surprised myself, too. But you make me happy, Serafina, far more so than I ever expected. And I want that happiness to last.'

'I do too,' I told him.

'A girl who will walk halfway across Rome for a particular gelato must surely know her own mind. So are we to think of a future together – you and me?'

'Are you asking me to marry you?' I asked unsteadily.

'I have no ring with me ... I hadn't planned to do this tonight at all. But if we love each other, why wait?'

All the world slowed: the people with their handfuls of

coins blurred away, a dribble of melting gelato dropped un-
heeded to my skirt, my heartbeat sounded in my ears. Pepe
was looking at me, waiting for my reply.

'You're not sure?' he asked gently. 'That's fine, I understand. You shouldn't rush a decision like this.'

Tossing the rest of his gelato to the ground, he got to his
feet and stood with his back to me beside the low wall sur-
rounding the fountain.

'No, Pepe, I'm sure, really I am.' Jumping up, I gripped his
arm. 'I do want to marry you.'

'So why did you hesitate?'

'Because there are things … things you might …' Lost for
words, I stopped.

'What things?' he asked.

Remembering my mother's smile at seeing us hand in hand,
I knew how happy she would be to meet him. But I wasn't
certain enough of his love, not yet.

'Never mind … but could we take our time?' I asked.
'Surely there's no hurry? When Betty and Mario were
engaged it was months before people knew. They even got
married without telling his parents.'

Pepe frowned. 'This has nothing to do with Betty and
Mario,' he began, then stopped and shook his head. 'Is that
really what you think we should do?'

'No, but I'd prefer to wait and for things to stay like this a
while longer. Can they, please? I like the two of us together
every evening. I like the walking and the talking.' My hand
stroked his arm, touched his cheek. 'And the kissing, especially the kissing.'

The Fontana di Trevi is the very best place in Rome to
kiss. When you close your eyes you hear the sound of rushing
water, and when you open them again the sky has darkened
and the fountain is brightly lit. There is an old stone bench
where you can sit when your legs grow tired of standing.
Slowly the crowds begin to thin and the street cleaners come

to clear the mess, then it grows quiet. Above the noise of water you hear church bells sounding that the hour is late but still you kiss because there is no reason to stop unless it is to whisper how in love you are and that is only an excuse to begin again.

Memories

I took a photograph on the deck of the ferry to Capri. It shows Mario with his arms encircling his four children. The girls are in headscarves because it's wintry and there's a brisk breeze. Damon and Marc are wearing matching gap-toothed smiles. All of them are holding onto their Papa, looking safe and happy. I've always liked that picture. For years I kept a copy of it in a frame, as though it might help me reach back and touch that time.

We were all so hopeful then and excited about the new movie. Betty even made a gaudy mascot and took it to the set to bring good luck to its cast and crew. All her talk was of fresh starts and future plans, as if she didn't dare speak of Mario's ill health in case she jinxed him and he sickened again.

After Capri we joined him in Berlin, and there they clung to each other. There was talk of renewing their wedding vows, even of having another baby. Mario's co-stars in the film were beautiful women but every chance he got he reminded them he belonged to his wife. 'My love for her is like an atom explosion,' he declared passionately one day and everyone seemed charmed by how open he was, how very Italian.

I knew how fierce love could be by then, that it could fill or empty you in a moment. It was like that for them, I think, for Mario and Betty. But there was something else, too – an intensity, a kind of hurry to get enough of one another that seemed strange in such a long-married couple.

Berlin wasn't an entirely happy time. It was there Mario

learned his friend, the actor Tyrone Power, had died of a heart attack and the news upset him greatly. Right away he had Betty help him compose a letter of condolence, although he kept breaking off from writing it to put his head in his hands.

'I won't die ... I won't die like Tyrone,' he repeated hoarsely.

'Of course you won't, darling, don't even say it,' Betty told him.

'But it happened just like that.' Mario clicked his fingers. 'He was in Spain filming a duelling scene for his new movie, went to take a rest in his trailer and then he was gone.'

'Oh, poor Deborah.' Betty looked pained. 'They've only been married a few months. Isn't she pregnant?'

Mario nodded. 'I heard she begged him not to do this movie, asked him to slow down ... Isn't that what you've been saying to me, too?'

'You're not the same,' Betty insisted. 'You've taken a good long rest and you're looking after yourself properly now. Not the same at all.'

'Ty was a good guy.' He put down his pen, his head dropping into his hands again. 'My God, I can't believe he's gone.'

Betty stroked his hair. 'Mario dear, let's finish this letter and have done with it,' she said, picking up the pen. 'Then we can think of more cheerful things. What about having a big party at home for Christmas and the kids' birthdays? All of our friends, lots and lots of children. You could play Santa and hand out gifts. Wouldn't that be neat? What do you say?'

Tiredly Mario smiled at her. 'Why not? Let's party while we can.'

He drank quite a lot that night and, although Betty seemed tense, she didn't try to stop him. A few evenings later he threw a cocktail party in his hotel suite, asking along all his co-stars. I was there to take the coats and hand round drinks but still found time to watch and listen.

Mario seemed fond of all his guests on that occasion but most especially the blonde actress, Zsa Zsa Gabor, who was all brash glamour and quick wit. As she leaned in for him to light her cigarette he teased her about her reputation as a femme fatale and she had a ready reply no matter what he said. Her eyes were sparkling and I could tell she enjoyed sparring with him.

Later I overheard her talking to Betty, the two of them with their heads together like they had been confidantes for ever.

'You know before I met your husband I heard such terrible things about him,' Zsa Zsa admitted. 'That he was rude, used bad language, everything. But he's the nicest, kindest man I ever met. I adore him and you, too, darling.'

She was so highly polished, with a false sweep to her lashes and brightly lacquered fingernails, she didn't seem at all the sort of friend Betty might make. But we saw a lot of her while they were filming, she was entertaining and a welcome distraction for Mario who was always far gayer when he was in company.

For me the best thing about that movie was it took me away from Rome. Yes I missed Pepe, although I only had to close my eyes to see his face, his olive skin and black eyes, his slightly hooked nose. I missed my city, too, the places we had walked together. But to have an excuse to be apart from my family was a blessing. I didn't want to answer their questions.

Since the evening we had encountered them near Piazza del Popolo I had been home only once to pack a suitcase for the trip to Berlin. As ever, Carmela was full of talk about herself. She had met some new man who worked at the big film studio Cinecitta and both she and Mamma seemed impressed by him. They were out at all hours now, paying a babysitter for poor Rosalina, and the little apartment had lost its homely feel entirely.

I packed hurriedly, piling in my clothes without a care for them creasing. As I was closing the lid my mother handed me a woollen scarf the colour of raspberries.

'Take this, too; it will be cold in Germany, I think.'

'Thank you, Mamma,' I said gratefully.

'You're travelling to some places with this family you work for,' she remarked. 'London, Capri, Berlin ... Who knows where they will take you next?'

'We go wherever Mario's career takes him,' I said, repeating words Betty had once spoken to me.

'And what about your suitor? The one you looked so happy with the other night. Doesn't he mind you leaving him?'

'I'm not sure,' I said awkwardly.

'Most men want to be the most important thing in a woman's life, the centre of everything,' she remarked.

Carmela gave a dry laugh. 'That's true, Mamma. Very true.'

'But he isn't like the men you know,' I told them. 'He's completely different.'

My sister laughed again. 'They're all the same, you just don't realise it. That man you work for, Mario Lanza, you think he's so special. But I've heard things about him from girls I know, all sorts of rumours you wouldn't believe. He isn't what you think. I don't expect your suitor is either.'

'You don't know anything about him.'

'No, because you ran away instead of introducing us.'

My mother tried to stop her. 'Carmela, leave it—'

'But it's true, Mamma. She won't even let us know his name. She thinks she's so fine now working for this family. Much too good for us.'

'That's not true,' I argued.

'Well, let us meet your man, then ... at least tell us what he's called.'

I wound the raspberry scarf round my neck and picked up my suitcase. 'I have to go,' I said. 'I'm sorry, Mamma.'

'Take care of yourself,' she told me, kissing my cheeks. 'Send a postcard. Let us know you're all right.'

Closing the door, I was relieved to think it might be weeks before I need see them again, and then I felt bad for it.

I never asked my sister Carmela to tell me more about those rumours she had heard nor did I find out who had told Zsa Zsa Gabor such terrible things. It felt disloyal to want to know. Who were these people with their gossip, anyway? Did they know Mario as I did? Had they lived inside his house, inside his life? It was me that helped to teach his children Italian. I rode in his car and ate at his table. I saw him when he thought no one was there. I witnessed the small kindnesses and quiet moments. I knew the real Mario, the man who loved to make people happy, who sang his children to sleep each night and could be so funny that Betty laughed until it seemed she'd never stop. Those weren't the things people wanted to believe. They didn't make good stories to tell.

In Berlin, after the news about his friend Tyrone Power, the drinking crept up on him again and we saw his other side. But for every low there were highs, and Mario was as wonderful as he was difficult.

It was late November by the time we returned to Rome. A new recording deal had been signed and movie offers were being juggled. All of the talk was about what Mario would sing and who he might work with next. At the Villa Badoglio there were endless meetings; people coming in and out, papers being signed, dinner parties thrown. All of us worked late and long, making it easy for me to find excuses not to go home. I sent my mother a note to tell her I was back, along with a gift of some hand-stitched leather gloves I had bought in Berlin. But I stayed away from Trastevere and spent all my spare moments with Pepe.

Much of my time was taken up helping Betty prepare for

the party that was to be the most spectacular they had ever thrown. We sent out scores of invitations, bought new outfits for the children, wrapped gifts and supervised the decoration of a Christmas tree more magnificent than the last. Betty wanted American food: fried chicken and hamburgers wrapped in soft white bread with sauces and pickles. There was an awkward afternoon spent in the kitchen while she showed Pepe the best way of preparing them. He held his temper in check, but only just. Later as we paced through Rome, kitted out in hats and scarves against the cold, he steamed with it for an hour or more.

'Does she think I cannot flatten a meatball, fry it up and serve it with onions, cheese and tomato sauce? Did you hear she has sent out for a cake, four tiers high? What will that be costing? I could have made it for a quarter of the price, less perhaps.'

Pepe's mood was bleaker than I had known it for a while, his face often set in a grimace. He seemed angrier about this party than he ought to have been.

'Money isn't short at the moment,' I told him. 'Why shouldn't they have some fun?'

'If they didn't spend every last bit of money he earns perhaps he wouldn't have to work himself so hard.'

'I suppose they enjoy the parties.'

'I expect they do,' Pepe said joylessly.

Despite what he had said, I thought that party was wonderful. There were magicians and circus clowns, so many children in their dress-up clothes and everyone hungry for Pepe's hamburgers. At the very end Mario appeared dressed as Santa Claus. Beaming beneath a cotton-wool beard, he handed out the gifts I had wrapped as everyone filed past him.

We had a second celebration, just for family and staff, once again opening our gifts beneath the tree and finding special little things for everyone. The next day we travelled by train to Switzerland for a holiday in the snow. Pepe was left behind, gone to see his own family, and might have preferred me to join him but Betty wanted my help: Colleen was learning to ice-skate, the boys were longing to go sledging, Mario needed a rest before the busy new year.

The place we stayed – St Moritz – was glorious. We were there for such a brief time but it was peaceful and Betty as carefree as I had known her. 'It's so good to be away from them all,' she told me. 'The reporters, the fans, the people that are always hanging around Mario. I feel as if I've got him to myself at last. We must do this more often. It's so good for us all.'

Mario was as excited as a boy with the place. 'It's incredible,' he kept saying to anyone who would listen. 'You look at a view and can't believe it ... and then the next view is even better.'

He bought postcards of the vistas he admired to send home to his parents in Los Angeles. I mailed them all and, although I struggled to read the English words, saw he'd signed each one Freddie. Up until then I'd never realised it was his real name and it seemed odd there was a part of Mario I didn't know – a person he had been before his voice made him famous, who grew up in another country with a different name.

I took more photographs in St Moritz, of a family playing together in the snow, Mario handsome in a Russian fur hat, Betty rugged up in sheepskin.

If I had known it was the last Christmas then the holiday would have been spoiled. But by then I felt as though we were cemented in their lives: me and Pepe, the housekeeper, the two maids, the driver, the governesses, the janitor, the animals they had collected.

They had no plans to leave us. In the past few weeks I had heard them both say they would be spending at least another three years living in Rome. 'I love it here,' Mario had told his friends. 'My children love it. Even Betty is speaking Italian now. Why would we go?'

If I had known how close we were to the end then I might have taken more pictures, stolen more memories. I should have photographed him showing Damon how to make a snowball, holding Betty's hand to help her over an icy patch of ground or laughing at the beauty of it all.

But I had no idea and I'm glad of it.

Softly, As In A Morning Sunrise

All winter and into early spring Pepe's moods changed liked the weather. At times there was nothing that would cheer him. Every morning, as we heard Signore Lanza begin to warm his voice, he would grow tense; once the singing began, its quality rarely pleased him.

'Where has the sweetness gone? And the feeling? It sounds strained, as if he's forcing it,' he complained.

'Maybe he's tired or his leg is bothering him again,' I suggested.

'More likely it's the Moët & Chandon he finished last night or the half bottle of brandy,' Pepe responded darkly.

Anyone could see Signore Lanza was nowhere near as well as he had been. Ever since we returned from St Moritz there had been too much work and too much drinking. Now his face was pouchy, his body growing fleshy again. To me he looked exhausted.

Often there were outbursts of anger when he got home from a long and unhappy day in the recording studio. Once he threw a phone against the wall and it shattered; doors were slammed and glasses broken. It put everyone on edge, Betty most of all, and I think the entire household was relieved when in April he announced he would return to the Valle Giulia Clinic for another bout of treatment.

He didn't seem a great deal fresher when he left the clinic but even so he pitched straight into more rehearsals. 'I have no time to be ill,' he kept repeating. 'There's too much work to be done.'

Betty had stopped talking to me about his health but I overheard her on the phone to Dr Silvestre and thought her tone sounded despairing and the words she spoke ominous: blood pressure, blockage, chronic.

She and Mario argued constantly, their anger just as fierce and unrestrained as their love could be. Everyone was tired of the atmosphere. Meanwhile, I had my own reasons for feeling tense. Holding Pepe and my family apart hadn't been an easy task and daily I worried how long I could continue.

I had a ring by then, a sliver of a diamond on a gold band that I kept in its velvet box. Who knew how many weeks of wages Pepe had spent on it or how disappointed he felt not to see it on my finger? 'Not yet,' I kept telling him. 'Soon, but not yet.'

Thankfully, as the skies blued everyone's mood warmed a little. We were preparing for summer visitors – this time family from America – and Betty wanted everything in the Villa Badoglio spruced and polished, for her own mother was to be among them. Accompanying her would be Mario's mamma Maria Cocozza, his aunt, and his grandfather Salvatore.

'It's been two years since we've seen any of them,' Betty told me, fizzing with excitement. 'My mother's never been to Italy in her life. We have to make this stay an unforgettable one. Show them all a good time.'

For Betty the family visit might have been about showing off their new lives in Rome but for Pepe it was only ever the food that mattered. His bleak mood was swept away by a surge of energy as he planned and perfected the dishes he would make to impress the new guests. There was always something to taste if you passed through the kitchen, always pans hissing and sizzling on the stove and Pepe hovering over them.

'I'm going to give them food they will remember for the rest of their lives,' he promised. 'Flavours that will always make them think of Italy. Signore Lanza tells me his grand-father left to go to America more than fifty years ago. I want to show him what he's been missing for all that time.'

'No hamburgers, then?' I teased.

'Ach no, that's child's food,' he said dismissively.

That summer was one of the hottest I remember. All of us dripped with it, even in the Villa Badoglio with its marble floors and high ceilings. Down in the kitchen Pepe felt it most, but rarely did I hear him complain. At times he stood outside beneath the trees, wiping the sweat from his face with an old towel but mostly he worked, turning out feast after feast for the crowds of people invited to the Villa to meet Mario's family. That was the best food I remember: giant trays of baked pasta, huge bowls of *caponata*, delicate fish soups, dressed spider crabs, squid stewed in its own ink.

One party followed another, with all sorts of guests, famous and important, enjoying the hospitality. Even the Mafia man Lucky Luciano turned up one evening, although Betty would have kept him on the doorstep if she had been able.

Mario's mother, a short but forceful woman, wasn't fond of holding back her opinions. 'Why don't you stay away from all those people, Freddie?' she demanded to know when she heard Betty's whispered worries. 'We always stayed away from them in California.'

'Mom, they'll never do anything,' Mario insisted. 'They're all right. The guy just likes my voice so he comes over.'

No matter who was there, Mario made sure his grand-father Salvatore was respected as the head of the family. At dinner no one lifted a fork until the old man's was raised or left the table unless he was ready. He was old but still proud and upright, with a shock of white hair and a neat moustache and I wondered if one day Mario would be exactly like him.

That was a busy time, but also a surprisingly calm one. While his family were present, Mario knew when to stop drinking and how to control his moods. There were no raised voices or shows of temper with his mother close by, calling him 'My darling Freddie' every second moment. He presented her with the very best of himself and took her almost everywhere – to the recording studio to hear him lay down tracks, to his favourite cafés. He was thrilled to show her Rome, you would have thought it was his own city. When she told him it was time for her to return to America, he was so upset he hid her passport, only allowing her to go when she agreed to leave his grandfather Salvatore behind and promised faithfully to be back in time for Christmas.

Once his mother went so did all of Mario's good spirit. Within days of her leaving he seemed dejected, dissatisfied with his voice and crushed by the long sessions in the recording studio. There was constant bickering between him and Costa, complaints about the quality of the orchestra and the pace of the schedule forced on him. Of course, it was Betty who bore the brunt of his drinking and the sudden rages that followed. I hated to hear them argue, all of us did. We would creep through the villa, subdued and unseen, until they'd finished tearing holes in the silence.

In July they had the worst fight ever. It was late evening and Pepe and I had been hoping to find a breeze somewhere in the stifling city. Just as we were about to leave, the insults started flying. As usual, it had begun with Mario drinking and Betty begging him to stop. He responded by blaming her for all that was wrong in his life – it was her fault he had never had an opera career, that he had taken roles in unworthy movies, toured and recorded his way to exhaustion, sung when his throat was sore. The more he shouted, the louder Betty became and I heard him crashing his fist against the door in fury and frustration.

'Let's wait a while,' I suggested to Pepe, reluctant to abandon Betty with such a fight in progress.

'No, we should go,' Pepe urged. 'I don't want to hear any more of this.'

'I'd prefer to stay and make sure everything is all right,' I insisted.

'Why? We've heard it all before and know how it will go. Signore Lanza will smash something; then she will cry and lock herself in the bedroom. He'll drink for half the night and in the morning he'll have his head in his hands and be sorry. We can't do anything to stop it.'

'I suppose not.' Still it didn't feel right to leave the Villa while their voices were raging.

We took a taxi to the top of the Gianicolo Hill, arriving in time for the Pulcinella puppet show. We planned to buy fresh fruit and cool drinks from one of the snack stands and find a bench looking over the city. But that night the dry spell broke and a cold rain fell heavily. It grew windy up on the hill and we were soon driven back down to the city for shelter. There Pepe bought tickets to a Marcello Mastroianni movie we had both seen before and we sat at the very back of the theatre kissing in the flickering light as the audience laughed up at the screen.

We stayed for two showings and then Pepe walked me back to the Villa Badoglio before returning to sleep in the small room he rented not far from Stazione Termini. It was late and the Villa was silent as I let myself in, creeping to my room, careful not to disturb anyone.

I woke several times that night to hear the summer rain drumming against the windows. The next morning I rose early and dressed quickly, thinking I should look in on Betty, for often a fight with Mario was followed by one of her great lows and she might need her pills fetching or the windows of her room thrown open.

I found her door ajar instead of being locked as I had expected. Peering inside, I was surprised to see the bed covers smooth as though they hadn't been slept in. There was no sign of anyone there so I went to check the guest rooms and sure enough found Betty deeply asleep in the bed her mother had used during her visit.

Leaving her to rest a while longer, I went downstairs to make coffee. Outside it was still wet and I stood for a moment in the empty kitchen watching the rain drip from the magnolia trees. Sipping my espresso, I listed the day's tasks in my head. I was to help Betty draw up the guest list for yet another party, sew a tear in one of her evening gowns, pick up a bracelet that had gone to the jeweller's to have a broken clasp mended. It was a dull sort of day but I decided to make a start on it. Finishing my coffee, I went up to Betty's empty bedroom to find the damaged dress.

I only realised the door to the terrace was standing open when I was rummaging through her wardrobe and felt a cool draft on my neck. Noticing the curtain billowing in the breeze, I moved to close it. That's when I saw a dark shape slumped on the marble walk as the rain sleeted down on it. For a moment I didn't understand what I was looking at and then, once I did, I was stilled by shock for a few seconds longer.

He was lying quite motionless. He must have fallen into a drunken sleep and been out there on the terrace all night long, for his clothes were soaked through, his lips blue and his skin cold to the touch. I couldn't tell if he was breathing.

'Signore Lanza,' I cried, fearing his heart must have stopped beating as he lay unconscious in the cold rain. I pressed my fingers to his neck, trying to find some warmth there. 'Signore Lanza, can you hear me?'

When he made no sound or movement in reply I panicked, slapping at his face with my hands, pinching his cheeks, shouting his name even louder. I was certain we had lost him.

'Serafina?' His voice was faint and shaky but he was alive and relief flooded through me.

'Yes, Signore, it is me.'

His eyes seemed to open with a great effort. 'What am I doing out here?' he croaked.

'I'm not really sure. Let me help you inside. Can you sit up?'

He was too confused and weak to get to his feet and too heavy for me to move. The rain was running off my hair and down my face as I struggled.

'Help ... can somebody help me?' I called back into the house. 'Pepe ... Antonio ... Liliana ... Is anyone there?'

No one came. Somehow I managed to force my hands beneath his shoulders and tried my best to pull him towards the door as he groaned and shivered.

'Help me,' I kept shouting. 'Please ... someone.'

It was Betty who came running, wild-eyed and pale-cheeked. 'Dear God, Serafina, what is it?'

I think she thought he was dead, for she screamed when she saw him lying there. Dropping to her knees, she threw herself over him. 'Mario, Mario. Is he breathing? I can't tell. Oh my God, Mario, please don't leave us. Please, God, no.'

'He is breathing, Signora,' I reassured her quickly, 'but he's terribly cold. We must get him inside and out of these clothes.'

Between us we managed to help him out of the rain. While Betty stripped off his sodden clothes and wrapped him in as many blankets as she could find, I went to call an ambulance. The other servants had begun arriving and the housekeeper ran to see if she could help while Pepe went downstairs to make hot drinks. I stayed at the front door waiting for the medics, my stomach rolling with the shock still.

They took him straight back to the Valle Giulia Clinic and told us he had pneumonia. There must have been something else wrong, too, because Betty held a lot of low-voiced conversations with the doctors but she never repeated them to me.

'He's out of danger, that's the important thing,' she said. 'Thank God you found him when you did. Thank God, Serafina.'

I heard her crying a lot in the days that followed and her eyes looked reddened and swollen. I suppose she felt guilty, blamed herself for what had happened because of that terrible argument. Every time she returned from the clinic she needed to take a rest with a cold flannel on her forehead. She might have slept all day if she could but I was careful to wake her and make sure she ate her meals, for I didn't want her to be the next one to sicken.

Costa visited the clinic one afternoon and returned to the Villa looking shaken. 'He looks at least ten years older,' I heard him telling Betty. 'Yet still he's full of talk about singing at the Rome Opera and San Carlo in Naples. He must think he's indestructible.'

'Does he have any voice left?' Betty wondered.

'I don't know. We'll have to see what he sounds like when he begins to work again. But, Betty, his health is badly damaged now. Even if he did want to sing an opera I don't know if he's got the stamina left to do it.'

'Did you tell him that?'

'I told him it could kill him,' Costa admitted.

'And what was his reply?'

'He only laughed and said, "You know, Costa, none of us lives for ever." Then he promised me the usual things, that he'd stop drinking, lead a healthy life, lose weight again.'

For the rest of the month, Signore Lanza stayed at the clinic and I almost dreaded his return. I kept remembering that dark shape on the terrace, slumped and still, and I wondered how I might find him the next time, if he failed to keep his promises.

The summer heat had returned and the house was unbearable. Whenever there was a chance I went and sat alone in the shade of the trees hoping for a hint of breeze, often taking Pepe's engagement ring from its box and slipping it on my finger.

I liked to move it so the stone sparkled, to feel its unfamiliar weight and dream of what it promised. I liked to think some day I might find a way to tell Pepe who I really was and he might love me still, and then we could be married.

The Lord's Prayer

The last thing I ever heard Mario Lanza sing was the Malotte Lord's Prayer. I had gone with Betty to the Cinecitta Studio and we were sitting in the control booth while he and Costa finished recording the songs they'd been working on before his last stay at the clinic.

Mario kept insisting he had rallied. He was trying to follow yet another diet, often surviving on little more than sips of iced water, in his struggle to lose weight for his next movie. But he had changed such a great deal. To my eyes he looked used and broken, far older than his thirty-eight years and so very frail.

Only his voice still blazed. As Costa directed him, he summoned whatever energy was left and sang with power and passion. Some songs were recorded in a single attempt; none took more than two tries. By the end of the morning there was only the Lord's Prayer left to record.

He sang it with such purity, the familiar words heartfelt, his voice whole and haunting. Closing my eyes, I thanked God for letting him keep his gift in spite of everything that had happened.

Once he had finished he lowered his head, rubbing at his eyes tiredly. Then he glanced up at Costa who smiled and nodded.

'Beautiful,' he said.

'Do you want to take it again to be sure?'

'No need. That was the best you ever sang in your life. It gave me chills.'

Mario laughed and there was a hint of the old sparkle in his eyes. 'Twelve years of working together and I can still surprise you, eh, Costa? That's not bad, is it, my friend?'

'Not bad at all,' Costa agreed.

'You know I couldn't have done it without you. Any of it.'

Costa shrugged. 'There are other conductors and accompanists,' he said gruffly.

'Yes, but you're the only one that understands me,' Mario insisted. 'You know my way of coming into a song, of breathing. You work the way I work. Thank you for making this morning so easy, my friend. Thank you for everything.'

Perhaps Mario was emotional because Costa was to leave for America later that afternoon and the thought made him homesick. As we were driving back to the Villa the three of them spoke nostalgically of the people and places they missed; a man called Terry and a house on Toyopa Drive that Costa promised to visit.

Pepe had readied a wonderful farewell lunch for Costa, made all his favourites: a *timballo* of macaroni, platters of seafood and grilled meats, salads dressed with lemon and olive oil. Once the new recordings had been toasted with champagne, I helped bring the dishes to the dining table, careful to catch snatches of their conversation as I moved in and out. They were planning Costa's return, the next albums they would record, all sorts of future projects. Already they were talking of Christmas.

'This will be the best one yet,' Mario declared. 'I want all my family to be here. Bring them back with you, Costa – my mother, Papa too this time, and Terry. It's time that man got himself a passport.'

'I won't let any of them change their minds,' Costa agreed. 'But in return I want you to promise me something. Swear you'll rest as much as you can while I'm away. When I get back I'd like to see my friend looking like himself again.'

Mario shrugged off the words with a laugh. 'Don't worry so much. I feel fine,' he insisted.

When Costa left, we lined up at the door to wish him Godspeed, waving as his taxi drove away from the Villa. Once he was out of sight I helped clear the table and got on with the normal chores of the afternoon, expecting the weeks of his absence to go in a flash and for him to be lunching with us again before we knew it.

That September continued warm and dry and the Villa bustled with activity as Mario prepared for his new picture. People arrived at all hours; meetings went on for whole afternoons. On several occasions I heard him muttering to Betty about pains in his chest, but still he refused to slow down.

'Remember your friend Tyrone?' she warned anxiously. 'Remember how you didn't want to be like that.'

'I won't be filming any duelling scenes in heavy costumes, just singing as usual,' Mario replied. 'Don't worry so much about me.'

Yet only a week later he cancelled a trip to London, not feeling well enough to travel. A family outing to the opera was cut short after a crowd of fans recognised him despite his dark glasses and besieged him for autographs. Once that sort of attention had pleased him; now he was far too frail to deal with it.

'The thing that's really bothering me is my right leg,' he told Betty one morning, stretching out in the chair beside their bed, his stick balanced against its arm ready for use.

I was in the room, busy removing curlers from Betty's hair, but as usual they talked as though I wasn't there.

Betty seemed anxious. 'You should check in to the clinic straight away,' she told him. 'Your leg, your chest, you keep complaining about them … You need more treatment, Mario. You mustn't try to go on without it or you really will be like your friend Tyrone.'

'OK then,' he conceded, sounding reluctant. 'Once I've sung at that charity concert in Napoli I'll go back.'

'No, no, cancel the concert,' Betty urged. 'It will be exhausting. You're not well enough.'

'I can't cancel. I didn't want to do it in the first place but … well, you know how it is.'

Suddenly aware of me, they exchanged a glance and then Betty frowned. 'I hate the hold these people have over us. Lucky Luciano and his friends. When will we ever be rid of them?'

'It's only one night and when it's done with I'll go to Valle Giulia,' Mario soothed her. 'I'll do exactly what the doctors say, take all the treatments. Everything will be fine, you'll see.'

That evening I went home to Trastevere. I had hardly visited the apartment in the past months and then only if I thought it might be empty. The few times I had seen my mother and Carmela, I offered them little in the way of news about myself and they had given up asking questions.

The room I used at the Villa Badoglio felt more like home to me; I had placed a photograph of Rosalina on the nightstand and hung my mother's raspberry scarf over a chair-back. But that evening for some reason I missed my family. I wanted to know how Rosalina was doing at school, to look into my mother's face. I longed for the comfort of how things used to be. So once I had finished work, instead of sitting beside the Fontana di Trevi with Pepe, I took a tram across the river.

I found Rosalina at the kitchen table, drawing doodles on the cover of her schoolbook instead of doing her homework. Happy to see me, she jumped up straight away and then held a finger to her lips.

'Don't make any noise,' she whispered. 'Mamma is in bed with a headache. We have no aspirin left so she's trying to sleep it off.'

'Where's Carmela? Couldn't she have fetched some?'

'I don't know. She went out ages ago.'

'I'll do it then,' I said impatiently.

'Bring back a treat,' Rosalina begged. 'Some chocolate or a little cake?'

'Perhaps. We'll see ... Finish your homework first.'

Rosalina pulled a face but when I left the apartment, her head was bent over her books and she seemed to be concentrating. Out on the street, it was the busiest time of the evening. Wives were returning home with their baskets laden with food to cook for their husbands' dinners, little knots of people were clogging the narrow passages and exchanging the day's gossip, cars hooting their horns as they tried to force a way through. My mother's friends were enjoying the last of the evening sun outside the corner bar, my sister Carmela among them, her lips painted bright coral and her hair cut shorter and teased around her face. Barely bothering to break from her conversation, she offered me a curt nod.

'Carmela, what are you doing? Mamma is sick in bed. She needs aspirin,' I said, exasperated.

'Yes, I know, and I've bought some for her, see?' Carmela reached into her bag. 'I only stopped for a quick drink on my way home. Now you're here you may as well take them back so I can stay out longer.'

She gave me a look, as if daring me to argue. Taking the aspirin bottle from her, I turned on my heel and without another word, went straight back to the apartment.

Rosalina was disappointed to see me so quickly. 'No treat?' she pouted.

'Later maybe,' I told her. 'Let me give Mamma something for her headache first.'

My mother's room was stuffy and smelt stale like a sickroom. Even with the curtains drawn against the light I could tell her colour was sallow, her hair unbrushed.

'Carmela, is that you?' I heard her murmur.

'No, Mamma, it's me.'

'Oh, Serafina.' She sounded croaky. 'I've run out of aspirin and my head is splitting.'

'I've brought some for you.' I pressed my palm to her forehead. 'But, Mamma, you're burning hot. How long have you been feeling like this?'

'A couple of days, I think. All I need is more pills and to sleep a while longer and then I'll be better.' Gratefully she reached for the water glass I offered. 'I'm sure I've never had a headache like this before.'

Sitting beside her on the bed, I wondered whether to call a doctor. 'Has it really only been two days?' I asked.

'I think so.' She furrowed her brow. 'What day is it today?'

'Friday,' I told her.

'Really?' She sounded surprised. 'Well, then I've been ill for longer than I thought.'

'Has Carmela been looking after you? What have you eaten?'

She screwed up her face. 'I couldn't face any food. I just want to sleep and sleep like I never have before.'

'You must try to eat. I've brought some leftovers with me, a little *peperonata*, some veal meatballs with capers and lemon. If I fetch it, will you take a few mouthfuls?'

'A little, perhaps,' she agreed. 'Just a taste or two.'

I went to the kitchen and made up a tray, just as I would have for Betty, arranging the food carefully and wrapping the cutlery in a coloured serviette.

'You're so good at looking after people,' my mother said when she saw it.

The meal pleased her and she managed a little of the peppers and almost a whole meatball. 'I wish I had some appetite and could do it justice,' she said. 'It's very good. Did you make it?'

'No, Pepe cooked it. He wanted me to bring it home for you.'

Her eyes searched my face. 'Pepe?'

'The chef at the Villa Badoglio ... my friend—' Feeling my cheeks flush, I broke off.

It dawned on her then. 'Ah, do you mean your young suitor?'

I nodded. 'That's right.'

'So at long last I'm allowed to know something about him.' Setting the plate aside, my mother took my hand. 'Tell me more, Serafina. Are you happy with this man? In love?'

'Yes,' I said awkwardly.

'Does he treat you well?'

I toyed with a tassel on the bed cover. 'Mamma,' I said without meeting her eyes. 'He's given me a ring.'

'What sort of ring?' she asked sharply.

'It's in my bag. I'll show you.'

My mother seemed disappointed when she saw the diamond. 'It's a small stone, isn't it?' she couldn't help saying.

'This is all he could afford,' I told her. 'But it's genuine.'

'Why do you carry it in your bag instead of wearing it?'

'I was waiting until I'd told you ...' Sliding the ring onto my finger, I held out my hand nervously. 'There, does it suit me?'

Mamma frowned. 'Are you sure he's the right man? I don't even know him ... This feels as if it's happening very fast and I'm not sure I'm pleased.'

'We haven't set a wedding date,' I reassured her. 'We've been taking our time. But yes, I'm sure. And we're ready.'

'My little girl is to be married,' she said wistfully. 'I suppose that must mean I'm not so young any more.'

Pepe's ring caught my eye every time I moved. It was bright on my finger, and I felt self-conscious. Yet at first Rosalina didn't notice. She was too distracted by the discovery I did have treats for her after all: a thick slice of rich chocolate tart that Pepe had baked. Only when she'd sated herself with sugar did the sparkle of the stone attract her attention.

'Is that a real diamond?' she asked.

I nodded awkwardly and held out my hand so she could see it properly.

'It's very pretty. Even Carmela doesn't have one of those yet.'

'I only have it because I'm going to be married,' I explained.

'Married? Will I be a bridesmaid? Will I get a pink dress and carry a posy of flowers?'

'I expect so.' I smiled. 'If that's what you'd like.'

'And will Carmela?'

'I don't know. I'm not sure if she'll want to.'

'She'd like a diamond,' Rosalina told me.

'Yes, I expect she would.'

Although its weight felt strange still, it was a relief to be wearing the ring, to see it safely on my finger. I tried not to think much further ahead. Some day my mother and Pepe must meet but I planned to delay that for longer if I could. Until then there was a pleasure in this feeling of belonging to him, and of having him belong to me.

I Walk With God

In the last week of September Signore Lanza prepared for his return to the Valle Giulia Clinic. I helped Betty to pack a bag for him. We were so used to this by now, it had become almost a routine. It was to be his sixth stay and an entire wing in the most secluded part of the building had been reserved for him with a living room where he could meet visitors, spare bedrooms for guests to stay overnight and a nurse dedicated solely to his care.

The story Betty was telling everyone was that Mario was going there to lose weight for his next movie but from careful listening and casual questions, I knew his health was precarious again. All those days and nights of drinking had damaged his liver, hurt his heart and blocked his arteries. Now he needed a great deal of rest and medication. It was treatment that couldn't be rushed and he wasn't expected home again for a good long while. No wonder he drew out his goodbyes, shaking Pepe's hand, hugging both the governesses, smiling over at me. 'Take care of the children and of Betty too,' he told us. 'I'm relying on you all, you know that.'

'We promise ... of course we do,' we reassured him.

His friend Dr Silvestre had come by that morning to pick him up and was waiting in the car outside. 'You ought to go now,' Betty said, clinging to Mario for one last kiss.

Turning for the door, he hesitated as though there was something else he wanted to say. Then he shrugged, lowered his head and, without another word, headed for the car.

We all knew how much he hated clinics. A restless patient,

exasperated by the empty days and endless treatments, he was always desperate to return home. This time must have been especially difficult because he would have known things weren't good at the Villa. Almost the moment he left, Betty took to her bed suffering from a high fever and a dry cough, not well enough to visit him even once.

After no more than a week he was on the telephone complaining he'd had enough of being jabbed and prodded by doctors, that he wouldn't stand for it any longer. Betty tried to argue but he refused to listen, vowing to come back no matter what she said, declaring he would continue his treatment in his own house surrounded by his family.

'I can't stop him,' she said helplessly. 'And anyway, I'd rather have him home and see him everyday.'

We were preparing for him to arrive the very next morning. Pepe had been busy cooking light vegetable soups and stocking the refrigerator with lean beef and white-fleshed fish to help him stick to his diet. It was early October, a wan autumn day and we were in the kitchen eating the staff lunch when we heard the telephone ringing in the upstairs hallway.

'I'll go,' I said, but the ringing stopped before I was out of my chair. Next I heard a scream and then a loud crash. Hurrying upstairs, Pepe close behind me, I found Betty collapsed on the ground, the telephone beside her.

'What is it? What's wrong?' I asked, dropping to my knees. Her eyes were wide and staring, her mouth hanging open but she had no words. 'Signora ... Betty, Betty.'

It was Pepe who picked up the telephone. 'Hello, hello.' He held the receiver to his ear. 'Who is this calling? ... Dr Silvestre? ... No, sir, she has fallen. I'm sorry what is that you said? ... What? ... No ... no—'

Pepe's voice broke. He found the wall for balance or else I think he too might have swayed and collapsed. Before I could ask what had happened Betty began making a terrible noise, a sort of keening. Rocking her body, she beat her head against the floor.

I tried to use my weight to hold her still but her strength was stubborn and her head kept hitting the marble. 'Tell the doctor we need him right away,' I cried at Pepe. 'For God's sake, get him to hurry. She's going to hurt herself.'

Thankfully the children were out, for the sight of their mother in such a state would have been terrifying. The rest of the staff surrounded us, staring helplessly, at a loss for what to do. 'What's happened? Why is she like this?' they wanted to know. 'What's wrong?'

Pepe looked at me but his words were for everyone. 'Signore Lanza is dead,' was all he said.

First there was disbelief and then a rush of grief. I remember one of the maids sinking to the floor and holding her starched white apron over her head to muffle the sound of her sobbing. It couldn't be true, we kept saying. Surely Dr Silvestre had got it wrong. Mario dead? Impossible. But the maid continued heaving with sobs.

I stayed with Betty until the doctor arrived, lying beside her and cradling her with my body. In her fury of grief she shouted, 'Let me die too, let me die.' All I could do was hold on tight and pray for Dr Silvestre and his sedatives.

Only when the needle had sunk into her arm and we were certain the drugs had worked did I risk leaving her. By then everyone was back in the kitchen, gathered round the radio. Joining them, I heard the final notes of 'Be My Love' before the announcer broke in: *That was the voice of Mario Lanza who passed away today of a heart attack in the Valle Giulia Clinic in Rome.* Only then did it seem real.

'It is true? He is really dead?' I sat down heavily.

'Yes, it's true,' said Pepe. 'We have lost him ... the world has lost him.'

Shocked, we sat round the table, some with tears falling, the housekeeper setting up a wail, the maids holding on to each other. In our great grief none of us remembered Mario's grandfather Salvatore who was still staying at the Villa. It was only when we heard him weeping in the hallway that we realised he had heard the news from someone on the street. The poor old man was struggling to believe it too. We helped him down to the kitchen, so he could hear the official announcements on the radio and know that it was true. *The tenor Mario Lanza passed away today in Rome*, the voice repeated gravely. *He leaves behind a wife and four children.*

I had never lost someone I cared for before. It felt as if my life had been torn in half; there was the part with Mario in it, and this new terrible piece of it without him. I missed him more than it seemed possible; missed his smile and his lively eyes; missed the sound of his voice and the way it seemed to wrap itself round me until I felt I was breathing with him. He had taken me into his family; had meant so much to all of us. Now he was gone, leaving nothing but sadness and pain. Those first few days were a blur. Someone must have talked to his mother in America, to Costa, to all the people who would never see him again. I never knew who did any of it. My life had closed in around Betty. It was my job to care for her and in that I never wavered.

To begin with Dr Silvestre kept her sedated but she couldn't escape into sleep for ever and there was always a moment when she woke, reaching for Mario, realising he had gone. Then her anguish was as if she were hearing the news for the first time. She would rock her body and thrash her hands, her voice raw and cracked, demanding to know why they hadn't saved him, blaming the clinic or Dr Silvestre, sometimes even the Mafia. 'They murdered him,' she cried once. 'Why couldn't they have killed me, too?'

It wasn't the worst of it though. For me that came when they brought the body home. It was laid in the centre of the living room in an open casket for everyone to see. The face was bruised and unshaven, the stomach bloated, cotton wool protruded from the nostrils and a strip of tape had been plastered across the mouth. This wasn't my Mario and I couldn't bear to look at it. But for hours I had to stay there, holding Betty's hand while she cried like an animal in pain.

People came to pay their respects but she refused to see a soul. Even when she wasn't sedated, she was dizzy with drugs and alcohol, often speaking about Mario as if he had just left the room, refusing to hear talk of funeral arrangements or consider the future. Coddled with barbiturates, she left the staff to manage as best we could.

No one seemed brave enough to break the news to the children. I had expected the governesses to do it or Dr Silvestre but perhaps they were hoping Betty would soon be well enough to tell them. They found out for themselves one terrible morning when Colleen climbed through the living-room window and discovered what lay inside. Poor little girl, to see her papa like that. The sound of her screaming brought us all running, but there was no comfort for her, nor her little sister and brothers.

The children's grief was pure and lusty. It must have been what broke the ice of my own. For days I hadn't been able to cry; now my eyes were rarely dry. Pepe kept a store of handkerchiefs, neatly pressed and lightly scented with whatever he had been cooking and, whenever he saw me, he would pull one from his pocket and press it to my hand.

Whilst we in the Villa were in mourning, so was the world outside. People came to stand at the gates, leaving behind bouquets with sad little messages. 'It's because they love him,' Betty said when I told her. 'Everybody loves him.'

It rained and the flowers rotted but still we couldn't bring ourselves to clear them away.

To our relief, Mario's mother Maria Cocozza flew back to Rome. While she too was distraught, her strength shone through and she took control of everything. She didn't spend too long in the room with her son's body, nor would she entertain the fanciful ideas some people had that Mario should be buried in Napoli near to his idol Caruso. 'We're taking him with us,' she said. 'My Freddie is coming home.'

First there was a Requiem Mass in Rome, and it seemed like half the city came to mourn with us that day. They began by gathering outside the Villa very early in the morning, some of them singing in soft, sad voices. When it grew light, the gates were opened and they were allowed to shuffle inside to sign their names in the book of condolence and file past the coffin. We heard the sound of their footfalls and the odd muffled cry but otherwise they passed through Mario's home in heartbreaking silence.

Closed up inside Betty's room I tried to concentrate on making her ready for the day ahead. Usually she cared so much about how I styled her hair and what we chose for her to wear, but that day she sat listless before her dressing table, barely murmuring as I powdered her skin and arranged her face. Her eyes were reddened and swollen so I hid them behind dark glasses, her face was covered with a black veil, her body swathed in a fur so no one could tell how skeletal she had become. Then I buttoned the boys into their smart blazers and helped the girls with their white lace headscarves and dresses. I'm not sure if any of them truly understood what was happening, although we'd tried to explain it. 'You look so pretty,' I whispered. 'Your papa would be so proud if he could see you now.'

Just before we left I covered my own hair with a black scarf and tugged on an old grey woollen coat. I was to go wherever Betty went, follow behind, carry her handbag, pass tissues, hold her up if I had to.

It was mid morning when Mario Lanza left the Villa Badoglio for the final time. Photographer's flashbulbs lit the way as his coffin was borne to the Basilica in a glass-walled carriage drawn by four plumed black horses. Thousands of people lined the streets as we passed; each of them silent and still, their heads bowed. They loved him. We all loved him.

At the Basilica there were more photographers waiting and hundreds of mourners overflowing the steps beneath the high, white columns of the entranceway. With his arm around Betty to support her, Dr Silvestre helped us press through the crowds.

It was a long and formal Mass with Betty denied the one thing she had requested – to hear the sound of his voice. Perhaps if the church had been filled with his 'Ave Maria' we might have felt close to him for one last time. But the pastor refused to play a recording, blaming church regulations, and instead an Italian baritone gave us the song accompanied by the choir. There was nothing wrong with the music but it wasn't Mario and it felt as if we had let him down.

Betty clung to her children, clutching Marc's hand, pulling Ellisa up on to her knee. All four were solemn and quiet, their cheeks shining with tears. Beside them sat Maria Cocozza, a handkerchief held to her face, and Mario's grandfather Salvatore, staring at the coffin in disbelief. 'Freddie, Freddie, my dearest friend,' he called out when the pallbearers came to carry it away.

Throughout that long and terrible Mass sitting on the hard wooden pews of the Basilica, I struggled to imagine a future. What would happen to Betty and the children? What would happen to me? To Pepe? Now that Mario had gone, what was to become of any of us?

Arrivederci Roma

The life Mario had made in Rome was wrapped and packed in trunks to be taken back to America with his body. I was in charge of Betty's things and treated them so carefully: layering the gowns in tissue, stuffing paper into the cavities of handbags and shoes to keep them from being crushed, folding and rolling the silks and woollens, locking up the jewellery. I tried to imagine the place they would be unpacked and kept in mind the American maid who would see how I had ordered everything. Not wanting to be judged and found lacking, I stored everything as though Betty might need it again tomorrow; although I couldn't imagine her ever joyful enough to wear those fine things again.

She watched as I worked, hardly summoning a word, only managing to nod or shake her head if she were asked a question. It didn't much matter because I followed Maria Cocozza's orders now and there was no shortage of them. Mario's mother stalked the marble corridors of the Villa Badoglio, list in one hand, ballpoint pen in the other. She was suspicious of the staff, convinced certain things had been looted: mementos of Mario, copies of his scores or recordings. I didn't believe anyone who worked there would have stolen from Betty, not then. Our hearts burned for her and our sorrow was still so fresh.

I removed only one thing from the Villa myself, a copy of the photograph I had posed for with Mario on the day of his daughters' First Communion. I had come across it in a drawer and spirited it home to store in the box of belongings still tucked beneath my mother's bed. It wasn't stealing, though, for hadn't he said I was to have it?

That morning when I slipped home unexpectedly my mother was still sleeping. She must have woken to the sound of my weeping and, finding me in the kitchen with the photograph on the table before me, she clasped her arms round my shoulders and rested her face in my hair.

'Years ago I used to imagine he was my father,' I admitted in a small voice. 'I wished it so much I even envied his children for belonging to him. I thought they were the luckiest children alive.'

She squeezed me tighter but said nothing.

'That was before he came to Rome, before I knew him at all. And now he's gone. All of us have lost him.'

'He had a wonderful voice your Signore Lanza,' Mamma said softly. 'A true talent. His death is a terrible waste.'

'It's a waste of a man, not just his talent.' I held up the photograph. 'This was taken such a short time ago. I could have reached out and touched him that day ...'

'It's so difficult to believe.'

'Impossible.'

My mother lit the stove to make us coffee, rummaging in a cupboard for the beans and sugar.

'Are you home for good? Have they let you go?' she asked.

'Not yet. But we'll be finished packing up the Villa soon enough and then there'll be no job for me.'

'What will you do?'

It was the question we had all been asking each other at the Villa Badoglio. The housekeeper and one of the maids had already found other positions, so had Antonio the janitor. Those who remained were looking.

'I have no idea,' I told my mother. 'None at all.'

She thought for a moment. 'You can come back and look after us like you always used to.'

It seemed a sorry ending to the life I had made in the

Lanza household. I had become so knotted up with them, so fond of Betty and the children, that saying goodbye would be another great loss, one more reason to grieve and feel hollow inside.

'I'll stay with her as long as she needs me,' I told my mother.

'You're very loyal, *cara*.'

'I promised him, that's all.' Lightly I touched the photograph. 'The first day I met him I swore I'd never let him down. And on that last day when he left it was the final thing he asked of us.'

'She'll be OK,' Mamma reassured me, taking her cup and settling in a chair by the window. 'She'll go home to America and be looked after by her own family and, while it may take time, some day she'll feel better than she does now. She'll find a new life, new reasons to be happy.'

'Maybe,' I said doubtfully.

'Grief is like any other sickness. You have to find a cure for it.'

'What happens if you don't?' I asked. 'Does it kill you?'

'She has her children,' Mamma reminded me. 'She'll stay strong for them.'

'You haven't seen her. It's like she's gone mad with grief. She thinks the Mafia killed him; that they'd been plotting to do it all along. There's this man called Lucky Luciano whose name she keeps mentioning. Pepe insists it makes no sense because Signore Lanza would have been worth much more to them alive than dead. But there was an appearance at a charity concert in Napoli that was cancelled at the last minute and she thinks they ordered a hit on his life because of it.'

'I agree with your Pepe. It makes no sense.'

'You see why I can't leave her, though? She's not in her right mind. I'm frightened she'll hurt herself.'

'If a thing like that happened it wouldn't be your fault.'

'But if I can prevent it, watch over her ...'

My mother put down her cup and came to wrap her arms round me again. I felt the warmth of her body, smelt her musky fragrance and a hint of last night's cigar smoke in her hair.

'She's not your family, we are,' Mamma reminded me.

The Villa itself seemed in mourning. Paintings had been stripped from the walls, mementoes cleared from mantel-pieces, furniture shrouded. All that was left was the bare bones of the place. Thanks to Pepe it still smelt like home. The food he cooked scented the empty hallways and cheered the rooms. There was a comfort in knowing that down in the kitchen there was a sauce of ripe plum tomatoes and basil leaves simmering, that garlic was being gently heated in a puddle of olive oil and peppers roasted until their skins charred and blistered. No one had much appetite, but still Pepe kept cooking for us.

Betty barely ate a thing, no matter how I cajoled her. If she saw me holding a dish of earthy mushroom risotto or a steaming broth of pasta and beans, she'd screw up her face and turn her head like a stubborn child. Every mealtime was a battle and I began to dread the rattle of pans that heralded another. Usually I coaxed her until she finished a few mouth-fuls but no one else had my patience. When Maria Cocozza tried to make her eat a dish of baked macaroni, the result was smashed crockery and raised voices.

'This has to stop,' Maria cried, furious. 'You must eat, get out of bed, start looking after yourself and your children. Pull yourself together.'

'Leave me alone.' Betty buried her face in the pillow. 'Just go.'

Maria was stubborn. Glancing down at me, on my hands and knees clearing up the mess from the floor, she demanded, 'Go back to the kitchen and fetch more food. I'll force it into her if it's the last thing I do.'

'Signora, let me try once she's calmed down,' I pleaded. 'In this state she will never eat.'

'I told you to fetch more of the macaroni,' Maria replied tersely. 'So do it, don't argue.'

Piling the spilt food onto the tray, I bit back the reply I wanted to make and followed her orders.

Pepe scowled when he saw what had happened to his pasta. 'It wasn't her fault,' I put in quickly. 'That woman keeps niggling and shouting – it's not the way to treat her but she won't listen.'

Pulling a foil-covered tray from the warm oven, he spooned out more of the baked macaroni, blushing with tomato sauce and stringy with melted mozzarella.

'I don't suppose it's easy for Signora Cocozza either,' Pepe observed. 'She's lost her only son and all the responsibility for his family has fallen on her shoulders.'

'In that case surely it makes good sense to let me care for Betty?' I reasoned.

'The poor woman will have to manage without you soon enough, won't she? I expect Signora Cocozza is worried, frightened even, and that's what makes her harsh ... and why she shouts so much.'

Pepe handed me the new bowl of pasta. 'Let's see how this one comes back,' he said drily.

Upstairs I found Maria sitting in the armchair, her head in her hands, looking worn out and defeated. Without a word to her I slipped into my usual place beside Betty, murmuring that she should taste a mouthful before it went cold, that it was delicious, Pepe had gone to so much trouble and would be happy she tried it.

'If you don't eat you won't be strong enough to travel home,' I reminded her. 'It's a long journey. That's why every-one is so worried about you.'

Still there was silence and Betty's face stayed hidden.

'I promised him I'd look after you,' I told her desperately.

'On that last day when he left us to go to the clinic, you and the children were all he cared about. I've done my best not to let him down. But what will happen in America when I'm not there? If you can't take care of yourself, who will?'

Betty rolled towards me and I glimpsed her face, creased from the pillow and ruined with tears. 'You're coming to America,' she said huskily.

'No, Signora. I'm to stay here in Rome.'

'You are coming,' she insisted.

'No, Signora—'

'Remember how we discussed this?' Maria interrupted tiredly. 'The children's governesses are to come back with us, but not Serafina.'

Betty sat up in bed, hair wild and eyes glittering. 'She is coming,' she said, her voice surprisingly strong.

'That's impossible. We haven't planned for it ... she would need tickets, papers ...' Maria tried to argue.

'Have Myrt Blum take care of it,' Betty snapped. 'He calls himself Mario's business administrator, doesn't he? Let him earn his five per cent.'

'Surely you can hire another girl when you get home.'

'I want this one. She's coming home with us along with the governesses and the children's pets no matter what you say.'

'The dogs yes, but not the canary,' Maria began.

Betty set her face: eyebrows drawn, lips pressed tight.

'You can't take the whole household back with you,' Maria said, exasperated.

'Mario bought that canary. He hired Serafina as well. He'd want them to stay with me, I know he would.'

'OK, fine. Take them all home with you if you like. Just for God's sake, eat some pasta, that's all we ask.'

Betty did force herself to swallow a few pieces of the maca-roni, although the effort seemed to half choke her. For half an hour I sat with her while she decided if she could tolerate another mouthful. When she declared she had finished with it, I dabbed the drips of tomato sauce from her lips with a napkin. Our eyes met then and she gave a half smile as if she was pleased with herself. For a moment I thought I saw a spark of the old Betty there. 'We're going home,' she said to me. 'Thank God we're going home.'

So many people dream of going to America, but never me. Why would I have wanted to? In America did they have a fountain on every corner and views over a sea of domes? Were there places you could buy an espresso so strong it shocked you? Was there music and history everywhere you walked? From what I'd seen of it in movies, it seemed fine enough but to me Rome was better. Rome was my home.

While I went along with all the fuss about procuring documents and tickets, I couldn't imagine truly leaving. Only when the last of Betty's belongings was packed in crates and shipped away, and my papers were in my hands, did I realise it was happening. I was going to America.

I told myself I had no choice. I couldn't abandon Betty now; she might not survive it. But I was determined to stay there only as long as it took to see her safe and settled. Then I would come back to Rome.

I was worried about breaking the news to Pepe, for I knew it wouldn't please him. That night we walked to the Fontana di Trevi. It was wintry by then so there weren't too many tourists but wound up in scarves we braved the chill together. Pepe had found work in a restaurant near Stazione Termini, a small basement place where they served traditional Roman dishes like tripe slow-cooked in white wine, slivers of veal rolled with crisped sage, plump artichokes fried in olive oil, fava beans simmered with pig's cheek and onions. He seemed pleased with the job, happy to have secured a future. 'But I'll be working long nights so we may not see much of each other,' he said regretfully. 'It won't be the same.'

'Pepe, there's something I need to tell you,' I began but he wasn't paying attention.

Through my glove he rubbed the spot where the engagement ring formed a hard ridge on my finger. 'I could ask them if you might have some waitressing work there?' he suggested. 'Perhaps not right away but once I see how things go. Then we'd be working the same hours, which would be much better.'

Letting my face sink into the prickly wool of his scarf, I breathed the familiar scent of him, earthy and slightly sweet, his skin warmed by a day in the kitchen. He pulled me closer.

'Pepe, you must listen for a moment.' I lifted my face to his.

'What is it, *cara*?'

'Betty wants me in America.'

'What?'

'She asked me to go with her.'

'What did she say when you told her no?'

I bit my lip and looked away, staring at the fountain with its soaring columns and winged horses, until I heard Pepe making a hissing sound.

'Tell me you said no, Serafina.'

'I can't refuse to go,' I told him. 'Not if she needs me.'

'What if I need you, too?'

'It will only be for a short while. Just until she's established and then I'll be back. You'll wait for me, won't you?' I squeezed his arm. 'I'll miss you so much.'

'If you go to America you will never come home.' He sounded certain. 'You'll make a new life there, one without me in it. You'll forget me.'

'I'll come back,' I said brightly. 'Of course I will.'

'People hardly ever do. America swallows them up and all anyone sees of them is a few letters and photographs. Look at Signore Lanza's grandfather. How long was it before he returned? More than fifty years, almost a lifetime. And when he did come back he felt like a foreigner.'

'Please understand,' I begged him.

'Surely there are other people who can care for her?' he said furiously. 'Or are you vain enough to believe yourself the only one?'

'It's not like that. I want to help her if I can. I care about her.'

'More than you care for me?'

'Of course not.'

'It must be true. Otherwise you'd put me first.'

I didn't hear any reason in his words, was too caught up with Betty's loss to see things from his point of view. 'Let's not fight,' I pleaded.

'You have to make a choice,' he insisted, pulling away from me. 'Her or me? Who is the most important? Who is it to be?'

I stared at Pepe. By then every part of his face was familiar, the curve of his lips, the hook of his nose, the tiny creases next to his ears that pleated when he smiled.

'Surely you understand I have to keep my promise?' I said.

'The promise you made to me ... or the one to Betty?'

'No, to neither of you ... My promise to Mario.'

Pepe scowled. 'Then it's hopeless for me. How can I compete with a man like him ... especially now he's dead and everyone speaks of him as though he was some sort of saint?'

'Don't be like that ... he was a friend to you.'

Pepe gripped my shoulders. 'Serafina, wake up. We worked for these people and they treated us well, but they were never our friends and we owe them nothing. Do you think Betty Lanza would give up her whole life for you? Of course not. And no one would expect her to.'

Those weren't words I cared to hear. Perhaps it was true the Lanzas weren't ever my friends but I had made myself important to them. During our time together they grew to rely on me, to need my help; and I was so much a part of everything they did. How could Pepe not see that? Why was he being so unreasonable when all I wanted was to accompany Betty to America and then come back to him?

'I made a promise. I can't break it ... I don't want to,' I said.

'In that case, you've made your choice,' Pepe said, uncompromising. 'You are going with her ... and we are finished.'

'Please, let's not do this now. Can't we talk about it later when we've calmed down?'

'Later I will feel exactly the same way.' His eyes looked hard. 'Nothing is going to change.'

Now I was furious too, wanting to hurt him as he had hurt me. Peeling off my glove, I took the ring from my finger and held it out. 'In that case, have this back,' I said. 'If it's what you really want.'

I didn't expect him to reach for the ring, to curl his hand around it and slip it in his pocket. I didn't think he would turn his back on me, saying 'Goodbye, Serafina, good luck', then walk away without another word.

'Pepe,' I called after him, disbelieving. 'Pepe ...'

I watched till he rounded the corner. For a long time I couldn't move. Around me tourists threw coins into the fountain, hoping to return some day. I had never felt the need to do the same, but now, reaching into my pocket, I found a few lire and dropped them into the water one by one.

'*Arrivederci, Roma*,' I whispered to myself.

I'll See You In My Dreams

Never had I felt so unhappy, and now there was another sadness lying ahead – saying goodbye to my family. Whenever I felt myself beginning to waver, Betty would hug me, remark on how I was such a blessing, or tell me she would never have the strength to go on without me.

What else was there to do? I had no other future waiting for me, no place I had to be, no person who needed me more than she did. And it wouldn't be for ever, I kept reminding myself. My coin was in the fountain; some day I would come home.

I found gifts for them: a beaded purse for Rosalina, a silk scarf for Carmela, a beautiful comb for my mother's hair that was shaped like a starfish and covered in rhinestones.

'It's not Christmas yet,' Mamma said when she saw the parcels wrapped in bright paper and tied with red ribbons.

I had waited outside the Basilica di Santa Maria, knowing Sunday-morning Mass was a ritual they continued to keep. Surprised and happy to find me there, we walked to my favourite café where I insisted on paying for crisp pastries filled with ricotta and dense cakes dripping with rum syrup. Beneath the table Rosalina kicked her feet with pleasure and even Carmela licked the stickiness from her fingers like a child.

When I broke the news, my mother pressed the tears away with the palm of her hand and tried to seem happy. 'America! What an opportunity. Of course, you must go.'

Rosalina pestered me with a hundred different questions

and I struggled to answer any of them. All I knew was that we were to travel to Los Angeles. No one had told me where we would stay or what sort of life to expect there.

'Will you be able to come home for dinner?' Rosalina wondered. Pulling her onto my knee, I explained how far away America was. When she understood at last she held onto me tightly, blowing sugary breath in my face, begging me not to go.

Carmela greeted the news more coolly, leaning back in her chair, without a word to offer for once.

'Perhaps you could come and visit,' I suggested, for I knew how much she had always wanted to see America.

With her finger Carmela scooped a curl of chocolate from the crust of a tart and smeared it onto her tongue. 'I really don't know when I'd have the time,' she said. 'I'm singing three nights a week now at a nightclub near Piazza Barberini. You should come to see me before you leave.'

'I'll try,' I told her, knowing there wouldn't be time.

'Did you hear Luisa Di Meo is still having to sing on the streets?' she asked. 'She thought she'd made it after she was in that movie, kept telling everyone Mario Lanza was going to take her to America because he didn't want her voice to go to waste. And now she's back where she always was.'

'Poor Luisa. She must be so disappointed.'

'I expect so,' Carmela said lightly. 'For me things have worked out so much better, haven't they? It's a very good nightclub, beautiful inside, with a chandelier and marble tables. You must come, you really must.'

I wound the comb into my mother's hair, showed Rosalina the secret pocket in her beaded purse and admired the silk scarf Carmela knotted at her neck. I made every moment with them count, for who knew how long it might be until we saw each other again?

Before we parted, my mother took my hand, rubbing her

thumb over my bare finger. 'You aren't wearing your ring,' she observed.

'I gave it back to him,' I told her. 'It's all over between us.'

She only nodded. 'That makes sense. Why tie yourself to a man here when you'll be making a new life there?'

'But I'm not going for ever. Some day I'll be back,' I insisted, still believing it to be true.

She squeezed my hand. 'I hope so, cara. I'm going to miss you.'

I saw Pepe one last time. He came to the Villa Badoglio on the morning of my final day there. He must have worked late at the restaurant the night before because his eyes were shadowed and there can't have been time for him to shave. The relief of seeing his face again was tempered by the knowledge this really was goodbye.

'This is yours,' he said, offering me the diamond ring wrapped in a clean handkerchief. 'I want you to keep it. I won't be giving it to some other girl and what else would I do with it?'

'If I take it will you wait for me?' I asked hopefully.

'For how long?'

I hesitated. 'I'm not certain.'

'Then like I said before, you've made your choice. But take the ring. It was always yours and that hasn't changed.'

'I have nothing to give you in return.'

'I know that.'

Pepe kissed me but so briefly I barely tasted his lips, our bodies hardly touching. 'I'm still angry with you for leaving,' he told me. 'Still, I don't want us to part badly. This is a better way to say goodbye.'

It was impossible not to cling. 'Can I write to you?' I asked.

Regretfully, he shook his head. 'Best not, I think. But I won't forget you or the times we had together … I'm not sorry for any of it.'

I saw him look back as he walked through the gates of the Villa. I was standing on the steps but he seemed to gaze up at the building rather than at me, as if saying goodbye to the life he'd had there. For a second or two he stood still and then he was gone.

In America we lived a life without music. No one played Mario's records or dared turn on a radio in case we heard one of his songs. We lived such small lives in that great country. I saw only glimpses of what lay beyond the walls of the houses where we stayed. The cars were bigger, the highways wider, the light so much brighter. The food tasted of nothing and there was so much of it. The days were long; they moved too slowly and tasted of nothing too.

The people were good to us, though. To begin with we had nowhere to live and Betty was grateful to be taken in by a friend, the movie star Kathryn Grayson. Recognising her from so many films, I was shy but she welcomed us into her home with its vaulted wooden ceilings and rolling lawns. She was kind to us all and especially sweet with the children. When Damon introduced me as his Zia Serafina, she shook my hand and said she was so pleased to meet me, sounding warm and gracious.

For a long time the children seemed bewildered. They kept speaking in snatches of Italian and asking to visit places they'd left behind in Rome: their favourite shop for a gelato, the gardens of the Villa Borghese, the Excelsior Hotel. Damon was the most reluctant to understand how life had changed.

'If we're not home by Christmas will Santa Claus know where to come?' he asked Miss Grayson one afternoon as she comforted him with sweet milky tea and oatmeal cookies. 'Will he find us here in Santa Monica?'

'Well, my dear, I'm not entirely sure if you'll be living here with me by then,' she said. 'But I'm certain Father Christmas will find you wherever you are.'

'Will Papa come and find us, too?' Damon wondered. 'Does he know where we are?'

Then Miss Grayson tried to explain what all of us struggled to grasp, that there was no more Mario, that somehow he'd disappeared from the world and left us all. 'I miss your papa too, so much and every day,' she told him. 'He was my good friend.'

It hurt like a bruise this missing people. Brushing against the smallest thing could make it sore. The fragrance of onions turning golden in olive oil reminded me of Pepe's kitchen. The chemical reek of nail lacquer or a delicate breath of Nina Ricci's L'Air du Temps took me to my mother's side. Even the sight of the empty crystal decanters lined up on the sideboard brought a memory. And I dreamed of them constantly. Carmela stalked through my head while I slept, Mario sang. They haunted me and I woke each morning sorry to leave them.

The mourning for him seemed to go on for ever, with two more Requiem Masses held in his memory. In Philadelphia, his birthplace, the outpouring of grief was said to be easily as great as in Rome. We were told thousands queued to view his body and when at midnight they tried to shut the doors of Leonetti's Funeral Parlor there was such a fuss the police were brought in to control the crowds.

Thankfully we had remained in Los Angeles, waiting for him to be flown home for the final farewell. On a bright autumn day in the Blessed Sacrament Church on Sunset Boulevard, Betty sat before his flag-draped casket one last time. She was very still at that Mass, hardly looking about her at the congregation. I saw people I recognised: Zsa Zsa Gabor the blonde actress who starred in his final film, other faces I was certain I had seen onscreen. Costa was there, of course, so full of sadness, and Mr Teitelbaum, too. Betty showed no sign of knowing any of them. Wrung out by grief, she was dry-eyed and withdrawn.

All the extravagance of sorrow fell to other people. Mario's father was inconsolable, crying out, 'Take me, me. Not my poor boy', and collapsing at the casket. Maria Cocozza kept repeating softly, 'My baby, my baby.' Their pain must have sliced into Betty, for she reached out a black-gloved hand, gently touching Maria's arm. 'Mamma, Papa, please. It'll be all right,' she whispered helplessly.

When they took the flag from the casket, folded it and presented it to Betty, I was glad. Enough prying eyes had seen the wreck of his body, enough prayers had been said over him and tears shed. It was time for Mario Lanza to be buried and for us to learn to be without him.

There were photographs of him everywhere in the house we rented in Beverly Hills; they were framed and hung on walls, propped up on mantelpieces and sideboards. Some were family portraits, others movie stills or shots of him singing. Walking down a corridor or into a room felt like moving through his life.

Betty may have had the pictures hung there but she can't have seen them clearly. Her days were softened by Seconal and vodka; she lived in a daze and hardly ever left her room. There were friends who came and tried to tug her back into the world. The one I liked most was the man the children called Uncle Terry. Anyone could see he was just as ruined by grief for Mario; yet every single day he came to the house to check on Betty and the children.

'How is she today?' he'd ask me.

'Much the same,' I'd always say.

'Is she dressed? Out of bed?'

'I tried but she refused.'

He was a powerfully built man, fit and strong. On blue-sky days he'd lift Betty and carry her to the sunroom, settling her with a blanket across her knee and usually bringing some small gift – a fashion magazine or a book of puzzles – to try to waken her interest. At times he grew impatient, especially if the drugs had muddled her words or if her head drooped and she fell into a doze while he was talking.

'If Mario could see you like this it would break his heart,' he told her once. 'You need to clean yourself up, get into a clinic. Promise me you'll try.'

By then Mr Terry was the only one who could rouse her from her apathy. 'Oh go to hell,' she snapped angrily at him. 'You should have been a priest. You're always telling people how to live.'

'I mean it, Betty; you can't go on like this.'

'What if I don't want to go on? What then?'

'The children need you,' he pointed out. 'You're all they've got left now and yet you seem to have abandoned them.'

'They're doing OK ... the girls are looking after them. There's no need for you to worry.'

All the children loved Mr Terry. He'd take them to the drugstore for a soda or run about in the garden, playing ball games for hours. Often I was reminded of how Mario had been with them, except Mr Terry was stricter: insisting on church every Sunday, scolding if they were thoughtless or threw tantrums.

He became the person all of us leaned on and I was always glad to see him. The day felt a little better as soon as Mr Terry arrived. He loved to talk, often stopping to tell me stories of the past and things he had done with Mario: training him so he was fitter for movies, driving him around, even helping him find places to live. He seemed to have been more a brother to him than a friend, and many times I wondered if things might be different had he been there with us in Rome.

Whenever there was a problem we called Mr Terry and he did his best to help – sorting the accounts, dealing with the stacks of condolence cards and letters, talking to the bank if we ran out of housekeeping money.

It was him I telephoned the day I couldn't get Betty to open her bedroom door. For all that week she had been ill with a bad cold that had settled on her chest and her cough was noisy and nagging. That morning, though, I arrived with her breakfast tray to find all was silent and her door locked tight. I knocked then rattled at the handle, but there was no response at all.

'Signora, it's me – Serafina. Your coffee is growing cold. Let me in,' I called. 'Betty, can you hear me? Are you there?'

I'm not sure how long I stayed there knocking. Ten minutes? Half an hour, perhaps? Until my knuckles were red, there was a skin over the milky coffee and her eggs had congealed. Until the housekeeper and maid heard my cries and came running.

I grew angry, then afraid, and angry again. Pressing my ear to the door, I strained to hear if she were moving about. 'Betty, are you all right? Answer me, won't you please.'

The housekeeper shook her head. 'This is no good. Best call Mr Terry and see if he knows what to do.'

I hated to bother him so early in the morning but couldn't think what else to do. He must have heard the panic in my voice, for, while he sounded terse, he came straight away. I had been certain Betty would open up when she realised he was there, when she heard his fist beating against her door and his familiar voice. She might tell him to go to hell but surely she'd open up. Yet still there was nothing.

'Something is wrong,' I said. 'She must be ill, unconscious even. I'm sure of it. What will we do?'

'I'll have to break down the damn door,' he said impatiently. 'I don't know what else to try.'

He had us stand back and in a moment the lock was splintered and the door swinging open. Inside the room her curtains were drawn back and sunshine poured in. We found

Betty lying face down, her robe askew and her legs bare.

Mr Terry touched her shoulder. 'Betty, wake up.'

She didn't move. He patted her arm. 'Betty? Betty?'

Then he shook her, once, twice, the third time more roughly. 'For God's sake, Betty. Oh, dammit no, no ...'

I had known it was too late as soon as I laid eyes on her. Her skin was waxy and pale; there was no rise and fall to her chest. And she would have let me into that room if she had been able. She almost always let me in.

Sinking down beside her, Mr Terry covered his eyes with his hands. 'Call an ambulance, get the police. Quickly, Serafina,' he said hoarsely.

They came with their sirens and all their equipment; went through the motions of trying to bring her back but it was pointless. There was no breath left in Betty's lungs, her heart had stopped beating, she was gone for good.

Once everyone had left and her body had been taken, the house felt empty but strangely calm.

'The children?' Mr Terry asked, weary and beaten.

'Still at school.'

'Pick them up and take them to Maria Cocozza's place. She'll know what to do.'

Later I blamed myself; wished I'd called an ambulance sooner or tried to break down the door myself, regretted not locking away the Seconal or pouring the vodka down the sink. Later the guilt held me for a long time; I had made a promise and then failed her. But that morning everything felt unreal.

'At least she's peaceful now,' I said, trying to find some consolation. 'The sadness is over for her. She won't have to bear it any longer.'

Mr Terry stared at me. 'Do you think she did it on purpose?' he asked.

I was shocked at the idea. 'No, of course not.'

On her nightstand was the Seconal bottle, lying on its side with pills spilling out, next to it a half-empty bottle of vodka. From habit, I began to make things tidy.

'There'll have to be an inquest, a coroner's report; they'll be all over the newspapers again.' Mr Terry looked defeated. 'Dammit, Betty, what have you done? How could you leave us?'

The day Mario died had been all clamour and hurt, but with Betty it was different. There were no screams, no one sobbed. It was a quieter sort of grief, perhaps because she'd been frail for so long.

'She'd never have chosen to leave the children. Never,' I said fiercely.

'How then ... a mistake?'

'Maybe it was the Mafia. Perhaps they sent someone to get her. It's possible,' I said, falling back on Betty's old fears as I tried to find some sort of reason.

'No, Serafina ...'

'She's been ill,' I added quickly. 'Bronchitis ... her lungs so bad. Maybe she couldn't catch her breath.'

'What about the pills ... the drink?' he said heavily.

'She can't have meant it to happen. I know she didn't.'

'Either way, she's gone.'

'What will we say to people?' I asked. 'How will we tell them?'

'Just say she died of a broken heart,' Mr Terry told me. 'It's true ... more or less. There was no life for Betty without Mario. No life at all.'

One Alone

Every dress held a memory. A string of pearls took me shopping with her on the Via Condotti, a satin shoe to one of her parties. As I packed each item for the final time, I said goodbye to Betty. The gown she had worn for Mario's triumph at the Royal Albert Hall, the shearling coat that had kept her warm in St Moritz, the sunglasses that shielded her eyes at his funeral. I sorted through it all: saving keepsakes for the children, filling bags for the thrift store.

Most of the clothes still held her perfume and I imagined she was in the room, lying in bed or at her dressing table. I talked to her, sometimes out loud, more often in my head. I told her how hard it had been arriving on the doorstep of the house in Toyopa Drive with four bewildered children in tow. I described how Maria Cocozza had taken us in and how we had prayed together for the strength we needed. Often I whispered that I missed her face, the sound of her voice, her laugh. I promised we would hold her in our hearts and minds for ever.

'She's with Mario now,' people kept saying, perhaps thinking it a comfort. But I knew she would never have chosen to leave those children, not even for him, and I told her so.

I stayed at the house in Toyopa Drive because there was nowhere else for me to go. Maria Cocozza was kind. She said she had been lost when Mario died but now she knew what God meant for her. 'I am to care for his legacy – the children, his music, all he left behind. That's what is important now.'

I felt lost, too, but God's plan for me wasn't so clear. I

was lonely and far from all I knew. Only in the kitchen of Maria's house did I find some cheer. There I breathed the familiar scent of garlic and onions, the sharpness of dried oregano and the resinous tang of rosemary, the hot-fat smell of crisping pancetta. It was a reminder of how life used to be when there was still some joy left in it. And I knew what I had to do.

I had no recipes, only the memory of taste but still I began to cook the food Pepe had made. First I made a simple dish of tender steamed clams in a nest of spaghetti, then macaroni baked in the oven, stringy with melted mozzarella and crunchy with breadcrumbs. I made soups of white fish, tomatoes and oregano, and dressings of pulped anchovies and lemon juice – anything he had cooked I did my best to recreate. And as I tried each dish I thought of him.

Even the equipment I pulled from the cupboards reminded me of him. The stone mortar and pestle Maria's mother had brought all the way from Italy to pound garlic and herbs to a paste. The scarred wooden spoons and metal ladles. The ravioli press identical to the one he'd used. But Pepe's cooking had been infused with energy and filled with noise: with the ringing of metal, steaming and hissing, surges of temper. I liked to feel easier in the kitchen, to order my ingredients and equipment, work quietly and be soothed.

Shutting out the grief, I focused on what I cooked: appreciating the colours on a plate, bringing flavours together; sweet, sour and salty.

I stayed with Italian food because those were the flavours I understood and they reminded me of home. For the children, too, each mouthful must have brought a memory. They were calmer when their bellies were heavy with a buttery risotto or a good spaghetti; slept better and had fewer nightmares. I was glad to have made a little happiness for them.

Out of habit I still listened at doors, although I involved myself far less with the things I heard there. Even the bitter battle waged between Maria and Betty's mother for custody of the children failed to engage me as much as it might have. There was nothing for me to do, no way to change the outcome. The only way to help was feeding people well.

'Serafina, you must miss Italy a great deal,' Maria said as I shaved Parmesan over bowls of pappardelle cradling a gluey ragu. 'Your food tastes of it. Every mouthful reminds me of being there.'

'I do miss Trastevere and my family,' I agreed.

'Why don't you go home? Return to your old life? We'd miss you but we'd understand.'

I couldn't, not then. I still wasn't ready to admit everyone was gone and it was over. And the children needed me. 'I can't leave them until the court case is settled,' I told Maria. 'Until we know for sure they're safe staying here with you.'

It took a whole year for the wrangling to be finished. Worn out by endless meetings with lawyers, Maria seemed glad to leave the running of the household in my hands. Often at the end of the day, we'd sit over a bottle of red wine and she'd repeat stories from the past when Mario was still only Freddie Cocozza and his fame lay ahead of him. She liked to talk and lead me through her memories.

'His voice belonged to us alone,' she told me. 'We'd listen to him singing along to his Caruso records in our little house on Mercy Street. We were so proud of his talent. Nothing could have held him back. My Freddie's voice was always going to take him places. In the end, I guess it's what took him away from us.'

'To Hollywood?' I asked.

'Yes, there. And then to Italy ... and finally it carried him to the grave. It wasn't the Mafia that killed him, like poor Betty thought. It was his voice, nothing else.'

'But the doctors said it was a heart attack. How could that have been caused by his voice?' I was confused.

Maria sipped her wine and stared at the portrait she kept

in a frame on her dresser. In it Mario looked very young, deeply tanned and well muscled, laughing as he posed on a beach with a group of friends in their bathing suits.

'If you'd known him back then, you would understand,' she told me. 'He was a good boy, such a big heart, always looking for fun, a simple kid from south Philadelphia. Then because of that voice he was pulled into a different life. It happened so quickly. Suddenly there were all these people wanting a piece of him – agents, managers, studio bosses – and he didn't know how to say no to any of them. He struggled, never knew who to trust, grew troubled. His life was no longer simple. My Freddie was an ordinary boy who found himself in a crazy business. Often I think if success had come a little later ... if it hadn't come at all ... he might still be alive today.'

'Perhaps it would have been better if his voice had always belonged only to you? Then it might not have killed him.'

Maria sighed and shook her head. 'His voice belonged to God who gave it to the world and in the end he took it back. Freddie walks with him now.'

I grew to like Maria more as I listened to her talk. It reminded me of the hours I had spent hearing Betty's stories. When at last the custody battle was finished and it was agreed the children were to be raised by her in the house in Toyopa Drive, I might have stayed there too. I had worked myself into the weave of their lives by then and felt safe enough. Both of the governesses had decided to make new lives in America; I could have done the same. But I hadn't forgotten another place that smelt of the sun baking on old stone buildings and was filled with the sound of water spilling from fountains. I wanted to feel its cobbles pressing beneath the soles of my shoes, to walk its streets and hear voices speaking in Italian. I wanted more of my mother than her hasty scrawl on a postcard, to see how Rosalina had changed, to listen to Carmela sing. I was homesick. And I couldn't help wondering about

Pepe – where he was, who he was cooking for.

More than a year after I had arrived in America I took Maria's offer of a ticket home. Hugging the children, I said goodbye to all that was left of the Lanza family. It was Damon I clung to until the last moment, for he had been there at the very start. 'Don't forget your Zia Serafina,' I whispered, but he was young and I would fade from his memory.

And This Is My Beloved

When you return to Italy you are meant to show your success, wear expensive clothes, have gold at your throat and
on your fingers, demand respect for what you've become.
I arrived in the coat I'd been wearing when I left, holding
the same cheap suitcase. I came home to no job, with little
to show for the past four years. With the Lanzas gone, the
world I had moved through had disappeared too. There were
no more parties, no trips to new places and no doors to listen
at. I was back in the drab story of my own life.

Even my family felt like strangers. Rosalina had grown
taller and was shy with me; Carmela seemed still more glamorous; Mamma looked older and had lost some of her lustre.
I tried to slip into my old routine, washing their clothes and
cooking meals, but I was different too and couldn't be content with such a life.

It was early summer and the days were sunny and long. I
seized on every chance to escape the tiny apartment. Eking
out my savings, I walked the city. Once I went all the way to
Parioli to stare through the closed gates of the Villa Badoglio;
several times I visited the Fontana di Trevi or looked at the
views from the Gianicolo. I returned to all the places Pepe
had taken me, always watching out for a tall man with hair
that fell in ringlets and the hint of a hook in his nose, disappointed when I didn't find him.

Once I even went to the restaurant near Termini where
I thought he worked, standing outside for while until a
waiter with dirty fingernails asked if I would like a table. He

frowned when I spoke Pepe's name. 'He left,' he barked at me. 'We haven't seen him since.'

'Do you know where he's gone?'

The waiter shrugged. 'No, and I don't want to.'

I was half-relieved not to find him. If he had emerged from the kitchen, what would I have found to say? That the best days of my life were when I knew him. Yet even so I could never regret the choice I had made to stay with Betty till the end.

After that I kept closer to Trastevere, sitting outside the corner bar each evening with my mother and her friends, trying to join their conversation. They talked of the same things – clothes, shoes, jewellery, titbits of news and scandal. Listening to them, I realised their life was still there waiting for me. Should I give in to it? Choose to follow them one night when they left the bar and went to work?

My mother thought I should take my time. 'Enjoy the summer,' she urged. 'Start looking for another job when the weather turns cold.'

Carmela seemed to agree. 'Rome is full of rich people,' she pointed out. 'They are everywhere. Surely it will be easy enough to find another family that needs a maid or house-keeper when the time comes.'

She was moving into a small apartment on the top floor of a building a few streets away. I helped her scrub it and cover the walls with a fresh coat of paint. She was very particular about the way everything was arranged, filling it with soft lights, coloured silk scarves and plump cushions. I enjoyed helping her and, working together, she warmed towards me.

'It would have been much more difficult when you had no experience or references. Now surely you could get work anywhere,' she reassured me as we lay side by side on her new firm-sprung bed.

'I can't imagine working for any other family after being with the Lanzas. I'm not sure I want to.'

'You must miss hearing his voice,' she said thoughtfully. 'Do you ever play his records?'

'No, not for a long time. Betty couldn't bear it and later Maria worried it might unsettle the children. Since I came back home I've thought about it but I never have.'

Rising from the bed, Carmela pulled a disc from its sleeve and set it on the turntable of her new radiogram. Together we listened to Mario singing the words to 'One Alone' and then to his lucky aria from *Pagliacci*.

We played another song, then another. It was bitter-sweet to listen. My scalp still tingled at the sound, but the thrill was mixed with such great sadness at what had been lost.

'I still miss him so much,' I told Carmela.

'You were in love with him, weren't you?' she said, sounding satisfied. 'I always thought so.'

I considered her words. 'Love? I don't think it's the right way to describe how I felt,' I said at last. 'He changed everything for me. Showed me a world I'd never have known otherwise. I admired his voice, was thankful for his kindness and cared about them all – him, Betty and the children. But I never loved him, not like I loved Pepe. It wasn't the same thing at all.' I shrugged helplessly. 'Still, it makes no difference now because I've lost every one of them.'

'It's Mario and Betty Lanza who are gone. You could find Pepe if you really wanted to,' Carmela said shrewdly and I hoped it might be true.

That night I played more of Mario's music, soaked myself in his singing for hours. The next day I found a theatre where they were screening his final movie, *For The First Time*, and I watched it over and over. When I got home I took the framed photograph of us together from the nightstand and put it away in the box beneath the bed. I had been there at two of those grand Requiem Masses but this was my real goodbye to him.

*

How do you find someone in a city as big as Rome? If they have cut themselves off from the past, left their job, moved from the place they were living, then it is very nearly impossible. For all I knew, Pepe had gone away, returned to his family near Naples, gone to another town to find work. Still I looked, walking every street, asking at each restaurant I passed. 'Do you have a chef here called Filippo Pepe? Have you heard of him? Everyone knows him just as Pepe.'

I grew used to seeing shoulders shrugged and heads shaken. Some tried to be helpful. 'Have you tried La Matricianella near the Spanish Steps? I heard they had a new man there. Or go to Checchino, they've been hiring lately.' Others flirted, told me to forget Filippo Pepe and take them instead. At every place it ended the same way. No one had come across him.

I tried every single bar along the Via Veneto, cafés close to the opera house, new places that had opened since I was last in Rome. I returned to the restaurant near Termini and begged the waiter with dirty fingernails to ask the other staff about him. 'Someone here must know where Pepe went.'

'I don't think so,' the waiter told me. 'He walked out one night. Lost his temper, started yelling and took off. Didn't even come back to collect the wages he was owed. That was the last we saw of him.'

It seemed impossible but he had disappeared just as finally as Mario. I didn't even have a photograph to show people.

Often I was drawn back to the Fontana di Trevi. If anywhere in Rome had felt like our place that was it. And I liked being there. The tourists seemed so happy and carefree. They came because they'd seen *La Dolce Vita*, and loved to throw their coins and pose for photographs with the fountain at their backs. I imagined their lives as being simpler and more certain than my own; I envied the lovers and ached at the sight of children. And I searched for Pepe but he was never there. Until one afternoon he was.

I almost walked straight past him. He was slumped on

the stone bench near the spot where he had proposed to me, looking thinner and unshaven. When I stopped in front of him he didn't look up.

'Pepe,' I said hesitantly, taking a step closer.

His eyes met mine. 'Serafina,' he replied.

Many times I had imagined this meeting but never the awkward first words nor the sense that Pepe had become a stranger.

'How are you? Where have you been?' I asked. 'I went to the restaurant near Termini looking for you.'

'That place,' he said dismissively. 'They were idiots, no idea about food, and filthy too.'

'Where do you work now? Where are you living?'

There was no reply to my questions. Instead, Pepe looked at me and said softly, 'So Betty Lanza died.'

'Yes.' I sat beside him and he looped an arm around me.

'I'm sorry ... after all you did ...'

'It wasn't enough,' I said regretfully. 'I couldn't save her. No one could.'

'I read about it in the newspaper and ever since I've been coming here,' Pepe told me. 'I hoped you'd return to Rome. I couldn't think where else to find you if you did.'

'I've been coming here too, looking for you.'

'Now we've found each other.' He tightened his arm round me.

We sat beside the fountain for over an hour, much of the time in silence. When I questioned Pepe about his life he avoided answering. When I talked about America he didn't seem to listen.

Over time I had grown used to the changes in his moods, the startling sunshine then the sudden thunder. But this was different. Something inside him seemed to have loosened while I had been away. Another person might not have noticed the change, but I was his friend and knew he was different.

'What's happened to you, Pepe?' I asked. 'What's wrong?'

'Nothing … I'm fine.'

'Do you miss them?' I asked. 'Mario, Betty and the children. Is that it?'

'They weren't my family. I never felt for them the way you did.'

'Still, you must be sad at how things turned out?'

'He never lived up to his promise,' Pepe said almost angrily. 'His voice belonged in the opera. He might have had an outstanding career, been a legend. It was what he wanted and yet he threw it away to be a film singer. He failed.'

'He thought he was still young, that he had plenty of time. If his life hadn't been cut short …'

'It's easier, isn't it, to shy away from your own talents?' Pepe observed. 'Any man can find himself doing it. Here at the end of it, looking back, I can see that.'

His tone alarmed me. 'But this isn't the end for you, Pepe,' I said quickly.

'Look at me. I have failed, too. I lost my job, lost my love of cooking … and worst of all I lost you. I never lived up to my promise either, did I?'

Suddenly it was clear what I should do. Standing, I held out my hand. 'Come with me,' I said. 'Let's walk.'

'Where to?'

'To Trastevere … to a place we've never visited together before. It's time now.'

We took a while getting there, stopping at a bar so I could buy something cool to drink and pausing on the bridge to catch the breeze from the water. Pepe seemed content enough to stroll. He took my hand, and I felt his mood begin to lift a little.

'This is where I live,' I told him as we entered Trastevere's tight-knit streets. 'It's not too far now.'

My mother was exactly where I expected to find her, sitting outside the bar with Carmela and her friends. I tried

260

to see them through Pepe's eyes and realised they seemed too bright – their colours, their jewellery and make-up – too bright altogether.

Mamma glanced up as we came down the street.

'I want to introduce you to someone,' I told Pepe. 'It's time to meet my family.'

It was my mother who called for champagne. She seated Pepe beside her and, turning from her friends, spoke only to him. At first I listened anxiously, but my mother knew how to talk to a man, how to make him feel interesting and attractive. She pitched the conversation perfectly, filling his silences with long-practised ease. Carmela joined in, at her most vivacious. They stayed with us much longer than I expected. The sun began to set; Mamma ordered more champagne and kept talking. When finally she stood and made her excuses, she put a hand on Pepe's shoulder. 'We will see you again,' she said.

'I'm not sure.' He looked at me. 'I have nothing to offer your daughter, Signora. Nothing at all.'

'Perhaps you think that. But shouldn't you ask her what she wants?' Mamma said.

We stayed to finish the last of the champagne. Slowly Pepe began to tell me what had happened in the year we had been apart. He walked out of two more jobs after the place near Termini. The reasons were always the same: the food was bad, the managers were fools, the kitchen badly run. Word got round and no one would hire him. Fast running out of money, he had been sleeping on the floor of a friend's room and soon would have no choice but to fall back on his family. 'So you see, it's true I have nothing to offer,' he finished.

'I still have the ring you gave me,' I reminded him. 'You could sell that.'

'No,' he said quickly.

'I don't care about jewellery. It's not what I need.'

'Every woman loves jewellery.'

261

'Not me.'

'What is it that you need, then? What do you want?'

Sipping my champagne, I watched people pushing their way up the narrow street and considered my reply. 'Pepe, I'm the daughter of a prostitute,' I began, watching his face for a reaction. When his expression barely changed I continued. 'I have no father, no family except my mother and my sisters. My life was nothing before I met the Lanza family and now they're gone and it's returned to nothing again. That's what I want, Pepe. A life … a life with you.'

'Are you sure?' His voice broke on the words.

I nodded. 'Yes, I am. Everyone says I loved Mario Lanza and perhaps I did in a way. I fell in love with him every time I heard his voice and I always will. But you are real, Pepe, and you are mine. He never was.'

262

Deep In My Heart, Dear

The sale of the engagement ring fetched enough cash to keep Pepe going for a while longer. In the meantime, I took action. First I wrote to Maria Cocozza begging her to supply us with references saying how faithfully and well we had served her famous son. With those in our hands I knew it would be easier to find good positions.

My mother and Carmela had connections and soon enough they heard of a woman in Parioli who needed a nanny for her children. Her house was only a few streets away from the Villa Badoglio but was only half as grand. She made me wear a uniform and boasted to her friends that she had hired Mario Lanza's most trusted maid. Still, she paid me well and I needed the money. My mother may have offered to pay for much of the wedding but there would be other expenses, the rent on a place of our own, furnishings to make it comfortable.

'Your Pepe is a good man but I think at times he may be difficult,' Mamma had warned me.

'Perhaps,' I conceded.

'You believe he's worth it ... that you can be happy with him. What if it's not as easy as you think?'

'We can make it work,' I told her, remembering how Betty's love for Mario stayed whole and true through all their difficulties. 'I'm sure of it.'

Pepe and I had nothing to offer each other except our love and that would have to be enough. In the life we made we would find the joy in small moments: cooking and eating together, listening to opera, walking through Rome. I had seen enough of the world to know those were the best parts of it.

I hoped to love just as fiercely as Betty and Mario had, but to live more quietly; have days and years together, some of them hard, perhaps, but others perfect.

Our wedding day was one of the perfect ones. We were married in Santa Maria on a sunny summer's day in 1962. Mamma had sewn me a dress in Chantilly lace and given it a full skirt, a sweetheart neckline and cap sleeves. In my hair I wore a brooch that sparkled with rhinestones and my shoes came from the smartest shop on the Via Condotti. Everyone said I looked beautiful and that was how I felt.

Our guests sat divided in the church: Mamma and Carmela on one side of the aisle, Pepe's family on the other. Standing at the altar I didn't have to see the looks that passed between them. Nor did I care about anyone's disapproval. All the people I loved most were there – all that were left anyway. My mother gave me away and I was so proud of her, my little sister Rosalina played bridesmaid. We had invited the housekeeper from the Villa Badoglio, Antonio the janitor, the chauffeur too. They were from the old life but I was happy to have them help me towards the new. And Pepe was by my side, promising to be faithful to me always in joy and pain, to love me and honour me all the days of his life. I knew the words came from his heart. My Pepe had his flaws but he never said a single thing he didn't mean entirely.

Our wedding banquet was served at Il Pastarellaro on tables lined up in the narrow lane that were covered in white linen and flowers. We ate artichokes cooked till they opened like flowers and saltimbocca flavoured with sage while we listened to a pianist playing.

'Isn't this perfect? We have music and food,' I said to Pepe.

'We'll always have those things,' he promised me.

More wine was opened and the divide between our guests

began to close. They clinked glasses when Pepe's father gave a toast and gradually Mamma's friends wove themselves like bright ribbons through his much plainer family. Voices grew loud; there was laughter and more drinking. The sky darkened but no one would leave to go to work that night.

'So you are married now.' Carmela patted my cheek and smiled. 'I wonder if the same thing will ever happen to me.'

'And Rosalina too,' I wondered. 'What about her?'

'I suppose she'll go her own way like we both did. Who knows what she'll choose.'

Then Carmela stood and tapped a spoon against her wine glass to silence the table, announcing she would like to give me a song. 'Which do you want?' she asked.

'"Deep In My Heart, Dear",' I replied without any hesitation.

'Are you sure? It's so sad.'

'Yes, but it's beautiful too.'

She sang with as much passion as Mario would have; each word she treated as precious. By the time she had finished there were tears in all our eyes.

Thank you, I mouthed, and she blew me a kiss.

My mother took flowers from the table and put them in her hair then did the same for me. Candles were lit and more wine brought. We got drunk that night, even Pepe who rarely touched more than a glass. He looked very handsome, his curls trimmed a little shorter than usual, his suit new and smart. He was attentive and tender. He was glad.

'I never thought this day would happen,' he whispered.

'I always hoped it would,' I replied.

The next day we woke with dusty heads and many things to do. We had found some shabby rooms to rent in a narrow lane not far from Santa Maria. There was a small, private terrace where Pepe could grow herbs and the bathroom was shared by only one other couple. We stayed there for a long time, he and I. We found a life together.

There were years Pepe worked but never again in a kitchen. He cooked only for me and found other ways to make a living – as a handyman, a guard on the trains, a ticket collector. It was easier for him that way.

My one great sadness was there were no babies. We tried so hard but they never came. Sometimes I remembered Ellisa squirming on my knee or Damon putting his hand into mine, and longed for a child of my own to do the same. Pepe might find me on the terrace shedding quiet tears into his leggy basil plants. He would pull a handkerchief from his pocket and wait while the mood stayed with me. Then he might lead me inside and find some sweetness to comfort me: a tart of orange zest and vanilla, a perfect white peach peeled and soaked in red wine, a sticky ripe fig and a piece of hard grainy cheese.

Most evenings we stopped at the corner bar and shared a dish of olives and a bottle of wine with Mamma and her good friend Gianna. They were to be found there at the usual time, dressed in their finery, all lipstick, polish and shiny things.

As the years moved on, Mamma's health broke and her looks began to fade. Always she held herself as if she were beautiful; her back stayed straight and her ankles slim. But when she had to give up her work, she turned seamstress instead. For years in those two small rooms in Trastevere, she sat stitching wedding gowns and evening dresses, made a tidy living from it, too.

My sister Rosalina found her own way, as we had known she would. She discovered she had cool hands perfect for making pastries and sweet confections. She married a baker from Napoli, a round and pleasant man who loved her *sfogliatelle*. Together they moved to America where she had many children and grew rather fat judging by the photographs that came with her letters.

And Carmela? There was always a wealthy man who wanted her on his arm and in his bed, always a bar or nightclub where she sang. She found the right life, the one for her.

And we were a family, all of us. We belonged to each other.

I never saw any of the Lanza children again but I followed their lives when I could. After Maria Cocozza died I made sure to stay in touch with Mr Terry. We exchanged letters if there was news, good or bad. Very often it was sad. Colleen, Ellisa, Damon and Marc, their lives were changed when their parents went. They shared so little happiness between them.

Marc was never strong. He suffered from agoraphobia and was only thirty-seven when he was felled by a heart attack, younger even than his father had been. Colleen was troubled too in many ways. Six years after losing Marc she was struck by a car and killed. Little Damon is gone now too, again it was his heart. I don't think he was ever especially happy either.

Only Ellisa is left, pretty Ellisa who I remember in her party dress eating honey cakes. Mr Terry sent me a photograph and her face is still the same. She has found a good life now, I think. I hope so, anyway.

Every night until the massive stroke that finally took him from me, Pepe and I used to sit out on the terrace. It was tiny and our chairs were jammed together side by side but we didn't mind. The work of the day was done and we were pleased to be together. I liked to talk about the past much more than he did. Pepe thought it wiser to look forwards. Still, he indulged me, especially when I spoke about Mario and Betty. He knew it kept them alive for me.

'What happened? How did it go so wrong?' I would ask now and then. 'They had everything then they were gone. Why did they have to destroy themselves? I was there and still don't understand it.'

Pepe would play music then; sometimes a Mario Lanza

song, later on arias by the newer tenors he preferred to hear: Pavarotti, Domingo, Carreras.

I wondered how it felt to hit those notes. Did it make any of them happy? Push away their problems for a time? I preferred to think so.

Our Lady Of Grace

There is no feeling in the music nowadays, only notes, and I gave up listening long ago. The songs I love most are in my head; the rest is noise and I don't care for it at all.

Why am I in this place? Because growing old creeps up on you and suddenly you are standing still as the world around you moves faster and faster. Because the day comes when you realise the people you care about are gone or far away.

Far easier to do as Betty once did: let it all go on without me. To lie still in my bed in this small room in the Our Lady of Grace Rest Home with the curtains drawn and my eyes half-closed so they think I am sleeping.

People come and go but they're shadows and only the past is real. It is where I live; with Pepe in two small rooms in Trastevere, in the Villa Badoglio, in a rented house in Beverly Hills. I dance at the parties, I cry at the funerals, I remember it all.

If only they were content to leave me alone. But always there is some well-meaning person trying to pull me from my thoughts. They want me to join in. They try to brush my hair and wheel me to the day room. They talk in cheerful voices. 'Signora, today there is a flower-arranging class. I'm sure you would enjoy it. Let's get you up and dressed, then you can be a part of things.'

I know their voices, can tell whether their hands will be rough or kind. I know the ones who will quickly grow impatient. I recognise them all.

Today, though, the woman who has come is a new one

and her accent a reminder of the past. It lifts and lilts in all the wrong places, it stretches vowels that ought to be short. She is soft voiced like Betty was and sounds the way she always did when she was trying to speak Italian.

'Signora, I am Jenny Butler,' she says. 'How are you feeling today?'

I ignore her but she doesn't seem to care. She talks on without pause. 'I was looking at the photograph you have on your door. I'm sure I recognise the man in it. Tell me, is that the singer Mario Lanza?'

I work to keep my face the way it is always arranged, my expression neutral and disinterested. But perhaps a flicker of something crosses it for Jenny Butler seems encouraged.

'It is him, isn't it? The great Mario Lanza. Oh, my nanna was such a fan. She used to play his records to me, all those wonderful old songs, "Because You're Mine" and "Ave Maria". It's years and years since I've heard them.'

I don't respond but Jenny Butler seems content enough with her own conversation. 'He was a big star in his day, wasn't he? Bigger even than Frank Sinatra. Is that right, Signora? Do you remember?'

I open my eyes. 'Of course I remember,' I tell her.

Now I have spoken it will begin, the forced enthusiasm and the kindly bullying. Jenny Butler will try to coax me from my room. There will be some activity she thinks I should take part in; some experience she's sure will be rewarding. I close my eyes again.

'I wonder how you came to meet him and have a photograph taken,' she says in that gentle American voice that reminds more of Betty every time I hear it. 'Would you tell me about it? About meeting Mario Lanza?'

Despite myself, I speak again. 'It's a long story.'

'Still, I'd like to listen to it.'

'There isn't time. You are too busy. You have work to do.'

'Oh no, I don't work here. I'm only a volunteer helper.

My husband moved to Rome with his business and I don't know a soul in Italy so I've got all the time in the world to hear your story. You know, I'd forgotten about Mario Lanza until I saw the photograph on your door. I watched one of his movies once, *The Great Caruso*. Did you ever see it?'

'Yes, many times.'

'That's what I love about this place,' she tells me. 'So many people, so many stories to hear. Some of them can't recall much, sadly. Their minds have let the memories go. But you're not like them, are you?'

'I remember it all.'

'Why did you pick that picture for your door?'

'It wasn't my choice,' I admitted. 'That photograph was in a frame, they must have thought he was my husband.'

'Still, Mario Lanza must have been special to you if you framed the picture.'

I look at her properly. She's settled in the chair beside my bed as though she has no plans to leave it.

'I know what you're trying to do,' I tell her.

She seems perplexed. 'I'm sorry?'

'You want to get me in that day room staring at the television with all those old people. There's no need for it. I'm happy resting here.'

'They told me you're depressed,' she admits.

'They know nothing.'

She laughs. 'Well, perhaps that's true. They say you're a bit of a mystery.'

I wait for her to leave but Jenny Butler is determined. We sit together in silence. She flicks through a magazine someone has left on my nightstand and pours a glass of water. Then she stands and I am hopeful but instead she comes closer, leaning down to help me sit up, plumping the pillows at my back as I once did for Betty.

'I'm not here to try to make you do anything,' she promises. 'But I'd like to pass some time with you. I'm lonely here in

Rome. It's no fun sightseeing by myself while my husband's at work.'

'You are homesick?' I ask.

'Yes, very, and a little bit aimless too, I suppose. It's as if I can't see the point of myself right now. Does that make sense?'

It has been such a long time since I've cared to look beyond my own life. This stranger showing me her sadness comes as a surprise. It moves me. 'Is that why you want to hear our stories?' I ask her. 'To escape your own?'

She is startled by my words. 'Perhaps,' she agrees. 'I hadn't thought of it like that.'

'Hearing about my life won't change anything for you.'

'No, I suppose not.' She settles down into the chair again. 'But I need a friend. I really do.'

My mother was right; I always did like to help people. For a long time there has been no one who wanted anything I could offer. Now there is Jenny Butler and her loneliness. Jenny Butler who needs a friend. I can feel myself weakening.

'I'd love to hear how you came to meet Mario Lanza,' she encourages me. 'Just tell me that.'

'It's complicated ...'

She looks at me expectantly.

'I didn't only meet Mario ... I knew him ... knew him very well ...'

And then I am lost and the story is there, demanding to be told. I can't resist it any longer.

'It doesn't begin with him, anyway,' I tell the new friend at my side. 'It starts with a woman leaning out of the window of an ivy-covered building in Trastevere and calling down into the narrow street below: "Serafina ... Serafina ... Serafeeen-aaaa."'

ACKNOWLEDGEMENTS

I fell a little in love with Mario Lanza the first time I saw him in *The Great Caruso*. That was years ago when I was a young girl with a passion for 1950s movies and handsome leading men. Every time I listened to his voice while I was working on this book I fell in love with him all over again.

I've taken some liberties for the sake of the story. While the Lanza family did have loyal staff in Rome, there was no personal assistant called Serafina and the cook at the Villa Badoglio was actually a woman. Here and there I may have stretched or contracted time but for the most part the details about the period Mario spent in Rome are based on fact. One note: the film *Arrivederci Roma* was released outside of Italy as *The Seven Hills of Rome*.

I am grateful to Lanza biographer Derek Mannering for his help, most especially for putting me in touch with Mario's only surviving child Ellisa Lanza Bregman whose memories of her father were invaluable and I thank her for sharing them. My other sources included three biographies: *Mario Lanza: An American Tragedy* by Armando Cesari (Baskerville); *Mario Lanza: Tenor in Exile* by Roland L. Bessette (Amadeus), and Derek Mannering's *Mario Lanza: Singing To The Gods* (Mississippi), as well as the BBC Four documentary of the same name. I also spent time on the many websites offering Lanza information, the most useful of which were www.rense.com and www.mariolanzatenor.com.

My thanks to opera singer Tiffany Speight for helping me

understand what it is to have a voice, and to everyone who has encouraged me in the writing of this book.

More than fifty years on from his death there remain Lanza fans around the world. This book is dedicated to them and to anyone who still feels a shiver down the spine at the sound of his voice.